THE COIN

A Novel

BARRY S. KAPLAN

An unforgivable family debt brings Jack Perle
from the shtetls of Eastern Europe to the docks of Philadelphia
where he plots to collect from those closest to him.

HALLARD
PRESS

Cover Design by Hallard Press LLC/John W Prince
Cover Image: "Silver Right Hand of God." Photo courtesy of GovMint.com
Page Design, Typography & Production by Hallard Press LLC/John W Prince

Published by Hallard Press LLC.
www.HallardPress.com   Info@HallardPress.com

Bulk copies of this book can be ordered by contacting Hallard Press LLC, Info@HallardPress.com

Printed in the United States of America   1

Publisher's Cataloging-in-Publication data

Names: Kaplan, Barry S., author.
Title: The coin / Barry S. Kaplan.
Description: The Villages, FL: Hallard Press, 2021.
Identifiers: LCCN: 2021910772 | ISBN: 978-1-951188-25-2 (paperback) | 978-1-951188-26-9 (ebook)
Subjects: LCSH Family--Fiction. | Immigrants--Fiction. | Jews--Philadelphia--Fic-tion. | Philadelphia--History--20th century--Fiction. | Europe, Eastern--History--Fiction. | Gangs--Fiction. | Historical fiction. | BISAC FICTION / Jewish | FICTION / World Literature / Russia / 19th Century | FICTION / World Literature / Ameri-can / 20th Century
Classification: LCC PS3611 .A6475 C65 2021 | DDC 813.6--dc23

ISBN Print: 978-1-951188-25-2
ISBN Ebook: 978-1-951188-26-9

"Rarely do I find a book I literally cannot put down. *The Coin* is a true page-turner... fast paced and the plot is riveting."

—Holly W. Schwartztol, Author of *Coming Around Again*

Originally a Jewish innovation, the convention of
using the hand of God—*Manus Dei* in Latin—as a
symbol for God Himself was embraced by Christian
artists. In late antiquity, the representation of
the full-bodied figure of God would have been
considered sinful, a grave violation of the Second
Commandment. The iconoclast campaigns of eighth
century Byzantium were inspired by fanatical
devotion to this prohibition on graven images. The
Hand of God was a compromise—a way to show
God without actually depicting Him.

The phrase "the right hand of God" appears
frequently in both the Hebrew Bible and the
New Testament. God's right hand is "full of
righteousness," used to vanquish enemies and guide
the way to the Promised Land.

This book is dedicated to my wife and family,
especially my daughter, Mindy, who has acted as
an ever available sounding board for my ideas
and helped me navigate the phrasing, plot, and
order of events in this book.

Prologue

"GO FORTH AND RESCUE THE HOLY SEPULCHRE. GOD WILLS IT."

Pope Urban II

26 November, 1095

27 May, 1096

Micah Ben-Pectres covered the five miles of dusty road to the town of Durenstein on foot, running much of the way. Durenstein was the home of the papal nuncio. Several times, he had to circumvent stragglers from the main Crusader mob without being spotted. This rabble would have liked nothing better than to capture and torture a young Jewish boy. Pretty soon, he knew, he would hear the trampling hoofbeats of Baron Emico and his band of Christian zealots searching for Jews who had taken refuge in the courtyard of the archiepiscopal palace.

The frightened thirteen-year-old boy could see the plumes of black smoke rising into the clear air and smell the acrid fumes wafting on the spring breeze.

Those ugly cinders used to be my house.

Until now, he and his Jewish neighbors had lived in peace with their German neighbors, as Jews and Germans had for hundreds of years.

Micah knew that his mother, Rizpah, his father, Yakov, and his two younger sisters were crowded into the compound of the local archiepiscopal palace along with three hundred other Jewish families. The episcopal structure was a sprawling red sandstone building modeled after St. Peter's cathedral in Rome, with three Romanesque spires and, on its eastern wall, a tall baroque tower. The central courtyard was surrounded on three sides by cloisters, and the front wall had a large gate that could be closed and barred with stout timbers. It was in this courtyard that the Jews had found refuge.

In a desperate move, Yakov, as head of the Jewish town council, had selected Micah, his fleet-footed son, to carry a message to Bishop Willebald, the papal nuncio, requesting help directly from the pope's personal representative.

"Here, Micah, is a silver coin to gain the attention of the bishop's assistant. It should help you get in to see the bishop a little more quickly."

Micah's father handed him a valuable and rare silver coin minted by the government of Mainz. The unevenly rounded piece of metal was decorated with the outstretched right hand of God, palm out, making a blessing gesture on one side. On the reverse side, there was a Christian cross. As terrified as he was, Micah was aware of the responsibility that had been entrusted to him. He was proud to have been chosen for this monumental, do-or-die mission for his entire community.

Little good that payment to the pope did to protect us. This crazy mob has already scared off Archbishop Ruart and called him a traitor for trying to keep us "infidel Jews" safe. He felt a tightening in his throat as this thought rose to his consciousness.

Micah arrived at the bishop's residence streaked with sweat and dust from the road. He had never seen so many marble crosses, statues, and large paintings as those that covered the walls and grounds of the edifice. He was intimidated by all of the activity going on around him in this strange place and didn't know where to find the bishop. At last, Micah spotted an elderly bearded man in a white robe with the scarlet cross of the papal insignia who seemed to be in charge.

Breathlessly, Micah approached the man and tugged at his robe. The bishop's aide turned, looked at the boy, and asked kindly, "What can I do for you, young man?"

"Please, sir," said Micah, placing the coin that his father had given him into the man's hand, "please, take me to see the bishop."

The aide smiled compassionately, looked at the coin, and returned it to Micah.

"I can see you've run a very long way in the hot sun. You don't need to bribe me to do my job. Have a drink. You may have to wait a while, but I'll make sure the bishop gives you an audience." Relieved, Micah placed the coin back in his pocket.

After about ninety minutes, the boy was led into the bishop's chamber.

"Yes, boy. What is it you want?" A tall, gaunt man wearing a long-sleeved white tunic covered by an intricately embroidered green silk cloak stared impatiently at Micah and tapped his right foot. He was sitting on a rough-hewn wooden bench and was obviously exhausted from his round of daily chores. He held a jeweled staff in his left hand, and his bishop's mitre lay on the bench next to him. A golden pectoral cross hung around his neck, and he wore a heavy gold ring with his coat of arms on his left index finger. Micah was his last petitioner of the day, and he was looking forward to shedding his heavy formal attire and sinking into a warm bath.

"Thank you for seeing me, Your Excellency. I have come to beg for the protection of the Holy See promised to the Jews of Mainz by his holiness, Pope Urban. Archbishop Ruart and the other church officials have fled the city, leaving us defenseless in the path of Baron Emico and his marauders. They have already murdered hundreds of Jews in other towns on their way to the Holy Land, and we will be next if nothing is done."

In a sharp tone, the bishop replied, "Boy, I think you exaggerate the danger. Baron Emico is a good Christian nobleman who has taken up the pope's call for a crusade to free Jerusalem from the hands of the Muslim infidels. He is merely passing through this part of Germany on his way to the Holy Land."

Micah knew differently. His father had received advance warning from friends in Cologne, Worms, and other cities along the baron's route. While the baron may have begun his Crusade as a religious quest with a holy purpose, his group of pious warriors had been joined by runaway serfs, ambitious businessmen, adventurers, and criminals. The group had deteriorated into an uncontrolled mob intent on grabbing whatever its members could get their hands on in the name of Christianity. They used every excuse to plunder, loot, and kill anyone and anything they came upon as part of their 'adventure.' The Jews were especially vulnerable because they could easily be labeled as 'infidels' even though the pope had made some half-hearted efforts to shield them by issuing letters of protection in return for large amounts of gold.

"But, Your Excellency, we will be slaughtered," pleaded young Micah. "Please help us!"

In desperation, Micah took the coin from his pocket and tearfully offered it to the Bishop.

The Bishop shook his head vigorously.

"Young man," he replied curtly, "even if I wanted to send help, I couldn't do it. All of my available guards are required to protect the citizens of Durenstein from the general unrest. I can't spare anyone to protect a group of frightened Jews worried about holding onto their possessions."

"It is their lives, not their possessions, that they are worried about holding onto, Your Excellency." Micah was surprised by the angry defiance welling up within him. "Please reconsider!" The Bishop shook his head again and flicked his wrist in a gesture of dismissal. Placing the coin once again in his pocket, Micah turned his back on the bishop and angrily left the palace, hoping to get home before the onslaught began.

Bishop Willebald was furious with what he considered Micah's irreverent behavior. With force, he threw his staff to the floor yelling at the aide who had come in to assist him with his bath, "Those damned Jews! First, they crucify our Lord. Then they stubbornly refuse to accept our generous offer of being baptized in His name. They deserve whatever misfortune God sends to them. It is a wonder we still permit them to live among us. The Holy Father has been far too lenient with them. And now they want us to save them from the consequences of their behavior. They don't deserve to be saved from anything. Let them sacrifice their lives on the altar of the great Crusade. It is only right that they should pay in this way for the death of our Lord."

Under his breath, the aide muttered, "I'll bet it would be different if it were your own family," but the bishop had already dozed off in the bathtub.

* * *

Five miles away, Yakov Ben-Pectres sat in the palace courtyard huddled with his wife and two small daughters on the grass by the stone wall of the courtyard. He tried to comfort the crying children by gently stroking their heads.

"Perhaps Micah will convince the papal nuncio to send us protection," said Rizpah, trying to reassure herself as much as her husband. "God knows we paid enough for it."

"It is a last-ditch effort, Rizpah. No one really expects it to work. The Christians tolerate us as long as we can provide them with goods and services they can't get anywhere else, like the spices and silks we bring them from the East. But, if they can use us for a more important political purpose, we are expendable. The pope wants to retake Jerusalem and needs to rally the masses to his cause. If we provide an outlet for their zealous thirst for 'infidel' blood before they reach the Holy Land, the pope is happy to let us be used that way, bribes or no bribes. It feeds their passion. And, in the bargain, they get to keep everything they can steal from us."

"But Yakov, what will we do?"

With a glance downward, Micah's father silently indicated to his wife to follow him a few feet away from the girls, who had now fallen asleep on the grass.

"The council of elders has discussed the situation," he whispered. "We know that these monsters stop at nothing. They rape and ravage the women in their path, often in front of their husbands and children. They torture the men and cut off their organs while they still live. We cannot allow that to happen. If there is no escape...." Yakov pulled a sharp dagger from under his cloak and made a motion with the blade across his neck.

"No!" gasped Rizpah, eyes wide with fear, stifling a scream. "Kill ourselves and our children?"

Yakov looked sadly and lovingly into his wife's clear green eyes. "It's better we should martyr ourselves than allow those savages to torture and mutilate us."

* * *

Returning stealthily from the bishop's residence, Micah was just about to leave the protection of the woods and make his way across the wide meadow to join his people in the church courtyard. As he stepped out of the shadows of the trees, however, he saw a cloud of dust rising not far away.

I'll never make it to the church, he realized. *I don't want to leave them alone to face the mob, but getting killed trying to join them doesn't make much sense. I'll go back into the woods until whatever this is passes.*

In the courtyard, the barricaded Jews heard the thunder of hoofbeats approaching. They could see a multitude of men and horses sweeping in bands across the countryside until their entire view was filled with them. A group of young Jewish youths had strapped on their armor and attempted to stop the horde, but they were no match for the twelve thousand men arrayed against them.

The families in the courtyard knew that they had little time left. The wooden gates of the palace would not hold up much longer against the heavy logs that were battering them.

* * *

Yakov removed a dagger from his beneath his cloak. The girls were still sleeping. He moved behind them, readying himself to carry out an act so terrible that he was unable even to bring himself to name it.

"No, Yakov. I can't let you do it alone," his wife said. "I'll find the strength to help you carry out what must be done." Her eyes filled with tears but contained a steely resolve that Yakov had never before seen though he knew her so well. His heart overflowed with love and gratitude.

Thank you, Lord. I made the right choice when I married her.

Along with the other families in the compound getting ready to carry out the unspeakable, Micah's mother and father began to chant the ancient prayer of their forefathers, the prayer that, through the ages, expressed the deep, unquestioned commitment of a people to their deity.

"HEAR, O ISRAEL, THE LORD OUR GOD; THE LORD IS ONE."

When Rizpah and Yakov had accomplished their mission, she lay down on the ground.

"You have been a good husband, my darling, and I love you very much. We shall be together again in heaven."

Kissing Yakov on the lips, she arched her neck and closed her eyes.

Having quickly dispatched his wife, Yakov kissed her peaceful body gently on the cheek and plunged the dagger deep into the left side of his chest.

"Shit!" cried the leader of the Crusader mob when the battering ram finally knocked down the last remaining timber. "They're all dead."

The Crusader horde was disappointed. They had looked forward to the exhilaration of torturing, murdering, and mutilating these infidels. Now they would have to wait until they reached the next town, the next city where they could exercise their bloodthirsty passion against another defenseless group of people.

* * *

Micah waited for the mob to pass. He guessed why things were so quiet in the nearby churchyard but couldn't bring himself to believe his thoughts.

As evening approached, Micah entered the silent palace courtyard with dread. The angry mob had left. The sun was setting softly over the remains of the hundreds of martyrs lying in their final rest.

After a heart-rending search among the groups of corpses, navigating his way with unending tears, Micah found the bodies of his mother, father, and sisters. As he knelt over them, weeping and reciting the prayer for the dead, he vowed, *I will never live again in a place like this, one filled with hate and rage toward my people. I will search until I find a spot of peace and friendship where I will be left alone to live and work in peace.*

The boy-man buried the bodies of his family just outside the courtyard of the Christian church. There was no way he could do the same for the hundreds of other bodies there. He said another prayer for his neighbors and friends and began walking aimlessly from the city of his birth.

Absently placing his hand into his pocket as he walked, he felt the silver coin. A shock ran through his body as he realized, *THIS IS THE LAST THING MY FATHER GAVE ME. I'LL KEEP IT FOREVER.*

* * *

For two years, Micah wandered through the towns and cities of northeastern Europe.

From town to town, village to village, he sought respite and refuge. He was hungry and tired. Without his family, he felt adrift. Life became meaningless.

At first, in an effort to fill his stomach, he would approach a farmer, "Sir, can I help with the harvest?" he would inquire. Or he would say to a shopkeeper, "Sir, can I clean your shop? All I ask in return is a place to sleep and something to eat."

"Where are you from?" the farmer or shopkeeper would ask.

At first, Micah's answer would be, "I come from Mainz, and my people were killed by the mob of Crusaders on their way to the Holy Land."

"Ah! You are a surviving infidel, probably a Jew dog. Get off my land before I call the church officials!"

How stupid of me to think they would sympathize with a Jew.

Micah learned fast. The next time he was asked that question, he replied, "I am an orphan. My mother and father died in the great plague. I am seeking lost relatives."

He survived by taking odd jobs, such as helping with the harvest, cleaning shops, and even scrubbing privies, a job that none of the villagers wanted to do. Often, he slept in the fields, but sometimes a kind merchant would allow him to huddle in the warmth of a barn or shop. He learned that he could judge the temperament of a town by counting the number of churches there: the more churches, the more dangerous for him. Hard-line religionists, with their inflexible and self-righteous behavior, were not inclined to come to the aid of strangers.

* * *

I can't take much more of this. Micah rubbed his sore and blistered feet. *I'm tired. I wonder what it would be like to be dead.*

My family isn't having to go through this pain. Please, God, help me find a place to rest!

A few days later, as if God were answering him, Micah noticed a remarkable change in the populace and landscape.

Where are the churches?

His eyes were greeted with magnificent vistas of seemingly endless rolling hills and ribbons of sparkling water running gently through. Along the banks of the narrow streams were houses of stone and thick wooden logs neatly surrounded by small gardens of colorful flowers. Micah could see smoke rising from some of the chimneys and make out the small figures of cows and goats grazing contentedly in the fields.

It feels like I am being called to settle in this place.

Walking into the small town, he was greeted by smiling faces. Though unable to speak the language, Micah sensed no tension, no fear of strangers among the townspeople. He noticed that, in front of most of the cottages, was a pile of large stones topped by figures of what appeared to be animals and other totems.

Those must be the gods they pray to.

He was surprised to see a continuing absence of the churches that were so ubiquitous in the other countries through which he had wandered. Though he was not aware of it at the time, Christianity had not yet reached this land and would not do so for another three hundred years.

Walking through the busy marketplace, Micah passed a stall from which emanated the delicious aroma of freshly baked bread.

I hear my language being spoken

He felt his heart skip a beat as he realized the speaker was a pretty young maiden.

"Good morning, miss. I've just arrived in town and don't speak the native tongue. I heard you speaking my language. Can you tell me what place this is?"

Smiling shyly, the pretty young girl replied, "You are in Jelcis, part of the Duchy of Poland and Lithuania. Where do you come from?"

With a stab of pain in his chest, Micah's thoughts raced back to that fateful day in the palace courtyard.

"I—I come from the city of Mainz in Germany," he whispered, and his eyes filled with tears as the words came tumbling out. "My family and neighbors were slaughtered by the Christian Crusaders, and I've been traveling for two years looking for a place to settle where Jews can live in peace."

"My family has been here for generations. Some say we came here originally from Babylonia. But many have also joined us from Germany over the years."

Gently taking Micah's arm, the girl said softly, "You've come to the right place. Tonight will be the Sabbath. I'm sure my parents will want you to stay and share our meal."

* * *

Unconsciously placing his other hand in his pocket and fingering his father's coin, Micah felt as if he had finally come home.

Chapter One

"**A**aron, get a move on."

"All right, father, I'm coming," answered Aaron in a shaky voice. *If I can ever calm down enough to move my feet. After thirteen years of wondering what goes on in that old bathhouse every Friday, I'll finally get to see it for myself.*

He forced his feet to catch up with those of his aging father, who could still move briskly. They tramped down the marble steps of the bathhouse, which had been worn smooth by generations of Jewish men and women practicing the cleansing rites of their religion. The men usually visited just before the Sabbath began.

Aaron saw a flight of stairs leading off to his right.

"Where does that lead, father?"

"That takes you to the women's mikvah, something you don't know much about." He continued, "Aaron, it's time you learned. Women have monthly cycles marked by bleeding, through which God intended to prepare them for having children. They are required by Jewish law to immerse themselves in the bath before being permitted to resume conjugal relations with their husbands."

"What are conjugal relations, father?"

"That's too long an explanation to give now, my son. Time will grant you appropriate knowledge." Yitzchak would later regret that he never followed up on this conversation.

Aaron didn't know what to do with this flood of new information from his father — the father who talked very rarely and never about sensitive or taboo subjects.

Aaron had just turned thirteen. Tomorrow, he would celebrate his Bar Mitzvah and be called up to read from the Holy Scriptures for the first time. He was shaking all over by the time the men undressed and entered the bath. Today's visit to the bathhouse was part of the coming-of-age ceremony. Aaron had never been naked among other naked men.

His father continued, "But know that this bath has been here, it is said, since the eleventh century—almost nine hundred years. Every day, fresh water is piped in from the River Mereczanka to this ten-by-twelve-foot tub, and every night it is pumped out, except for the Sabbath. Men and women are assigned different days on which to use the bath."

I'll undress facing the wall.

Aaron secretly glanced at the naked men all around him. He wondered whether they were as nervous as he was. Looking at the somewhat older youths, he couldn't help comparing himself to them.

Am I as developed as Jake? Do I have as much hair as Shmuel?"

After discretely glancing around, he concluded with relief, *I'm glad I'm pretty developed myself.*

Noticing Aaron's hesitation, Yakov yanked his son's arm, pulling him into the chilly water. Soon he was laughing and joining in the general chatter as if he had been part of it for years.

That wasn't as bad as I thought it would be, but I'm glad it's over.

As father and son approached their shop on the perimeter of the village square, they smelled the delicious aromas wafting from within. Aaron's mother, Rivka, had been cooking for days in anticipation of the midday Sabbath meal at which his new status as a full member of the adult community would be celebrated.

Aaron ran into the small living area behind the bakery and hugged his mother. She knew that he had been anxious about the visit to the bath and was relieved to see him in an exuberant mood.

"Hello, mama," he said as his mother rushed to hug him.

Thank God it's over and he's feeling good. Then Rivka returned to braiding the challah bread and taking the-fruit filled pastries out of the oven.

His mouth watering, Aaron asked, "May I have one?"

"No," she replied, and catching him trying to snatch a hot pastry behind her back, made him return it. "No!" she said, playfully slapping his outstretched hand, "these are for tomorrow."

Then she relented. "Well, maybe just one." And she handed him a hot pastry filled with apples and walnuts.

Aaron went to his bedroom and once again studied the Torah passage that he would be chanting tomorrow during the Sabbath service. He had already memorized it but was worried that stage fright would paralyze him during his performance. The thought was persistent.

What will my parents think if I screw up?

And Rabbi will not recommend me for yeshiva.

And Mrs. Cohen will never let mama forget that her son Victor did better than me in the pulpit.

A combination of excitement and anxiety kept him awake very late that night, but he finally fell into a fitful sleep.

Rifka did not sleep well, either. Tomorrow, Aaron, her only child and her life's work, would be on public display. She knew that, along with his performance, the community would also be judging her performance as a mother.

What will Mrs. Cohen think? I'm sure all the other mothers will see how well he's been raised. I know he'll do a good job and that everyone will love him. He'll make us proud. I'm so lucky that God gave me a son like Aaron. I only wish my mother could be here today to see what a wonderful grandson she has.

As Rivka thought about her mother, she began to cry. Not wanting to wake her husband, she got out of bed and sat rocking in one of the few pieces of furniture in their small domain. Rocking was a comfort. Her thoughts drifted back to her mother, Leah, who had died when she was fourteen. Leah had been a strong and capable woman who worked hard to make her home livable. She also had been married off at a very young age to a much older man who paid no attention to meeting the basic emotional needs of his unsophisticated wife and their daughter.

She tried to teach Rivka as much as she could about the world but had little knowledge or experience to work with. Rivka idolized her mother and had felt lost when she died, never resolving her grief. When her uncaring father sent her away at the age of fourteen to marry a man of forty whom she had never met, it was one trauma piled on another. Upon arriving in the house of her new husband, she had felt that she had nothing and no one. When Aaron was born, all of her unused love and energy was poured into her son, and he reciprocated her love in kind.

Two years after being sent away, Rivka learned from community gossip that her father had married a young girl just about her age and that his new wife had given birth to a baby girl who was just six months younger than Aaron. Thinking about this development made her cry, though, if you asked her, she would not have been able to articulate why. Her sorrow spilled over to include the baby half-sister whom she never met. Sometimes, as her hands almost automatically shaped the day's pastries, her thoughts would drift.

How odd it is that my sister is just six months younger than my son.

Then she shrugged off her gloomy thoughts and went to sleep.

* * *

Yitzchak, too, was pensive that night as he tried to sleep. *Aaron is a good son. I wish I could afford to send him to a better cheder. He is such a good student. But I can hardly even afford to send him to*

Mendel's second-rate school. Aaron would make a good rabbi. Thank the Lord for the few dollars my older sons send from America even though they've never met their brother. Without that money from Lemel and Simeon, Aaron would have to attend the community school with all the orphans and the least-educated teachers. I know he wants to go on to study at the yeshiva, but I don't see how I could pay for it. Aaron would have to earn a scholarship from the Jewish community league. I can tell that Aaron has no interest in staying here and running the family bakery. So this will be the end of the line for the business. Well, it's time. Everything changes. Such is God's way.

Yitzchak knew that he would never see his older sons again. Like thousands of others in Eastern Europe, they had chafed under the rule of the Russian monarchy. Some of these young Jews organized an attempt to establish a Jewish homeland in Palestine. Others joined the new Bolshevik party in an effort to overthrow the monarchy and improve the situation in their own country. Lemel and Simeon chose to join the thousands of their brethren who emigrated to the new world looking for a better life. Just after their mother died, they said goodbye to their father and grandfather and left for the new world of America. They had already managed to start their own small bakery in a place called Philadelphia. As far as Yitzchak could tell, they seemed to be making a decent life for themselves.

* * *

Aaron rose with the dawn. His excitement and anxiety grew as the time approached for the most important Sabbath service of his young life. After a small breakfast of fruit and tea, the

Pechtrowicz family walked to the synagogue, meeting many well-wishing congregants along the way.

"Good luck, Aaron."

"I know you'll do just fine."

Aaron wasn't so sure. He sat with his father, whose slightly hunched back was covered with a large white woolen prayer shawl. They sat in the front row of the sanctuary just before the altar. His mother, as required by custom, sat in the balcony with the other women; each woman's head was covered by a 'sheytl,' a wig of modesty. Aaron was wearing an elaborate prayer shawl that had originally belonged to his paternal grandfather.

As Aaron began his chanting of the Holy Scriptures, he worried that his adolescent voice would break during his performance. He was relieved that his newfound tenor voice rose robustly over the altar and carried to every corner of the house of worship.

His parents listened with tears in their eyes, both thinking similar thoughts. *Amazing. Just a few short months ago his voice was high and cracking. Now it is the voice of a man. Before long, he'll be leaving home, and we'll be alone again. I wonder how that will feel?*

Even Rabbi Roznowski was impressed with Aaron's stellar performance. *I must keep my eye on this boy. With the proper development, he may be a candidate for the yeshiva.*

Rivka had outdone herself in preparing the celebration feast. There was gefilte fish with horseradish, chopped herring decorated with rings of pickled onion, chopped liver topped with hardboiled egg, veal with green beans and potatoes, and a dish of broad noodles with raisins. She had even brewed the sweet cherry wine used to bless the momentous event.

After everyone had left, Yitzchak sat down with a sigh in his large old leather chair by the open hearth. The heat of the fire felt good. His bones were aching; he could feel the insidious tentacles of old age advancing upon him.

"Come here, son," he called.

Aaron knelt by his father's side as his mother watched intently from across the room. He knew that he would be receiving some sort of gift. He expected a small amount of money or a new book. He planned to put any money that he received into his yeshiva fund.

The boy waited expectantly as Yitzchak slowly drew something from the pocket of his black Sabbath frock. Aaron's eyes grew large as he focused on the richly textured, wine-colored velvet pouch that emerged. On one side, embroidered in golden silk thread, was a six-pointed Star of David; on the other side, stitched in the same golden thread, was his name in Hebrew letters. Glancing across the room, he saw his mother smiling sweetly.

It must have taken her hours to cut and embroider this beautiful pouch. He felt a surge of love and gratefulness rising within.

Aaron gingerly took the pouch. Rubbing the rich fabric between his fingers and thumb, he felt something irregularly round and thin inside. With great excitement, he untied the drawstrings and pulled them open. Inside, he saw a shiny object, which he carefully removed and examined in the glint of the setting sun. It was an ancient silver coin polished to a bright sheen by his father.

Aaron caught his breath. It was the oldest coin that he had ever seen. He knew that it must be extremely valuable. He ran across the room and gave his mother a hug. Then, stepping back to his father's side, he bent down and kissed his father's cheek.

"Thank you, papa," he said. "I'll save this to sell for tuition at the yeshiva."

Yitzchak leaned back in his chair and shut his eyes. His thoughts were conflicted. He wanted Aaron to remain in Jelzai. He knew that, if his son could somehow manage to become a rabbi, having achieved the highest status of citizenship in the Jewish community, he would be unlikely to leave his native shtetl. It would also fulfill the unspoken dream that Yitzchak once had for himself.

Yitzchak opened his eyes and gazed lovingly at the face of his son. As he smiled wistfully at the boy's lingering expression of surprise, his words came slowly but forcefully. "No, son. You must hold on to the coin. Even though your attending the yeshiva is an important goal for all of us, your mother and I have given this to you for a different purpose. It's an expression of our family tradition. It's an heirloom that has been passed down through our family from generation to generation. No one even knows exactly how old it is. My father told me it dates back many centuries to Germany. Our ancestors brought it with them when they left Germany because of religious persecution. They eventually settled in our little village of Jelzai."

"But why didn't you give this to Lemel or Simeon?" asked Aaron.

Yitzchak knew that this question was coming. He answered gravely. "Ordinarily, this coin would have passed to your half-brother Simeon, but he and his brother left for America before my father died, so the coin was not in my possession. I'll probably never see them again. I never expected to have another son, another gift from God to whom I could pass on this treasure. I don't want to wait like my father did. I want you to have it now. Eventually, it will be passed down to your own son and your son's son. With it will go the memories and stories of our family, for it is said that, as long as one person has memories of another, that person remains as if alive."

It's pretty funny to think about me being a father and having a son. Nevertheless, Aaron was flattered by his father's words. He felt he was finally being treated as a 'grown-up.' He had more questions. "But papa, we are Jewish. Why is the Christian cross on this coin?"

"That's a good question, Aaron. My father explained that, back in those ancient times, each region minted its own coins. Because the German government was connected to the church, all coins were hand stamped with religious symbols.

"Papa, please tell me more about our history here."

Yitzchak didn't know where to start, but he did his best to summarize for Aaron what he had been able to glean from conversations with his own father. As the evening faded into night, he talked, and his son listened eagerly.

"The Pechtrowicz family has run the bakery for as long as anyone can remember in this little village of Jelzai; as you know, it is called Jelcis by the Christians. Your ancestors lived through terrible periods when the land was fought over and divided by Russia, Austria, and Prussia. Up until the late seventeen hundreds, the Jews managed to thrive here. But, at the close of the eighteenth century, Russia took possession of vast territories in the Ukraine and Lithuania along with part of Poland. The government has always been antisemitic and has forbidden Jews to live in Imperial Russia. But, when it took possession of these new territories, it suddenly inherited the largest Jewish population in the world.

"You mean we are part of the largest Jewish population in the world?" asked Aaron. "Wow! I never knew that."

Yitzchak continued with great effort.

"To deal with this new situation, the Russian government created the 'Pale of Settlement,' a restricted territory outside of which Jews were not authorized to live. However, even here, the government severely limits our ability to function. We are prohibited from owning land and cannot practice law or medicine. Banking is also barred."

* * *

Yitzchak wondered whether he should go on with the next part of his narrative. *Aaron is old enough to handle the truth,* he decided. *He deserves to know what he will be dealing with.*

"To make matters worse, Jewish boys are required to serve in the Russian army, where they are mistreated and abused, often to the point of death. For years, the government has endorsed a policy of kidnapping Jewish boys, some as young as six or seven, and raising them as Christians in a military unit. Most of these boys die before they reach adulthood, and the ones who survive remember little of their early roots."

"Will that happen to me?" asked Aaron, frightened by the prospect.

"No, son. I have taken certain precautions to prevent that from happening."

Yitzchak didn't mention that he had made a point of befriending the local police chief and giving him a yearly 'gift' in order to make sure that Aaron's name would never be placed on the recruitment list.

Aaron was not only fascinated by his family's long history but also moved by his father's words. Before today, his father had never allowed himself to express so much emotion. It had never occurred to him that his father harbored such deep feelings about past and future generations.

Yitzchak kissed his son's head and then, as if embarrassed by such an open display of affection, pushed himself up from his chair and stood with great effort.

"Come," he said. "The sun is setting. It's time to milk the cow."

After completing his nightly chores, Aaron prepared for bed in the little cubicle that served as his sleeping area, which was just off the common room on one side of the great hearth that the family used for baking and cooking. He drew the flimsy curtain across the opening to the makeshift bedroom to give himself a modicum of privacy. The entrance to his parents' not much larger bedroom was on the opposite side of the common room so that they were as separated as possible.

He placed the velvet pouch with the coin in it under his pillow and rested his head directly above.

What a wonderful day.

Slowly, he drifted off to sleep.

Chapter Two

"**A**aron, get up!"

The shrill voice of his mother pierced the Sunday morning stillness.

"Aaron, this is the second time I've called you. You can't sleep your life away."

Startled, Aaron shoved his hand under the downy pillow to make sure that his treasure was still there. He was relieved to feel it's reassuring presence as he clutched it in his fist.

He willed himself out of bed and suddenly became acutely aware that his bladder was full. Quickly, he ran outside to relieve himself in the chilly outhouse before he wet his pants. He liked to watch the hot urine steam as it hit the cold air and disappeared into the hole in the ground.

Returning to the house, he washed his hands and face using the pitcher and basin, then donned his school clothing. Putting on his skullcap, he quickly chanted his morning prayers and raced out to the small yard behind the house to help his parents milk the cow and goat.

"Go inside and eat your breakfast!" he called to his mother and father, who were doing his chores as well as theirs. They were quite relieved to do as he asked.

His chores complete, Aaron gulped down a piece of bread with jam and grabbed the cloth rucksack containing his schoolbooks. His mother had put his lunch inside, a piece of leftover veal and an apple.

"I'm going to be very late for school this morning," said Aaron to his mother, "but I don't care. Sleeping late is worth getting yelled at in front of the class, even with Reb Mendel's bad breath in my face."

"Just don't make a habit of it," smiled Rivka. She was enormously pleased that her son so obviously appreciated the effort that she and her husband had expended to make the past weekend a memorable occasion. He was her pride and joy. For the first time in a long time, she thought about how disappointed her father had been that she was a girl and how much more disappointed he must have been that his second wife gave him yet another daughter. With that thought, she laughed inside.

It served him right.

Rivka had heard that her father had died from typhoid fever seven years after his youngest daughter was born, leaving the child to be raised alone by her mother. Ever the realist, Rivka wondered, What would I have done if that happened to me? I just can't imagine. At least I've had a husband who has taken care of me with love and tenderness. My life could have been much worse.

Aaron had been born just a year after their marriage. Rivka had to learn to be a wife, a baker, and a mother in a very short period of time. She was grateful for her husband's unending patience and tolerance of her inexperience. They had both worked hard to make the best of difficult circumstances, and she had grown to feel affection, if not love, for Yitzchak.

After all, what is love if not two people helping each other, taking care of each other, and easing life's burdens for each other as much as possible?

* * *

Rivka shook her head at the vagaries of life. She snapped back to reality as her son went flying out the front door, rucksack strapped to his back and shouting a running goodbye.

Aaron had already decided on a hiding place for his treasure. He would put it behind a loose brick above the hearth.

But first I want to show it to my friends at school. They'll be really jealous. He knew that such thoughts were sinful, but he couldn't help himself. Forgive me, God. I promise I'll never brag about it again after I show it to my classmates

The town was quiet as Aaron raced to school a distance that was ordinarily a fifteen-minute walk. He spotted a few Jewish shopkeepers beginning to open up, but there were no Christians to be seen.

Today might be the Christian Sabbath, but it's just another ordinary workday for the Jews.

The school was located in the teacher's rented house on the other side of the town square. It was just across the bridge that spanned the stream at the edge of the communal grazing meadow, a short distance along the road that led eventually to the manor house of Count Polonski, the Polish nobleman who owned the surrounding area.

Jelzai had about four thousand inhabitants, roughly half of whom were Christians and the other half Jews. The Jews were tradesmen, merchants, and artisans who lived mainly in the area around the central market square. Many, like Aaron and his family, inhabited small rooms behind their shops. The wealthier Jews usually lived further from the town center. They were the leaders of the councils and other organizations that developed the rules for the Jewish community and interacted with the local government. Most of the Christians lived outside the town and farmed or owned fruit orchards.

Aaron ran through the town square toward the bridge, one hand holding on to his skullcap and the other covering the pocket in which he had stuffed the velvet pouch. He liked the feeling of the cool spring wind blowing through his long, uncut earlocks. He knew that he did some of his best thinking when he was alone, running outdoors through the lovely countryside. He wondered how it came to be that Jews and Christians should be so different.

* * *

Once, about a year ago, Aaron had asked his father about it. "Papa, why do they make fun of us and hate us so?"

Yitzchak had sighed and sat down in his chair with a heavy heart. He remembered pondering those same questions as a boy.

When he summoned enough courage to ask his own father about it, the latter's face had reddened, his fists had tightened, and he had snapped angrily, "Don't ask so many questions! Things are what they are." Then his father had remained withdrawn and visibly upset for days afterward. Yitzchak was frightened and never brought up the subject again.

But I don't want to discourage Aaron's curiosity and search for understanding.

He had considered the question quietly for a few moments while his son sat next to him on the floor patiently waiting.

"I truly don't know the entire answer to that question. I suppose they hate us because we have such different customs and beliefs. We dress differently and pray differently. But, most of all, they believe their messiah has already come. And they don't understand why we won't accept that belief, especially since their messiah was one of us, a Jewish rabbi who lived centuries ago. I don't know for sure. It's a subject none of our people will speak of openly, but I think they hold us responsible for the death of this rabbi, and so they take it out on us."

Tears had filled Yitzchak's eyes and rolled down his face. Aaron was frozen in place, afraid to breathe and uncertain how to react to his father's unexpected show of raw emotion.

Rivka had realized that something unusual was going on and come over to listen, but Yitzchak silently dismissed her with a flick of his wrist. This was not a subject for women.

Finally, Yitzchak had pulled himself together and been able to go on.

"Wherever we go in the world, we're tolerated for a while, and then, when the country begins to have some troubles that aren't our fault, they blame everything on us and tell us we must accept their beliefs or else we must leave. It's happened in many countries over many years. Our family has been here in Jelzai for hundreds of years. My grandfather said that, until the time of my great-grandfather, we lived here in peace and prosperity with our neighbors. But when Russia conquered this country, everything changed. Things got worse."

"What happened, Papa?"

"The tsars are more interested in lining their pockets with gold than doing what's in the best interest of their citizens. And so they've heavily taxed their people and not treated them very well. When the Russian peasants begin to get angry with them, the government blames the Jews and encourages the common people to come after us. We've always been easy targets."

This was the first time Yitzchak had ever allowed himself to talk about these things with anyone. He had felt guilty about discussing it with his young son, but also enormous relief from finally being able to say the things that he had held inside for so long.

Yitzchak had continued, "Here in Jelzai, it hasn't been as bad as in some other places. A few years ago, in Kiev, soldiers stirred up the peasants, and they attacked the Jews in the city. They burned down Jewish houses and shops, stole Jewish property, and attacked Jewish women and children. Many were raped and murdered. Then the peasants went on to other towns in the area and did the same thing. So far, we've been lucky it hasn't happened here."

Aaron had learned that antisemitic sentiment peaked around Christian holidays, such as Christmas and Easter, when the churches preached sermons characterizing the Jews as 'Christ-killers.' The invective stirred up the masses, creating a tinderbox environment where any small incident might trigger an unexpected attack on Jewish shops and homes. He also realized that the Easter holiday, which usually occurred near Passover, was fast approaching and wondered whether this year would bring a dreaded pogrom.

At that moment, Aaron's musings were interrupted, for he spotted two figures ahead of him blocking his path across the bridge. They were laughing tipsily and pointing at him. Aaron recognized them as two loud young farmhands who often came to town on Saturday evenings, caroused all night at the local tavern, and then attended early mass before returning home to sleep it off.

* * *

Oh no! I know they're going to give me a hard time. It would have to happen today. What if they take my coin? Maybe God's punishing me for being so prideful.

Aaron noticed that he was more worried about losing his precious coin than he was about the possibility of being beaten up. He was somewhat surprised and pleased at this reaction. I'll handle myself like a man.

"Hey, Jew boy!" called the taller of the two, a blond youth, in slurred Polish. "Where ya rushin' to? Ya late for church?"

With that, the pair burst into another round of raucous laughter.

Aaron tried to ignore them and pretend that he didn't understand what they were saying, but they weren't put off. Everyone knew that, though the Jews spoke Yiddish as their mother tongue, most spoke the local dialect as well. It was the language of village commerce.

"Oh! Too stuck up to talk to us goyim," snarled the shorter one.

Aaron wasn't surprised that these bullies knew the Yiddish word for 'gentiles.' Most local Christians had picked up a few words from the Jews. Some even spoke fluent Yiddish.

Aaron tried to go around the youths, but they cut him off, blocking his movement in any direction.

"You need a haircut," said the taller one, yanking hard on one of Aaron's long earlocks.

"Yeah! And a new hat!" added the second as he grabbed Aaron's skullcap and threw it on the ground. "This one won't keep you very warm."

Aaron was frightened and unsure of his next move. Before he could think about it, the larger youth noticed Aaron's hand unconsciously protecting his pants pocket.

"What you got in there, Jew boy? Lemme see!"

Now Aaron was really scared. He knew that they would take his coin without a qualm and wished he hadn't been so stupid as to carry it to school.

Please, God, help me.

However, his body froze. It was too late to run.

"I said, lemme see," repeated the burly farmhand.

Before Aaron knew what was happening, the Polish youths pushed him to the hard ground. His nose struck a large rock and began to bleed, and his pants ripped at the knee. As one boy held him down, the other shoved his hand into Aaron's pants pocket and roughly yanked out the velvet pouch with the coin inside.

"What have we here?" sneered the youth as he removed the precious coin from the pouch. "You must have stolen this from a good Christian. I'll return it for you." Both farmhands laughed uproariously.

As Aaron lay on the hard, now bloodstained gravel, his mind numb with desperation and hopelessness, he heard a deep and unfamiliar voice from behind his line of vision.

* * *

"What's going on here, boys?" boomed the voice. Aaron painfully turned his head and saw a tall, well-dressed man standing behind him. He recognized the man as Count Polonski, the ancestral lord of the village, who happened to be walking to his manor house on the other side of the bridge.

"Oh, nothing," replied one of the farmhands. "We found this coin on the Jew and knew he must have stolen it."

The count examined the embroidered pouch and coin.

"This doesn't look stolen to me. I think you'd better get to church and go right to confession. And don't let me catch you doing anything like this again."

The two farmhands slouched off, muttering under their breath something about "traitor" and "Jew lover."

The count helped the grateful lad up from the ground, pulled out a white linen handkerchief, and used it to staunch the blood that was still trickling from Aaron's nose. Then he brushed the dust from the boy's clothing as best he could.

"I apologize for the terrible behavior of my countrymen," said the count. "Let me know if it ever happens again." He handed the velvet pouch and coin back to Aaron and, without another word, went on his way.

Aaron walked slowly to school thinking about what had happened. He endured a harsh lecture from his teacher without comment. He was unable to concentrate on the lessons. Most of the day, he silently prayed for forgiveness from God for the sin of pride. Then he thanked God for giving him a second chance. Even when Max, 'the fartzer,' was able to produce a record-breaking string of ten loud, gaseous blasts on command, he didn't join in the classroom laughter. He kept the pouch and coin hidden in his pocket until he returned home that evening, as usual, after dark.

I promise you, God, that I'll always obey your commandments. I've learned my lesson.

Chapter Three

Aaron was particularly subdued for the next few months. He was still shaken by the incident with the two Polish ruffians. Every morning on his way to school, he kept a watch for their possible presence, especially on Sundays. He was afraid that they might try to take revenge on him for being reprimanded by Count Polonski. He was also very embarrassed about how close he had come to losing the coin, which had been part of his family's history for so long. Moreover, he was at a loss to understand the different responses of the Christians he had encountered. Until now, he had assumed all Christians to be similar in their attitudes toward Jews. Now he was confused and didn't know what to think.

"Why are you so quiet?" his mother would ask.

"The classwork is difficult. I'm working hard to understand it, mother," he would answer. "How is your work going with the community relief society?"

"We've already had many births this month, and I've been present at every one. So many children born since we founded the society a few years ago!"

Aaron knew that she was proud of her work and liked to talk about it. Whenever he wanted to distract her from conversation about himself, all that he had to do was steer her into a conversation about the society. It worked every time.

By the time September rolled around, Aaron was feeling better. He was able to concentrate more on his schoolwork and was convinced that the rabbi would eventually recommend his entrance into the yeshiva.

In October, just after the High Holy Days, Aaron came home from class on a Friday afternoon as the entire Jewish community prepared for the Sabbath. The smell of gefilte fish being cooked permeated the village streets. Yitzchak had already left for his weekly dip in the communal bathhouse, but Aaron, who usually accompanied his father, was a bit late that day. Unlike most Friday afternoons, when the house was filled with the delectable aromas of Sabbath cooking, his nostrils rebelled at the acrid scent of something burning. A pot was pouring gray smoke while his mother paced obliviously back and forth in front of the hearth sobbing and shaking silently.

"Mother, what's wrong?"

Rivka didn't answer.

"Mother, what's the matter?" Aaron repeated in a louder voice.

Finally, Aaron's loud voice penetrated Rivka's emotional wall and she turned to look at him with a tear-stained face.

Trying to pull herself together so as not to alarm her son, Rivka said, "I received some upsetting news today." Then she fell silent again.

"What about?" asked Aaron, fearing that something had happened to his father.

Through her sobs, Rivka replied, "My stepmother died, and my sister Rebecca has nowhere to go. The community wants to send her here to live with us. She's only thirteen, and I'm her only living relative."

"But why are you so upset? Your father died years ago, and you didn't even know your stepmother."

With that, Rivka burst into another round of weeping.

"How can we afford to take in another mouth to feed?" she managed to gasp. "We can barely support ourselves."

Aaron placed his arm around his mother's shoulders.

"Calm down," he said, "When papa comes home, we'll sit down and think of something."

For the first time, it struck Aaron that he felt grown up. He realized that he and his mother had switched roles. It was a new feeling, but a good one.

* * *

Rebecca arrived at the Pechtrowicz household in early December carrying her belongings in a large woven basket. Her hometown community had paid for the coach ticket to Jelzai, a journey of sixty miles. Four to eight wagons caravanned once or twice a week between the towns, carrying freight as well as passengers. The journey took a full day including the three or four rest stops.

Rebecca seemed the epitome of a modest, well-brought-up young girl. She was of average height, with shoulder-length brown hair and clear green eyes. Her womanly features were already well-developed at the age of thirteen. She seemed happy in her new surroundings. She spoke softly but not very often. It simply seemed that she wanted to intrude as little as possible on the day-to-day lives of her sister's family. She spoke little about her former life and was careful not to do so.

I like it here. If they ever found out what things were like in my house, they'd kick me out without a second thought.

Rivka didn't press her to talk about herself, but, secretly, she had many unasked questions.

I wonder what her mother was like and how she managed to support the two of them. Did our father treat her as insensitively as he treated me? Did she hate him the way that I did?

However, Rivka felt awkward asking such personal questions of a virtual stranger. As Rebecca quickly became acquainted with the daily household routine, her eagerness to help diminished Rivka's initial worries. Soon, Rivka was feeling not only grateful but also dependent on the assistance she was receiving. She had forgotten how good it felt to be able to share household responsibilities with another woman. As winter melted into spring, the life of the family took on the rhythm of a pleasant, peaceful routine.

Rebecca had never felt so content. Her prior existence had been one of instability and intimidation by the men whom her mother brought into the house, the ones she was told to call 'uncle.'

I'm part of the family here. They don't fight. And Aaron is so cute.

Aaron felt quite self-conscious whenever he was around Rebecca, especially when they were alone in the house. He had no sisters and was not knowledgeable in the ways of young women. He wondered how much body covering he needed as he moved about the house or made a trip to the outhouse. He didn't know what kinds of things to say to her, and their verbal interactions were limited. Rebecca would smile at him and make small conversation, mainly during the evening meal and on the Sabbath. The rest of the time, they were rarely together.

He did notice that Rebecca would go out of her way to try to please him.

"Would you like another serving of meat?" she would ask at dinner, or "Can I get you a glass of hot tea while you study?"

Aaron wasn't quite sure how to respond to her politeness. He was not experienced enough to recognize the seductive nature of her behavior. Rebecca was an attractive young woman with shining eyes and a body that had already ripened. The pubescent young man began to notice his own body reacting physically to her presence, especially at night when he studied by the oil lamp near the fire. He could see her shadow as she undressed by candlelight behind the curtain of her cubicle. Rivka had set up a small bed and table for her on the other side of the hearth from Aaron's bedroom. Try as he might to stifle it, he began to experience new and pleasant sensations in his groin as he watched her movements behind the curtain. Sometimes, he imagined, she was deliberately moving and swaying for his benefit, but he knew it must be a product of his fantasies.

I should be ashamed of thinking something like that.

And he would cover his stiff, pointy lap with shirt flaps or an open book so that his mother or father would not notice if they happened to come out of their bedroom.

His father slept like a log once he retired for the night and never emerged until morning. Rivka, aware of the possibilities, would occasionally venture out into the common area to tell Aaron to go to bed. He learned to keep his jacket next to the chair so that when he stood up he could hold it in front of him to hide his tented trousers.

Three months after Rebecca's arrival, Rivka was called out one night by the childbirth society to help deliver a new baby. Aaron studied that night as usual but didn't feel the need to cover up his lap as he usually did. He unconsciously massaged himself as he watched Rebecca's shadow move behind the drawn curtain. He was suddenly surprised to feel a wetness on his pants and hands and panicked as he noticed it had also soiled part of the chair.

What will I do if mama comes home and sees this mess?

The boy grabbed a kitchen rag, wetted it, and cleaned up as best he could. He hoped that his mother wouldn't notice the wet marks on the chair and on his clothing.

Aaron went to bed that night wondering what had happened to him and vowing never to let it happen again. He felt terribly guilty. After all, Rebecca was his aunt, even though she was younger than him. She was part of his family. How could he have done such a thing? He wished he had someone to talk to about it, but these things were not to be discussed, even with friends, and especially not with his parents.

If she did notice anything, Rivka never mentioned it. The family went on as before. Aaron continued to study by the fire but was very wary of letting the same thing happen.

One night several weeks later, Rivka was again called upon to deliver a baby. Despite his vow, Aaron could not resist giving in to the torrent of adolescent hormones raging through his body. Once again he sat in the chair caressing himself and fantasizing with his eyes closed. This time he had put a rag nearby to clean up any mess. He imagined what Rebecca's body would look like if the curtain were not pulled.

Into his reverie came the perfumed aroma of newly washed hair. He felt a soft hand placed upon his own. Opening his eyes, he saw Rebecca kneeling before him in her nightgown. The swell of her young breasts was touching his knee. She put her fingers to his lips to prevent him from speaking. Before he knew what was happening, Rebecca had begun softly rubbing his body producing strange and wonderful sensations he had never before experienced. As his arousal grew, she took him into the moistness of her mouth. Aaron was so shocked he was mute. All he could do was remain passive as Rebecca stimulated him in ways he could never have imagined. As passion built within, he lost himself. Time disappeared. The eruption came suddenly. Before he had a chance to collect himself, Rebecca stood up, quietly slipped back into her cubicle, and closed the curtain. She knew that she had behaved impulsively and worried that she might get into trouble.

That was something my mother would have done. I hope he doesn't tell his parents.

Aaron could not think, let alone move. Luckily, his mother was out later than usual. It took him a long time to collect himself sufficiently to move into his bedroom. Just a few minutes later, he heard the squeaking of the front door signaling his mother's return. He lay awake most of the night trying to figure out just what had happened.

Aaron knew only a minimal amount about the rudimentary facts of sex. He had watched farm animals copulate and been present when the cow and sheep delivered young. Other than that, he was a complete innocent. As unsophisticated as he was, though, he knew that what had happened between him and Rebecca was not right. The biblical laws proscribed any carnal contact between a man and his mother's sister. Yet, somehow, this seemed different. Rebecca was his age, even a little younger, and he had never truly known her as a family member. He wondered how she had come by her knowledge. He suspected that her prior life had been a difficult one. Yet, astonishingly, it did not occur to him to think of her as 'bad' or 'immoral.' In fact, he began to think of her as grown up and mature in ways that he couldn't hope to match. He wondered whether his parents were aware of the scope of Rebecca's knowledge and activities.

The next morning at breakfast, Rebecca acted the same as usual. She helped with the morning chores and breakfast. She made no sly eye contact with Aaron that might tip his parents off to any unusual activity.

Aaron said nothing to his parents. He waited for the next evening when his mother would be called away with a mixture of dread and anticipation. He wondered what would happen next and how he would respond. He tried to prepare himself to turn away any contact Rebecca might initiate. Over and over he rehearsed his speech.

"No, this is wrong," he would say. "You're my aunt, and this is a sin."

But he would have to say it softly enough to avoid waking his father.

His opportunity arrived about one month later. There was a childbirth emergency, and Rivka warned her family she would probably be gone the entire night. When Rivka left, Aaron was about to commence his usual study practice in the common area but panicked at the thought of possibly having to face Rebecca.

* * *

I'll take the coward's way out.

He decided to skip his study session that night and on any other night that his mother might be away. Aaron visited the outhouse, then undressed in his bedroom and put on his nightshirt. He blew out the candle and tried to go to sleep. He couldn't help thinking about what had happened before and what might have happened if he had remained in the common area. Just to think about it was stimulating.

Rebecca had watched her mother, Zelda, struggle to eke out an existence. Zelda had been forced to marry an older man much like Rivka had been. But Zelda's husband, unlike Rivka's, was an uncaring, unloving, and selfish man who never made a sufficient living to meet his family's needs. With no one to help support them upon her husband's death, Zelda was forced into a life of prostitution to feed her daughter and herself.

Rebecca grew up with a series of men passing through her life. She did not attend school; education was only for men. The skills that she developed were those of a seductress.

With no man to provide the essentials for a stable life, Rebecca soon realized that her only chance for a decent existence was to find a man willing to marry her. Having no dowry or family resources, she had decided that she had better take advantage of her present situation while she could. Besides, she appreciated Aaron's childlike innocence, which gave her a sense of control over at least one thing in her life of which others had little knowledge. She had come to the conclusion that she wanted to marry Aaron and went after her goal in the only way that she knew how.

As Aaron hovered in that dreamlike state between sleep and wakefulness, he felt a warm hand sliding under his comforter and working its way beneath his nightshirt. The hand gently massaged his body as if it had a roadmap of its most sensitive areas. As he became more fully awake, Aaron tried to push Rebecca away. But by this time she had slipped off her nightgown and crawled into bed next to him. The smooth friction of her skin against his was electric—like satin against satin. The rhythmic movements of her body beckoned his into a reciprocal response. She slowly pulled herself astride him. He was learning another new dance—a dance which lifted him to a heaven that his holy books had never mentioned. As his tension burst within her after what seemed like eternity, he lay back trying to catch his breath—confused about what to do next.

Finally able to breathe again, he gasped, "You're my mother's sister. How can you do this"?

"I am in love with you, Aaron. I've loved you since the moment I walked into this house. How can love be sinful?"

Aaron was too spent to argue or think clearly. He rolled over and closed his eyes as Rebecca stood up, re-dressed, and left his bedroom.

I hope I'm doing it right, she thought. I think that's how mama did it.

* * *

Household life went on as usual, and so did the love trysts, whenever the opportunity afforded. Aaron wondered whether God would punish him for these transgressions but always ended up accepting Rebecca's statement that anything based on love could not be a sin. He knew that the argument didn't hold much water, so he kept telling himself that he would end it after each encounter. But the physical pleasure that he was receiving outweighed the guilt he was experiencing.

God will understand. I'll pray for forgiveness on the next Day of Atonement.

Chapter Four

"Aaron, you've been looking very tired lately," remarked his mother. "Have you been studying too hard?"

"I've been studying hard, but I've been learning a lot, mother," he replied smugly. *I wonder what she'd say if she knew what I've really been learning. And I'll bet I know more than any of my friends about sex.* Aaron had somehow found a way to compartmentalize his guilt in a corner of his mind.

"Rosh Hashanah comes next week, and I've barely started to cook for the new year holidays," Rivka continued. "I've asked Rebecca to help prepare the food, but she hasn't been feeling well and is spending a lot of time in her bedroom."

This information surprised Aaron. Rebecca hadn't said anything to him about feeling sick. He walked over to her curtained-off cubicle and asked if he could come in. He smelled vomit as he approached her bed.

"Please stay away. I'm not feeling well."

"What's wrong, Rebecca?"

She thought, *I think I'm going to die,* but she answered, "I'm sick to my stomach."

"Did you eat something that didn't agree with you?"

"I don't think so. This has been happening for a few days."

Rebecca truly didn't understand what was happening to her. She had learned the art of sexual seduction by secretly observing her mother. But the girl was ignorant about other matters of sex, including pregnancy and childbirth. She noticed her breasts becoming swollen and tender and her abdomen beginning to enlarge but didn't know why these things were happening. Her mind hadn't even registered the cessation of her menses. Between the nausea and the other changes, she was feeling miserable and lost.

What's happening to me? This never happened to my mother!

Aaron, of course, was even more ignorant than Rebecca.

"I think you should talk to mama," he said. "She'll know what to do."

* * *

Rivka was desperate. She blamed herself for taking Rebecca into the house and then for not monitoring their interactions more closely. She was very angry with the youngsters but even angrier with herself.

If I don't find a way to end this pregnancy, our lives will be ruined. Aaron will never attend the yeshiva, and I'll be to blame. Yitzchak's heart will be broken. He'll hate me for the rest of my life. And he'll be right! The child will be a bastard and will be rejected wherever it goes. Oh, what shall I do?

* * *

The fate of Rebecca never crossed her mind.

Rivka decided to keep the information from Yitzchak.

If I'm not successful he'll know soon enough.

"Don't say anything to your father about Rebecca," she warned Aaron.

Rivka was familiar with the folk beliefs of pregnancy and abortion. She prepared several large doses of castor oil.

"Drink this," she ordered, as Rebecca forced them down her throat, gagging. I don't want to drink that, but if I don't she'll make me leave.

"And," Rivka added, "lift as many heavy things as you can."

These actions resulted in increased nausea and vomiting, but Rebecca remained pregnant.

Rivka tried again. I need something stronger!

"May I please have some feverfew and quinine," she asked old lady Mentzer, who sold herbs in the marketplace. When the woman gave her a questioning glance, she replied, "I've been having terrible headaches and cramps." The seller seemed satisfied.

She ground the herbs into powdered form and concocted a hot, ill-tasting tea. Rebecca did not want to drink the bitter brew but could not stand up to her sister's demands.

Surely, this will be strong enough to bring on Rebecca's monthly cycle.

Once again, the result was nausea and vomiting but no bleeding.

* * *

Through her connections with the childbirth aid society, Rivka had occasional contact with the shadowy world of abortion. So far, she had not divulged her secret to any of her colleagues, but, by now, she knew that the pregnancy was past the early stages. In her desperation, she approached a Christian man who was reputed to have been a physician before alcohol and venereal disease ruined his practice and reputation.

"What can you give me that will guarantee the desired result?" she asked. She couldn't bring herself to use the words 'pregnancy' or 'miscarriage.'

"I can give you something that's very strong but may harm the mother,"' he replied. "It's called potassium permanganate and is used to counteract certain poisons. But it's very dangerous."

The state of Rebecca's health was, in truth, the least of Rivka's concerns. She occasionally caught herself hoping her sister would die from all this.

That would solve all our problems.

She paid the doctor for the small bag of pale pink crystals

* * *

Taking the crystals home, she prepared them as directed, mixing the tiny heap into a small glass of red wine. She instructed Rebecca to drink the solution.

"What is it?"

"Don't worry. It won't hurt you."

"But I don't want to drink it."

"You must, or I'll talk to Yitzchak, and he'll kick you out."

For the third time, against her will, Rebecca acquiesced to

her sister's wish. I hate her. That devil woman is trying to kill me.

About fifteen minutes later, Rebecca experienced the first pains in her abdomen. The burning pain grew worse. Soon she began to vomit copious amounts of purple-black material that resembled coffee grounds. Purple spittle ran down the sides of her mouth. She fainted and fell to the floor.

Rivka didn't know what to do. She was feeling quite guilty about the horror she had brought about. I'll be a murderer twice over."

She could no longer handle the situation by herself. She finally took Yitzchak aside and tearfully explained what had happened.

"Why have you kept this from me?" he demanded.

"I hadn't the heart to ruin your dreams."

"You may have killed your sister in the process!" he shouted as he hobbled out of the house, slamming the door behind him.

Though Jews were not permitted to attend medical school, in each village in which they lived was at least one man or woman with some medical experience who served as the doctor.

Yitzchak raced as fast as he could to the house of Kenchek, the local medicine man, and brought him back to the house behind the bakery.

The treatment consisted of forcing as much water as possible down Rebecca's throat to wash out the toxic chemical. Over the course of a few hours, her vomiting subsided, and she fell into an exhausted sleep.

"It's a good thing I got here when I did," said Kenchek. "Otherwise, she would have surely died."

Rivka thanked God that he hadn't granted her wish.

Aaron was terribly upset and, in his innocence, did not comprehend what was going on. All that he understood was that Rebecca was very sick. Rivka certainly did not discuss the situation with him. He was, at least, happy that Rebecca seemed to be recovering.

Yitzchak, with a heavy heart, knew that the family had reached a point that would change the future forever. Only he understood that any possible solution would be unhappy for all.

When Rebecca woke, she regretted bringing unhappiness into the family. However, once she realized that she was going to have a baby, she was secretly pleased that Aaron would now be bound to her in a physical way.

"Thank you, God, for saving my baby. I know you did this so Aaron will marry me. I know he will."

* * *

Once the medical crisis had passed, Aaron worked up the courage to confront his mother.

"What's wrong with Rebecca, and why have you been giving her horrible things to drink?" he demanded.

Rivka knew that her son understood next to nothing about sex. She toyed with the idea of keeping the truth from him but, to her credit, realized that such a gambit would backfire and create more dissension between them. Nevertheless, Aaron couldn't miss the anger in her voice.

"Rebecca is pregnant. She is going to have a baby. And you are the father. Do you understand what that means?"

Aaron was stunned into silence. He walked to the fireplace, slumped into a chair, and stared unblinkingly at the dancing flames.

Finally, he said to no one in particular, "I'm going to be a father? How can that be?"

"Go to bed," said his mother. "We'll discuss this in the morning.

* * *

That night, Aaron, like Jacob centuries before him, wrestled with the angels.

I'm too young to get married. It's as much my fault as hers. I could have stopped it if I really wanted. I'll never be able to attend yeshiva. I don't want to stay here and run the bakery. But, if I don't marry her, she'll be sent away with the baby. To where? To what? I can't let them do that.

Aaron fell into a fitful sleep. He wondered whether God was angry enough to strike him down while he slept.

That might be the best solution.

He drifted off to sleep.

The next morning, Yitzchak and Rivka called Aaron into their bedroom where they could speak without being overheard by Rebecca.

"We have decided that Rebecca must leave. She can't stay here any longer," said Rivka.

"But where will she go?"

"We'll give her some money and buy her a ticket to Vilna. From there on she'll be on her own."

"What will happen to the baby?"

"We can't worry about that. That's her problem."

"That's my problem, mother. How can I allow my own child to die or to grow up without a father? I'll marry her."

"That isn't possible, even if we agreed to it," chimed in Yitzchak. She's your mother's sister and you know that the law won't permit such a marriage. There is no other recourse but to send her away."

"Aaron, do you understand the seriousness of this situation?" Rivka began again. "If she doesn't leave, you'll have to give up the yeshiva and all the other things you want to do with your life. You can never marry her. Your children will grow up as outcasts. They will be mamzers, bastards. No one will want to have anything to do with you or them."

For the first time in his life, Aaron turned his back on his parents, walked out of their bedroom, stormed outside and slammed the front door. His father and mother made no move to force him to go to school.

All day, he lay in his bed staring up at the inside of the tin ceiling.

Lord, I know you're punishing me for all the sins I've committed. And I know I deserve it. But must I choose between giving up Your work and casting away this girl bearing my child to a solitary life of grief and sorrow with no one to take care of her? Please, Lord, help me find another way.

"It's dinner time," called Rivka outside his closed door.

Silence.

Aaron fasted and prayed in his room until the next morning. After a tortured night of struggling to find an answer, he left his bed and pulled open the curtain to his cubicle. Exhausted and sleepless, he emerged from his bedroom and moved wearily into the sitting area. With a surprising determination that he had not shown before, he called together his mother and father.

"I know you love me very much," he began, "and only want what's best for me. But I could never live with myself knowing that I was responsible for destroying the life of Rebecca and my child. I can't just throw them away and pretend everything is all right. We'll go away to a place where no one knows us and somehow make a life together."

"Aaron, you can't do that. It will kill your father," cried Rivka. She was shocked at the next words from her husband's lips.

"We'll do whatever we can to help," he said.

Although Yitzchak was grieving, he respected his son for making an honorable but difficult decision. It seemed to him that his son had changed overnight from a wide-eyed innocent boy into a self-aware and determined man of action.

Rivka ran from the room.

Although Rebecca was not part of the family discussion, she could overhear everything as she cowered in her tiny bedroom area.

What have I done? Where will we go? What will happen to us?

* * *

Over the next several days, Aaron and Rebecca packed their

belongings while Yitzchak made arrangements for the carriage that would carry them to Vilna, the big city one hundred and twenty-five miles away. Rivka closeted herself in her bedroom. Just before they left, Aaron slowly walked to the hearth, removed the loose brick, and retrieved the pouch and coin that had given him so much joy just a year and a half ago.

I placed it there as a child, and I'm removing it as an adult.

He felt the weight of the world upon his shoulders and almost changed his mind, unable to bear the loss he was about to suffer.

Dressed in her long-skirted black mourning outfit, Rivka dragged herself from the bedroom, hugged Aaron for a last goodbye, and kissed him tenderly on the head.

"Goodbye, my son. May God be with you."

Ignoring Rebecca, she dragged herself back to her bedroom and softly closed the curtain.

Rebecca watched, gloating secretly. My mother was right. She told me what to do to get a man. He's choosing me over his own mother.

Then, she suddenly became aware of the mean-spiritedness of her thought and felt a sharp stab of guilt.

How can I do this to my own sister, who took me in when nobody else would?

Tearfully, Yitzchak embraced the broken dream of his future and slid what remained of his life savings—seventy-five rubles— into Aaron's pocket.

"Take care of each other, and God will take care of you."

While he mouthed the words of that old Yiddish truism, he secretly wondered how they could possibly survive. He thought he would never see his beloved son again.

I might as well die now. My life is over.

Each carrying a large, tightly packed wicker basket, the child parents-to-be trudged to the carriage that would carry them to their new life.

Chapter Five

"**A**aron, I'm scared," whispered Rebecca as she huddled in the corner of their seat. "I feel sick from the rocking, and I have a terrible headache. I think I would be better off dead. I can't take this anymore."

The horse-drawn coach with its twelve passengers was pulling into the outskirts of Vilnius—the Jews called it 'Vilna'—after an exhausting journey of two days. The seats were uncomfortable, and the constant bumping from the rutted dirt roads made their bodies ache. Despite occasional rest stops, the passengers were hungry and had gotten little sleep.

"Don't worry, we're almost there," answered Aaron. "It's almost Sabbath. When we arrive, we'll go to the synagogue and ask if someone can put us up overnight until we find a place to live."

Rebecca didn't answer but secretly thought, *I wonder if he knows what he's doing. What will happen to us?*

These words were the most that the couple had exchanged since embarking on their journey. They were still very uncomfortable in each other's presence and felt like strangers.

Neither innocent had an inkling of what was expected of them or how they were going to manage their lives. There was no one to guide them. Each felt frightened, lost, and unsure. The reality of the situation was just beginning to hit them, and Aaron wondered why he had made the decision to go away with Rebecca.

I must be very stupid or very brave.

Rebecca didn't know what to expect of her pregnancy. She had no idea how long it would last or what care she might need. Her childlike ignorance and utter dependence belied the seductress image that she tried to convey to Aaron.

I know he won't let anything bad happen to me. My mother told me that, if you please a man in bed, he'll do anything for you.

* * *

Vilna was a large city where Jews made up almost half the population. It had begun as a small town at the confluence of the Neris and Vilnia rivers in the twelfth century and flourished as a city of tolerance and freedom in a country of tolerance and freedom. Because of this, Jews flocked to Lithuania, and especially Vilna, from all over Europe in order to escape persecution. The city became affectionately known as the Jerusalem of the West because of its growing tradition of Jewish cultural, educational, and charitable activities. The Jews of Lithuania called themselves Litvaks and considered themselves a notch above other Eastern European Jews. Even after Russia gained control of the country in the late seventeen hundreds and antisemitism became blatant, the community managed to thrive.

The heart of that community was in the Old City or Jewish Quarter, where the Great Synagogue was located. Around the synagogue and its affiliated schools was a network of narrow cobblestone streets. The two- or three-story buildings were built with no separation between them, mostly of wood or brick covered with dirty white plaster. Jewish businesses and homes were clustered in this web of alleyways that radiated out from the synagogue.

The coach disembarked its passengers on the perimeter of Synagogue Square. Aaron spent several moments simply staring at the Great Synagogue, which he had heard so much about.

"Isn't it beautiful?" he asked, his voice filled with awe. "It must be wonderful to pray in a place like this. I know I'd feel closer to God."

How can he think about that at a time like this? Rebecca wondered. Aloud, she replied, "All I feel is sick and tired. I want to lie down and rest."

Not knowing what else to do, they picked up their heavy baskets and lugged them toward the enormous building.

Since the massive iron front gates had not yet been unlocked for the Sabbath, Aaron circled the property until he found a plain brown wooden door located just under a turret of the building. He knocked loudly.

"Who is it and whaddaya want?" came a gruff voice from inside. "Don't you know it's almost Sabbath, and I have work to do?"

"Sorry to bother you, sir, but my wife and I just arrived in town. She's pregnant, and we need to find lodging for the night."

Muttering under his breath, Shmulka the shammus opened the squeaking wooden door. He had been the caretaker of the synagogue for many years and didn't like his routine interrupted.

Shmulka glanced at the two youngsters standing in front of him, the boy so young and the girl with her belly just beginning to swell. He asked no questions. Compassion flooded his crotchety old bones. These children looked so lost and forlorn.

"Come in. When did you last eat?"

"Yesterday, sir."

"Well then, come with me."

Shmulka led them through a dark musty corridor that ended at the door to his small apartment at the rear of the synagogue and opened the door.

Rebecca was frightened. *Where is he taking us? Are we in danger?*

"Sit down," he said, pointing to a small, rickety wooden table and chairs in the kitchen.

Aaron and Rebecca did as they were asked.

The old man brought out the remnants of his lunch and added more bread and cheese to the platter.

"Here. You must be starved."

Rebecca's nausea had abated, and she gulped down a piece of rye bread with cheese. Aaron tried to be a little subtler, but quickly consumed three pieces of bread and cheese and washed the food down with a glass of milk.

"Thank you, sir. Please let me pay you for what we have eaten."

Shmulka didn't bother to reply to Aaron's statement.

"Where will you sleep tonight?'" he asked.

"I don't know sir. We're looking for a place."

"Tonight is the Sabbath. The whole city will be coming here to welcome her. I'll make some inquiries for you. In the meantime, rest here in my bed until I return."

He showed the tired couple into the little cubicle that served as his bedroom. Still in their clothes, they lay down.

"See? What did I tell you?" said Aaron. "We'll be okay."

"I hope you're right. We are truly in God's hands."

The young couple was asleep within a few minutes.

The next morning, they awakened confused and disoriented to banging on the bedroom door.

Shmulka fed Aaron and Rebecca a breakfast of cold hardboiled eggs and milk and then commanded, "Come with me."

The old caretaker walked at a surprisingly rapid gait as he marched the couple through the winding alleys of the ghetto area. After fifteen minutes, he stopped at an old, rundown house on the periphery of the Jewish quarter across the street from the cemetery.

"This is our shelter," he explained. "It's run by the hospitality society for travelers passing through or new residents who need temporary lodgings. The rooms here cost only two kopecks a day, and, if you don't have the money, you can pay the society back after you've found some work."

Aaron knew that the Jewish community taxed itself in order to provide such services for the poor.

"We have money," replied Aaron indignantly, pulling some coins from his pocket. He didn't want to be thought of as a poor drifter who would depend on community charity.

"Put that away," growled Shmulka. "Today is the Sabbath, and you shouldn't even be carrying money."

Aaron sheepishly placed the coins back in his pocket.

Already I've forgotten my Jewish training. He'll think I'm ignorant. What's happening to me?

Shmulka went on. "After you're settled here, you're invited to join Meir Kemelski and his wife for the midday meal. Meir operates a tavern not far from here and lives within walking distance. They would be honored if you accept their invitation."

Aaron knew that inviting strangers to the Sabbath meal was considered a good deed. It was a rare occurrence in his parents' home not only because they could not afford the extra food, but also because few strangers passed through their little village.

"Of course we'll be there! We're also honored."

After Shmulka left, Rebecca asked, "What will we tell them about ourselves and why we're here?"

"We'll just say all of our parents are dead and we wanted to start a new life in a new city."

"I hope they believe us. I don't know where we'll go if they don't let us stay here."

Just after noon, Aaron and Rebecca, having been guided by Shmulka's precise instructions, knocked on the Kemelskis' door.

"Come in, come in," said Meir Kemelski. "We've been looking forward to your arrival."

As he stepped inside the door, Aaron became immediately homesick. The fragrances redolent of the Sabbath meal hit his nasal passages and caused an immediate, physical reaction so strong that he had trouble speaking and almost started to cry.

Mama, I want to come home.

Meir Kemelski was a short, balding man in his mid-thirties. His left leg being two inches longer than his right, he walked with a distinct limp. He wore a heavy gold ring set with a two-carat ruby on his right hand. His three-story, well-appointed house reflected his considerable business accomplishments.

Malka Kemelski stood behind her husband at the doorpost. She was a painfully thin, scarecrow-like woman with pursed lips and widely separated teeth whose forehead seemed to hold a perpetual scowl. She had a large wart on her right cheek, and her black hair was pulled back in a tight knot. She didn't crack a smile and seemed uncomfortable with people. Her demeanor was intimidating, and Rebecca sensed that she was not happy with her husband's decision to invite guests for the Sabbath.

"She is a bitter woman. I don't like her at all," Rebecca whispered to Aaron.

* * *

"Thank you for your hospitality," Aaron said, directing his comment to the lady of the house as the meal began.

Malka simply nodded her head as she stared down at her plate of mostly untouched food.

"My wife is a woman of few words," Meir chimed in swiftly, "but she welcomes you as well."

Aaron nodded. *He's being polite to excuse her rudeness. I'd hate to live with her.*

At that moment, Annabel, the Christian housekeeper who ran the Kemelski household, brought in the main dish, a crispy roasted duck surrounded by steaming potatoes and green beans. After not eating much for almost a week, Rebecca and Aaron devoured their portion and asked for seconds. For the moment, things seemed perfect.

When Meir asked about their past, Aaron delivered the story that he and Rebecca had discussed. Their host tut-tutted appropriately during the sad parts.

Rebecca remained mostly silent. *If I say the wrong thing, Aaron will be furious with me, and they might make us leave.*

"So, what will you do now?" asked Meir.

"I don't know. I'm looking for work. I've got to find a way to support my wife and child."

* * *

Aaron had trouble even forming the word 'wife,' let alone speaking it.

"What can you do?"

"Not much. I have no real work experience. But I know my Torah pretty well," said Aaron honestly.

"Let me think about it," replied their host. "Come see me at my tavern tomorrow evening."

* * *

The following night, Aaron found his way to the tavern, which was located in a dilapidated neighborhood directly on the main route out of town. It was already dark when he arrived, and the dimly lit interior was filled with shabbily dressed, tough-looking characters who laughed raucously and used obscenities. Many of the customers were Christian, but there were also a number of Jews who obviously lived on the fringe of Jewish society. A tall bar made of rough-hewn wood with two or three high stools overlooked five or six tables, each circled by four chairs, which, this night, were filled.

Meir Kemelski stood behind the bar pouring the drinks. A worn-out-looking blond girl, stray locks of disheveled hair hanging over her face, served the customers, slapping the hands of drunken men who tried to pinch her rear whenever she passed.

"I see you've never been in this kind of atmosphere before," smiled the tavernkeeper as he observed Aaron's expression of surprise and discomfort. "You'll get used to it."

I don't want to get used to it, thought Aaron.

After the latest round of orders had been filled, Meir showed Aaron to a small table in the back of the room.

"I talked to Reb Kaganowicz, who runs the elementary school for orphans and sons of the poor. He could use an assistant, who would be in charge of cleaning the school and could help teach the boys their alphabet in his spare time. For that, he'll pay you two kopecks a day. In the evening, you can help me dispense drinks here in the tavern. I'm getting older and more tired. In return, you and your wife can live in my attic and eat food from my kitchen. After you settle in, Rebecca can help out cleaning the tavern. She can work until the baby is born. After that, we'll see."

Aaron didn't know what to say. The man was trying to be

helpful. Working at the elementary school from dawn to dusk five and a half days a week would be grueling. But an additional three or four hours in the tavern? He didn't know if he could handle it.

What choice do I have? I guess I'll have to try it for a while and see how things go. We've got to have a place to live and to raise the baby.

"All right. I'll talk it over with Rebecca. I'm sure she'll agree."

* * *

Aaron liked Reb Kaganowicz. The daily chores of sweeping and washing the floors of the house of learning were not difficult. In fact, Aaron looked forward to the solitude of his work every morning. He used the time to meditate and pray.

After lunch, which usually consisted of bread and cheese, he would join the reb's class of fifteen spirited and giggling boys aged five to nine. It was the custom of every Jewish community to run an elementary school for those who had no fathers or whose fathers could not afford tuition at a private school. Aaron had a natural flair for teaching, especially children with short attention spans who didn't respond to the older instructor.

"Aaron, you're doing a fine job," Reb Kaganowicz commented one afternoon. "How would you feel about taking over the class for an hour or so while I rest?"

"Of course, reb."

Aaron felt pleased that his talents were being recognized, though he was making a pitiable amount of money.

The worst part of the job for Aaron was observing the many students in their black frocks and fur hats who passed by every day on their way to and from the neighboring yeshiva. Aaron would think, That should be me, and the bitterness of his situation would once again engulf him.

For Rebecca, whose belly was swelling every day, the adjustment was more difficult. She spent her first days alone in the attic bedroom not knowing what else to do, with tears her constant companion.

Because Malka Kemelski passed the bulk of her time locked in her bedroom, even taking most of her meals there, Rebecca's only available companion was Annabel the housekeeper.

Annabel was a warm, friendly woman who was happy to have some company in the lonely house and gossiped with Rebecca between household chores.

"They haven't slept together in the same bedroom for years, and she doesn't even want to ever see his face," Annabel confided to Rebecca about Malka. "And I know he is lonely and wishes he had a child to bring some joy into the house. Maybe your baby will bring smiles into his life."

Meanwhile, Rebecca's feeling of isolation drove her increasingly to thoughts of self-destruction.

I can't stand being alone another second. How can I live like this? I've got to get out of this room.

* * *

"How would you feel about working in the tavern?" Meir asked Rebecca a few weeks after the couple had moved in.

"I would love it. I'm feeling very lonely alone here in the house."

"All right. If you start at nine a.m., you should be finished by noon."

Rebecca was disappointed. She had thought that she would be working at a time when other people would be around with whom to converse.

After work each day, Rebecca would take a walk alone around the city. Sometimes, she would venture outside the Jewish quarter and gaze at the many architecturally distinguished buildings. Vilna was a city of old palaces and churches. Once, intrigued by a beautiful multi-domed Orthodox church, her curiosity moved her to step inside hesitantly. She was awed by the colorful gilt icons hanging on the walls and frightened by the figure of a mostly naked man hanging on a cross.

"Hello, daughter. Can I help you?" The voice behind her was deep but friendly. She turned to see an elderly man in a black robe wearing a red cap. "I'm Father Ignatius. Who are you?"

"I'm new to the city and stopped by to see your beautiful building."

"Thank you. Would you like to return for services this evening?"

"Oh no. I'm Jewish," she replied, then bit her tongue in panic, wondering whether he would cause her trouble for revealing her religion.

However, his face reflected only kindness.

"I'm pleased that you visited us today. If I can ever be of any help to you, please let me know."

"Thank you, sir."

Rebecca hurriedly exited the building, feeling guilty that she had betrayed her religion but surprised that a Christian priest would be so nice to her, nicer than any rabbi she had yet encountered.

* * *

The days fell into a routine. Aaron would leave the Kemelski's attic as dawn was breaking to go to the school, where he emptied the trash, cleaned the floors and windows, and took care of any other janitorial duties. At eleven, he would eat his simple lunch. At noon, he would join the reb in the classroom and tutoring the children on their daily lesson, thus allowing the teacher to take some time off for a restful lunch. As night fell, he would rejoin Rebecca at home and have dinner with her in the Kemelskis' kitchen. Rebecca usually helped Annabel prepare the household meal so that the quality and quantity of food were ample. After dinner, Aaron would rest for a short time and then walk over to the tavern, where he assisted Meir as bartender. The tavern owner increasingly depended on him.

"You learn fast," said Meir one evening four months after Aaron and Rebecca arrived.

"Thank you." Aaron basked in the compliment. It was a rare positive moment in the wretched situation in which he found himself.

"How would you feel about managing the tavern alone for the two hours before closing? It would give me a chance to go home early and rest. I'm getting too old to keep putting in these kinds of hours. I'll add two kopecks a day to what you are receiving from the community school."

Aaron considered the offer. *I'm already spending that time here anyway. I might as well make the extra money, meager though it is.* "I would like that very much," he replied.

*　*　*

Aaron's only time off was from Friday at noon to Saturday night after dark, when the tavern re-opened after Sabbath. He was so tired that he needed a good bit of that time to catch up on his sleep.

One Saturday morning, he awoke to Rebecca nestling herself close to his body, at least as close as she could get with her pregnant belly pushing into his crotch.

"Are you going to synagogue this morning"?

Though he enjoyed tutoring the little boys, it suddenly struck Aaron that he had lost his passion for Torah and had no desire to pray.

What kind of God are you to do this to me, Lord? Have my sins been so great? Must I suffer for the rest of my life? You're an unjust and merciless father. Perhaps you don't even exist.

He surprised even himself with the vehemence of his thoughts.

"I'm too tired," he said.

"Oh?" said Rebecca, beginning to rub his leg seductively, "I'm happy to have you here with me." When Aaron pushed her away in disgust and guilt, she quietly sobbed, *How can he treat me this way?* and cried herself to sleep.

The next Saturday, though, Aaron's need for sexual release

was so great that it overcame his guilty self-loathing and anger. As much as he tried to control himself, when Rebecca again began stroking his thigh, he involuntarily responded. He allowed her to gently mount him and guide him inside her. With increasingly powerful thrusts she brought both of them to climax, her swollen belly somehow making the contact between them even more stimulating. Yet not a word was spoken.

Aaron was guilt-ridden. *I'm a terrible person. How can I let this happen after all the evil it has wrought? I'll never be worthy of studying the holy books. I'm a sinner whose life will always be a living hell.* Tears ran down his cheeks as he got out of bed, put on some clothes, and left the room in silence.

Rebecca, who had imagined that Aaron's acquiescence signaled a change in his attitude, was heartbroken. Again, she felt lost, alone, and without direction.

During the last few months of her pregnancy, Rebecca felt the strong need to interact with others. Annabel worried about the upcoming birth and Rebecca's seeming unawareness of her situation. She decided to bring Rebecca to meet with Chaya Rozinberg, the leader of the local childbirth aid society.

"Tell me, my child, how far along are you?"

"What do you mean?"

"I mean, when are you expecting the baby?"

"I don't know. How am I supposed to tell?"

Chaya was astonished at the extent of Rebecca's ignorance. She estimated that Rebecca was about six months pregnant and would deliver sometime in late spring or early summer. She tried to give Rebecca a short primer on childbirth but, frustrated by the girl's childlike confusion, cut her explanation short.

"In about three or four months you should have this baby. You'll know it's coming when you begin to feel contractions in your belly that get stronger and stronger. When that happens, send someone to fetch me, and we'll come to help."

Not really understanding what Chaya was talking about, but grateful for someone who offered to help her, Rebecca felt better. Other than occasional back pain and tiredness, her pregnancy was not a problem for her.

* * *

"Mr. Meir," she said one day to her employer, "would you mind if I did my work when the tavern is closing instead of the next morning? That way, I could be with Aaron a little more and have a chance to talk to other people. I'm feeling very lonely."

"As long as you get your work done, I have no objection," he said, "but be careful. There are some rough characters in that place."

"I can take care of myself. And besides, Aaron will be there to protect me."

So, Rebecca began to accompany Aaron when he went to work.

"Hey, lassie. What's a beautiful girl with a big belly doing with that little tight-assed kid behind the bar?" They would say. "I didn't think he had it in him."

"He's a better man than you," would be her flirtatious retort.

"You should see him in bed."

Laughing, the men would rub her belly and order another drink.

Rebecca was elated at the opportunity to be with people and engage in back-and-forth chatter with the customers.

"You've got to be careful around here," said Aaron at one point. Pointing to a fat, bearded man loudly telling a filthy joke, he whispered, "That one runs a band of young pickpockets." And pointing to a mustached man wearing several gold rings and bracelets, he said, "that one runs a bordello around the corner. I heard it's frequented by many Jewish husbands and even some of the girls are Jewish."

Just then, the mustached whoremonger, who particularly enjoyed Rebecca's spunk, shouted to her, "If you ever need a job, come and see me." Then, chortling heartily, he turned back to his drinking partners.

Aaron was ambivalent about these interchanges. He was embarrassed by the way Rebecca invited these kinds of interactions, but he felt a certain pride in the way that she built up his sexual prowess and made him look powerful in the eyes of the rough clientele.

As the tavern began to empty out for the night, Rebecca would begin her clean-up duties, pacing her work so that it was complete by the time Aaron was ready to lock up.

Walking home together that night, Aaron said, "Did you see the whoremaster this evening? He must have drunk almost a whole bottle of vodka by himself."

"Yes," replied Rebecca, "I wonder how much his wife knows

about what he does."

"I can't believe he's a Jew," continued Aaron. "Jews don't act like that."

Rebecca put her arm through Aaron's, and he didn't pull away.

As the weeks went on, there seemed to be a partial thawing of Aaron's coldness toward her. He gave in to her sexual advances more often, though he never initiated them. Still, there was almost no casual conversation between them beyond short questions and answers involving the practical issues of living and working in the same place.

* * *

A few months later, Rebecca was finishing up washing the bar glasses when she felt a gush of warm fluid splash onto the floor.

"Aaron," she cried, "something is happening to me!"

Aaron looked at the wet stain on the tavern floor. Not knowing any more than Rebecca, he replied, "You just had an accident. Get to the bathroom and dry yourself off."

The couple locked up the tavern for the night and walked to their attic room.

As she reached the top of the attic steps Rebecca suddenly doubled over in pain.

"Aaron, I'm in bad pain!" she screamed. However, as the initial contractions eased up, she felt less frightened.

Moments later, Aaron heard Rebecca scream more loudly.

"Something bad is happening!" she yelled at the top of her

lungs. "I think I'm dying."

As Aaron tried to figure out what to do next, there was a knock on the door. Meir Kemelski had heard Rebecca's scream and stood at the threshold, wondering what was going on. With a look at Rebecca's contorted face, he knew at once. He gave Aaron some brandy to help Rebecca with the pain and took off down the street to find Chaya Rozinberg.

Before long, Chaya and another middle-aged woman arrived bearing blankets, sheets, knives, and scissors. They instructed the men to bring boiling hot water and then ordered them to leave the room.

Aaron paced the living room downstairs where Meir waited with him. Mrs. Kemelski was nowhere to be seen. A few hours later, they heard a loud baby's scream coming from the attic.

Chaya Rozinberg stuck her head out the door and yelled downstairs, "It's a boy!" Then she slammed the door and began cleaning up.

"That one has strong lungs," smiled Meir shaking his head knowingly. "You'll have your hands full with him."

Aaron didn't answer.

Unconsciously fingering the coin, which was now hanging around his neck, Aaron thought, "I wish mama and papa were here."

Chapter Six

They did, indeed, have their hands full with the baby. Aaron decided to name him Jacob—Yaakov in biblical Hebrew—because he himself, like the biblical Jacob, had spent so much of his time leading up to the child's birth "wrestling with the angels." A ritual circumcision was held when the baby was eight days old.

Jacob was colicky from the start. Rebecca was clumsy and inept in handling him, and the baby reacted to her tension. His strong lips and jaws chewed on her nipples, which were constantly sore. As a result, she would delay nursing him as often as she could, which only increased his hunger and crying. She tried to ease the soreness by massaging herself with a paste made from soap and chicken fat, but it was of little help.

I never realized how bad this was going to be. I am a terrible mother. Sometimes I want to squeeze his neck until he stops breathing. Please, God, forgive me.

Jacob cried constantly, and Rebecca could sometimes barely keep herself from shaking him and slapping his little face, though, to her credit, she realized that such an action would be physically harmful.

Annabel sensed when Rebecca was reaching her breaking point.

"Rebecca, Jacob is going to fall off that chair! You left him too close to the edge." Or, "Rebecca, the baby's diaper hasn't been changed all day." "Why don't you leave the room for a while?" Annabel sometimes suggested, "I'll keep an eye on him" as Rebecca tried unsuccessfully to rock the baby to quiet him.

Even at night, the baby woke every few hours and interrupted the precious little sleep that Aaron was able to steal.

"Why are you coming home so late at night"? Rebecca would rant. Aaron ignored her questions and complaints. He was trying to find ways to spend as little time as possible at home

Rebecca was so tired and worn out that she had no energy left to even think about sex, for which Aaron was simultaneously relieved and disappointed. The new mother was so exhausted she thought she was going to have a nervous breakdown.

I can't go on like this. I think I'd rather die.

Finally, after two months of what seemed like endless torture, one of the ladies from the aid society made a home visit and gave Rebecca some soothing ointment for her breasts. She also instructed her in techniques of bottle-feeding. This advice gave the harried new mother some relief, and her disposition improved considerably. The baby quieted down some and began to thrive. This boy was clearly going to be a survivor.

* * *

By the time Jacob turned a year old, he was walking and already speaking short sentences. Though he spent most of the day with his mother, it was his father whose attention he sought. He would refuse to go to bed until Aaron returned home for the evening meal and stayed awake until Aaron left for work at the tavern.

"Da-da stay!" the toddler would demand.

And when Aaron left the room, Jacob would run to the closed door and pound on it screaming "Da-da, da-da!" at the top of his lungs. It took a long time to distract the child from that door.

On the Sabbath, when Aaron was home all day, Jacob stuck by his side—which both pleased Aaron and exhausted him. The tired father would recite for his son the Hebrew alphabet and the prayers of thanksgiving. Jacob was a fast learner and reveled in the time spent with his father. He relegated his mother to a second-class position, which infuriated her since she was the one who cared for him on a constant basis.

Why does he always want to be with his father when I am the one taking care of him?

Rebecca increasingly began to resent the position in which she found herself. She was alone most of the time. Annabel was her only companion, but she was busy doing chores and had little time for idle chit-chat. The lady of the house continued to spend all day in her bedroom, avoiding any contact with Rebecca—or anyone else, including her husband. The young mother was beginning to feel that she was going crazy with no adult companionship and nothing to do but keep her little son entertained. Her fantasies of a happy marriage and a loving husband who would take care of her forever had given way to the reality of her situation. She finally realized that her feminine wiles were simply not enough to keep Aaron satisfied with their relationship. He now repulsed every sexual advance that she initiated, and their interactions were limited to trivial one- or two-word conversations. She was a lonely, needy child taking care of her own needy child.

Aaron doesn't care about me or how I am suffering. All he thinks about is himself. He's a selfish, spoiled baby.

Sometimes Rebecca would take Jacob for a walk in the broken-down stroller donated by the ladies from the charity group. She would walk by the old Orthodox church, the gilded domes of which she had come to love, and secretly look for the kind Father Ignatius. A few times, she ran into him, and he was always as friendly as ever.

"Would you like to stop in for a glass of tea?" he would ask.

"Oh, no, father. Thank you. I'm just walking my baby, and I have to get home."

I never thought a Christian priest would be so friendly to a Jew. He's the only person who treats me like a real person, like I really exist.

Aaron's hopes and dreams had likewise given way to the humdrum routine of his exhausting existence. He no longer thought about studying Torah at the Yeshiva. Not even the sight of the students passing by in their fur hats made an impact on him anymore. He saw no future for himself except more of the same.

Every Saturday morning, the only day on which he didn't have to get up early for work, Jacob would wake him at 6 a.m. Aaron was resentful that the boy let Rebecca sleep undisturbed.

"Eat breakfast, daddy," he would say as he tried to pull Aaron over to the table to make him breakfast.

"Go away!" he would yell exhaustedly. "Wake mommy. This is the only time I can sleep."

But Jacob, of course, paid no heed. He relentlessly demanded his father's attention.

I wish they'd disappear, Aaron would sometimes think. *It's me who should be home now sleeping late and having my mother prepare breakfast for me.*

Aaron often thought about his parents and old school friends, especially around holiday time. He thought of the wonderful food that his mother cooked and the days spent with his father carrying out the Sabbath rituals. Even his old teacher with his bad breath took on a rosy glow in the mists of Aaron's memory.

If I were home now, I'd be going to the bathhouse with papa, he would muse on Friday afternoons as he trudged back to his room in the attic and the demands of Rebecca and Jacob. He would try to picture in his mind praying with his father in the beautiful little synagogue and the warm glow that it used to give him. It was the feeling of belonging that he missed the most. Here in Vilna, he was an outsider, with no friends and no family, only a counterfeit wife and a made-up family history.

As time went on and Aaron's hopelessness increased, he toyed with the idea of leaving Rebecca and Jacob in Vilna while he returned home alone, but he simply could not picture himself abandoning these two helpless creatures. His sense of duty and morality was too strong.

* * *

Eventually, Rebecca's need for companionship drove her to take some action,

I'll wither away without some human companionship.

Once again, she got up the courage to approach Meir Kemelski.

"Sir, you've been very good to us, allowing us to live in your house and eat your food. But I've been very lonely. With your permission, I would like to go back to work at the tavern. I can bring little Jacob with me, and he can sleep on a mat behind the bar while I take care of customers. That way, I can get to see more of my husband as well."

Meir reflected for a moment. He remembered how Rebecca's flirtatious manner would encourage the customers to order more drinks. Having the baby around might be a problem, but he decided to give the young mother a chance.

"All right. I'll pay you two kopecks a day for your work in addition to your room and board. We'll see how it works out."

* * *

"A tavern is no place for a child," said Aaron when Rebecca told him of the new arrangement. "It's a rough atmosphere and could be dangerous for both of you."

In truth, Aaron was trying to avoid spending any more

time with Rebecca and the baby. He resented their constant neediness and the demands they placed upon him. As far as he was concerned, the less he saw of them, the better.

Rebecca sensed his feelings. By now, she was learning how to get around Aaron's excuses.

"But this way I'll be happier," pleaded Rebecca. "I'll have other people to talk to. I won't always be complaining to you."

Aaron actually agreed with her reasoning. *Oh well. If nothing else I'll have some extra help that I can use. And it'll mean another two kopecks a day.*

Rebecca loved going back to work at the tavern and bantering with the crude and boisterous customers, and they loved her playful, flirtatious manner. The men enjoyed her even more since she was no longer pregnant and had regained her richly endowed figure.

"That's no way for a respectable Jewish woman to behave," Aaron said to her on more than one occasion.

"But I do it to help you," she would reply. "They drink more that way."

In fact, Rebecca was right. When she was tending the tables, the consumption of liquor almost doubled.

"You can't handle another drink," she would tease Nafty, the rowdy bordello owner. "It will knock you flat on your behind."

"We'll see about that," he would shout. And he would down in one gulp his eighth or ninth drink of the evening.

"I'll bet you can't match Nafty," Rebecca would quip to Herschel the smuggler.

"I can outdrink that little nebbish anytime," Herschel would cry, taking up Rebecca's challenge.

Jacob became the tavern's mascot. When he was awake, he would be passed from table to table, customer to customer. He loved the attention. He ate up the time spent with male figures, and the men loved having him around. The presence of a young child somehow satisfied a need within them for a family that either didn't exist or was somewhere far away.

Aaron often had pangs of jealousy watching his 'wife' tease the other men, but he was not prepared to increase his own intimacy with her, sexual or otherwise. However, some sense of fairness within him recognized that she deserved attention from somewhere, and, if he wasn't prepared to give it to her, he knew that he shouldn't interfere with the harmless way in which she was gratifying some of her needs. The crusty clientele wondered why Aaron allowed Rebecca's uninhibited behavior to continue, but they loved both the reserved bartender and his family and never allowed themselves to cross a certain unspoken line in dealing with her. This group of tough, foul-mouthed characters on the fringes of society became a kind of family to Jacob and Rebecca. Aaron, on the other hand, though physically present, remained aloof from any emotional attachment.

Chapter Seven

On Jacob's fourth birthday, Nafty the whoremaster and Herschel the Smuggler threw a birthday party for him. By this time, little Jacob operated like an adult in child's clothing. He was talkative, bright, and treated the tavern customers not only as equals but also as friends. He would serve drinks, clean the tavern, and run errands for the customers. When he asked potentially embarrassing questions about their activities, more often than not, the men would give him straight answers, and Jacob was smart enough not to push too far or discuss their business outside the 'family.'

"Uncle Nafty, do you have any children?" Jacob asked in a typical query.

"Yes, little one, I have a wife and two little girls."

"Why don't you ever bring them to see us? Don't you like us?" continued Jacob.

"Of course I like you. Would I make this party otherwise? But they live on the other side of town, and this is a rough neighborhood. I don't want to take a chance on them getting hurt."

"So, then, why do you work in this neighborhood?" Jacob pressed.

"Because a lot of my customers live around here, and many of the others don't want anybody to know they are doing business with me."

"Why not?'

"Because it would embarrass them."

"What kind of business do you do with them?"

"I give them entertainment that they want but can't get at home."

"What kind of entertainment?"

"Spending time with ladies their families don't like."

"Why don't they like them? Aren't they nice?"

"They're very nice."

"So why don't they like them?" Jacob persisted.

Finally at a loss for words, Nafty sighed,

"Listen, boychik, when you're a little older I'll explain it to you. Right now, just be quiet and eat your cake."

In fact, Nafty was telling the truth about his wife and daughters. His wife was aware of his profession but chose never to discuss it. They had an unspoken 'don't ask, don't tell' agreement. Nafty was a major contributor to the synagogue, and on the High Holy Days was given the honor of sitting in the first row facing the eastern wall. He was always one of the first members of the congregation to be called up for the honor of reciting the blessing before the Torah reading.

"How do you manage to get to sit in the front row?" Herschel once asked Nafty.

Nafty answered by raising his arm and briskly rubbing his thumb against his second and third fingers.

"A little bit of this will go a long way."

* * *

For the past two years, Meir Kemelski had taken to leaving the tavern as soon as Aaron arrived. He was approaching his fortieth birthday and felt that he deserved to cut back even more on his working hours. Because Aaron had proved to be entirely trustworthy—there was never a kopeck missing from the till, and the liquor was completely accounted for—he had absolutely no qualms about his decision.

Meir had accepted the fact that his relationship with his wife was effectively nonexistent. Her isolation was increasing. She had stopped coming out of her room for any meals at all. She barely acknowledged his presence when he knocked on her bedroom door and attempted to give her a perfunctory greeting.

"Malka, it's me, Meir," he would loudly say each night after knocking three times. "I've come to say goodnight."

Nothing.

"Do you need anything?"

Silence.

"All right. I'll be back tomorrow"

Despite Malka's reclusive behavior, Meir continued to feel a sense of responsibility for her well-being owing to the generous treatment that he had received from her father, who had now been dead for five years. Though never very social, it was her father's death that had sent Malka spiraling into a deep depression that only kept getting worse.

"Malka, eat something," Meir would say when it first began. "You can't live like this. Your father would want you to be happy."

He called in the local doctor, a man with a reputation for getting results in these kinds of cases.

"Feed her lots of red meat cooked rare," was his advice. "And take her to the seashore for some fresh air."

Meir had instructed Annabel to follow the doctor's orders and made arrangements to take his wife to Riga, on the Baltic sea, for a vacation, but nothing seemed to work. Meir had hoped that, when Aaron and Rebecca came to live with them, Malka would take an interest in the new baby. Malka had never conceived, mostly because there had been almost no sexual interaction between them. For years before the young couple's arrival, Malka had shut her husband out of the bedroom.

Meir's hopes were never realized. If anything, the presence of Aaron and Rebecca served only to push Malka into greater isolation.

Meir thought about divorcing her and looking for a new wife, but the thought of exposing his handicap and vulnerability to a new woman caused him extreme anxiety. Besides, he had promised her father that he would always look after her, and his business affairs were closely tied to those of Malka's brother, who now handled the deceased merchant's far-flung business interests.

Meir had been born with a congenitally clubbed right foot and short leg. All his life, he had been teased by his peers and felt like an outcast among them. He became known to the neighborhood as 'the cripple,' a name that he detested. He cringed whenever he had to pass a group of others his age. Even the adults began to refer to him by that awful name, which seared his soul, degraded him, and made him want to crawl into a closet and never be seen again. The worst part about it was that he began to think of himself that way, and it became part of his identity.

When he was nineteen years old, Meir went to work as a bookkeeper for Abel Holzberg. He was a conscientious worker, reliable and steady. He had few social relationships, and work was his only interest in life. No woman would give him a second look. But Abel, unlike the others, recognized his intelligence and potential and never exploited his handicap as a way to denigrate or take advantage of him.

Abel was a widower with two children. The eldest, Beryl, a man then in his mid-thirties, was married with two children of his own. He was second-in-command at the warehouse and clearly had been designated to take over the thriving business eventually.

Abel's second child was a daughter—Malka. His wife had died when the girl was twelve years old, and Abel had never remarried.

"Too much trouble," he would say when pushed by the local matchmaker to find another wife.

Abel was worried about what would happen to his daughter when he died. He did not want to burden his son with the responsibility of taking care of her. He knew that his daughter-in-law would never tolerate that. Malka was difficult to be around. Her craggy, unsmiling face, with the large wart on her cheek, gave her an angry, witch-like appearance. She rarely left the house. All attempts at finding a husband for her had been fruitless.

After observing Meir for four years, Abel decided that the young man, now twenty-three, would make a suitable groom for Malka, who was approaching thirty. He concluded that Meir's physical problem would encourage him to tolerate her shortcomings and provide an anchoring influence in her life. Malka knew that she didn't have much choice in the matter and reluctantly accepted her father's decision to approach Meir. She knew that she couldn't expect much more and didn't want to be dependent on her brother, whose wife she hated. Her sister-in-law Bella was all that she was not—attractive, outgoing, and social. She couldn't bear the thought of having someday to live in her brother's house in Bella's shadow as the old maiden aunt.

And so, one evening, as the working day drew to a close, Abel approached his head bookkeeper.

"I'd like to talk to you, Meir," he said. "Come into my office."

Meir's first thought was that he had done something wrong and was about to be fired. Anxiously, he slid off his stool with difficulty and limped to the office.

* * *"I

I have a proposition for you," said Abel.

Meir fidgeted in his chair and listened.

Abel got right to the point. "Meir, I won't be around forever, and I want someone I can depend on to take care of my daughter when I'm not here. I believe you to be a man of honor and responsibility and feel you would make a good husband for Malka. If you agree to my proposition, Malka will come to her marriage with a dowry that would make any man envious. It will include a fine house, furnishings, clothing, and twenty thousand rubles. I'll help you start out in the business of your choice. Working here with my son would not be in anyone's best interest."

Meir thought that he had just died and gone to heaven.

Now that Meir was leaving the tavern at dinnertime, requiring Aaron to come to work earlier, Aaron asked Reb Kaganowicz for permission to cut back on his hours at the elementary school.

"For anyone else, I would say no, the reb replied. "But you're such a good worker, and the children love you so much, that I cannot refuse you. Of course, you'll have to take a cut in pay."

Meir had foreseen this probability and had already generously increased Aaron's salary so that it significantly exceeded what he was earning before.

Aaron would arrive home about 4:30 in the afternoon, and Rebecca would feed them all dinner, after which the three of them would arrive at the tavern at 6, as Meir was leaving. Rebecca and Aaron would finish up any of the day's remaining cleaning chores—with help from little Jacob—and prepare for the evening crowd. This new routine pleased Rebecca immensely. She had all of the social stimulation that she needed, and Jacob was kept busy by the customers, which relieved her of dealing with his usual demands. She would put Jacob to bed on his pallet in the small kitchen at 10 p.m. When the tavern closed and the final clean-up was finished, Aaron would carry his sleeping son home to bed.

Even Aaron was pleased with this new arrangement. He was making more money and was able to save some for special purposes, though he wasn't sure what those might be. Rebecca and Jacob were happier and made fewer demands on him. He even enjoyed the camaraderie of interacting with the same customers over time, who indeed began to feel like family.

The tension between Jacob's parents had decreased to the point that Aaron once again began to accept Rebecca's sexual initiatives, though, as usual, the initiative was never his. By this time, both parents had learned a lot more about sex and childbirth. They took the precautions available to them to avoid conceiving another child that neither of them wanted. Life seemed to settle down.

That spring, Aaron began to notice a change in the customer base. More strangers began to frequent the tavern. They would gather in groups of three or four at the back tables and whisper among themselves. This behavior was disconcerting to Aaron as well as his usual customers, for whom open, bawdy revelry was the essence of the establishment.

It soon became evident that political turmoil was once again brewing in the country. Because the tavern was located on the outskirts of town at a major crossroads, it was the perfect meeting place for revolutionaries hatching secret plots and wanting to avoid the notice of the authorities.

"I don't like what's going on here," Aaron would confide to Rebecca, "but there's not much I can do about it."

"We have no reason to throw them out," Rebecca would reply. "They're not causing any problems for us."

"We'll see what happens. I have a bad feeling about this."

* * *

One Sabbath afternoon about 1:00 p.m., someone knocked on the attic door. The family was cleaning up after their midday meal and preparing to nap.

"Who could that be?" asked Rebecca. "Annabel isn't working today."

"We'll soon find out," answered Aaron as he pulled open the door.

Meir Kemelski was standing on the landing outside.

"May I come in?"

"Of course."

Meir looked around the room, obviously pleased with what he saw. The attic was neat. Rebecca had decorated the room with several cheap drinking glasses filled with dried flowers. There were a few knick-knacks on the small table, and on the wall were tacked two collages made of bits of colored paper and glass that she had collected and formed into a design. The result was quite attractive.

Meir limped over to where Jacob was sitting and gave him

a kiss on the head. The child accepted it without pulling away.

"May I sit down?"

"You know you needn't ask," said Aaron.

Meir, his hands on his lap with fingers tented, stared up the ceiling and began to speak. "You know I've come to love you both over the years. You have been good tenants and good employees. You've never tried to take advantage of me and have become trusted members of my family. I've become dependent on you to run my business. Now, I find myself in a position that might change the routine we've all gotten used to."

Aaron and Rebecca remained silent, waiting for him to continue.

"Annabel informed me yesterday that she is getting married and will be leaving my employ. I'll have to replace her with someone I can trust. I don't know anyone who can take over the job of dealing not only with the house but with my wife as well. Malka is not an easy person to get along with, and I would prefer someone she already knows and has a relationship with."

He went on.

"Rebecca, I know you love what you do at the tavern, and you're very good at it. But I'd like you to consider taking over as housekeeper. You've learned to cook well, and you already know the house routine. If you agree to do this, I'll double the salary that both you and Aaron are currently making. It will be worth it to me."

He paused and looked over at the couple, now no longer children but young adults able to make an informed decision.

Aaron and Rebecca were flabbergasted at this turn of events.

"Give us until tomorrow to think about it," said Aaron

* * *

"What do you think?" Aaron asked after Meir left and Rebecca was finishing putting the dishes away.

"I don't know. I don't like it." Aaron could see that she was trying to hide tears that were trickling down her cheek.

"But he'll pay us double. Look how much money we could make! Pretty soon, we could save enough to buy a place of our own."

Rebecca wasn't convinced. "For what? So I can be alone again every day and go crazy?" Her subsequent silence expressed more than any words.

Aaron tried again.

"And what if the new housekeeper is nasty and makes life hard for us? It would ruin everything. Besides, Meir has been kind to us, and he would be hurt if we refused. I would feel terrible after all he's done to help us."

This last argument made sense to Rebecca. She knew that Meir had gone out of his way to take care of them, and she didn't want to appear ungrateful. Besides, Jacob would be starting elementary school shortly, and her days would be free. She could spend evenings with her son feeling considerably less stressed. Her chief concern about the arrangement was having to deal on a daily basis with Malka.

What will she be like? Will she be horrible to me? I couldn't take that.

Chapter Eight

In August, two months after his fifth birthday, Jacob began elementary school. He was to attend the school for poor children and orphans—the school where Aaron worked. Because the community supported the school, it required no tuition. There, the children learned their alphabet and began their study of the prayers and rituals that comprised so much of Eastern European Jewish life. Although five seemed to Rebecca a very young age to send her son off to school, most children whose parents could afford regular tuition actually began school at age three or four, attending from early morning to dusk.

Friday at noon, school ended for the week, and the children were sent home to help their parents prepare for the Sabbath. They would carry their mothers' pots of stew to a common oven at the baker's shop. Since Jewish law forbade making a fire on the Sabbath—doing so was considered 'work,' and therefore unacceptable—the stew would cook slowly overnight on a fire tended by the 'Sabbath goy.' This Christian boy was paid to carry out the chores forbidden for Jews to do on the Sabbath, including delivering the stew to each household on Sabbath morning so that the food would be ready to eat for the midday meal.

Jacob was thrilled to be going to school with his father. As was the tradition, on the first day, Aaron wrapped his son in a prayer shawl, carried him to school, and placed him in the arms of the teacher.

"Let me down! Let me down!" Jacob began to scream, much to Aaron's embarrassment.

However, the teacher was prepared for situations like this. He handed Jacob an alphabet tablet smeared with honey, a small cake, and a hard-boiled egg with passages from the Bible written on the shell. Jacob fell momentarily quiet as the teacher whispered a few magical phrases above the boy's head to keep away the angel of forgetfulness. Then he allowed Jacob to eat the cake and lick the honey off of the alphabet tablet.

"Now let me down!" screamed Jacob.

"We're going to take a little walk," the teacher quietly said. He gently lowered Jacob and proceeded outside.

All of the students followed him to a small creek that ran through the city a few blocks away. Fresh running water was considered conducive to memory and study. As the group stood by the side of the creek, the teacher whispered a short blessing over the heads of the children. Then, they returned to the classroom. With this ceremony, Jewish boys left their carefree childhood behind to become schoolboys officially.

When Jacob returned to the classroom to find Aaron gone, he once again began to scream.

"I want my papa!" he yelled at the top of his lungs.

"Your papa is working in another part of the building," said Reb Kaganowicz. "You'll see him at lunchtime."

Before the teacher could react, Jacob jumped out of his seat and darted out of the classroom and into the hallway. He ran through the building screaming, "Papa! Papa!" The reb, trying to catch him, followed up and down the halls. The rest of the children, unsupervised, ran into the hallway behind their teacher, laughing and pushing each other and trying not to miss a minute of the wonderful show. They hadn't had this much fun in school for a long time.

"Go, Jacob, go!" they yelled. "Don't let him catch you!"

Finally, hearing the commotion, Aaron appeared and caught Jacob in his arms. He was angrier than he ever remembered being and slapped Jacob hard across the face.

"You are a very bad boy! Don't you ever embarrass me like this again! You will go to school like everybody else, and you will respect Reb Kaganowicz. If you ever do anything like this again, I'll take a strap to your tuchus and you won't be able to sit for a week!"

Jacob was stunned by his father's actions. Aaron had never acted like this before. He had certainly never slapped him, let alone in the face.

Aaron carried Jacob back to the classroom, sat him down, and marched out without another word. Jacob became aware of the other boys laughing behind his back. Now he was the one who felt embarrassed and humiliated in front of the whole class. He sobbed quietly and withdrew into his shell.

At lunchtime, the reb went home as usual, and Aaron took over the class. The entire atmosphere was strained. All of the boys were watching closely to see what would happen. Father and son avoided any interaction during the afternoon, even after the teacher returned from lunch and Aaron left at 4 p.m. to go home for dinner. By the time Rebecca picked up Jacob at school and brought him home for dinner, his father had already left for work. He picked at his dinner with his mother, who noticed that he was behaving differently.

"What happened at school today?" she asked.

Jacob, feeling hurt and rejected, just crawled into his bed and went to sleep. His face still burned from where his father's hand had met his cheek.

*   *   *

"Get dressed for school," said Aaron to his son early the next morning, "or else we'll be late."

Jacob ignored his father and silently continued to play with a spoon on the breakfast table.

"I said to get dressed," Aaron repeated in a strident, more threatening tone. Again, Jacob did not respond.

Aaron walked over to where the boy was sitting, picked him up, and shook him.

"You'll do as I say and will not disrespect your father!"

Jacob's facial expression of distance and impassivity finally broke. With his face contorted into an expression of rage and hurt, he screamed, "Let me go! I hate you! I'll never go to school again!"

"You'll never talk to me again like that again!" retorted Aaron as he smacked Jacob across the mouth once more. "Now get dressed!" He forcibly began to pull Jacob's shirt over his head as the child sobbed loudly.

Rebecca, who had not wanted to interfere, moved between her son and his father.

* * *

Aaron is behaving more childishly than Jacob. He reminds me of my father.

"Let me dress him," she said.

"Jacob. You're a big boy now. All big boys have to go to school to learn how to be good, Jewish men. Your father only wants what is best for you."

Jacob said nothing but allowed his mother to dress him.

"Take me to school," he said to Rebecca. "I don't want to go with him."

Fuming at Rebecca's perceived undercutting of his authority, Aaron stormed out and walked to work by himself. Rebecca finished dressing Jacob and walked him to school, which was fifteen minutes away.

* * *

From that point on, Jacob kept his emotional distance from his father, and Aaron refused to make an effort to end the rift between them.

"But he's only five years old," Rebecca would say, pleading Jacob's case.

"He's old enough never to disobey his father."

"But he loves you. Can't you see that? All he wants is for you to love him back. Give him a chance. He was frightened on the first day of school and was trying to be with you."

Rebecca was maturing gracefully into motherhood. She remembered how hard she used to try to please her own father and receiving nothing in return but displeasure and angry words. She also realized how important it was to Aaron that his child be perfect in every way. He was too dependent on the opinion of others to shape his own self-esteem, but she couldn't say that to him.

I'll try to reason with him from a different angle.

"It's good for a child to show some independence. That trait will serve him well in the future. You should not expect blind obedience," Rebecca wisely said to Aaron when he came home from work.

"Where would the Jewish people be if they did not blindly obey the Lord's word?" Jacob retorted. "They would have disappeared years ago. Sometimes, obedience is a matter of faith, and Jacob must learn that life will accept nothing less."

Working up her courage, Rebecca replied, "I'm not sure that's true. Blind obedience to archaic laws sometimes strangles people. Those kinds of laws are what prevent us from living a normal married life. I don't think God meant for his laws to create so much suffering for his people."

"What do you know"? shouted Aaron. "You're just a woman with no education."

As a result of making this open declaration about the necessity for blind obedience, Aaron began to feel guilty about skipping his prayers and religious observance. He started to attend Sabbath services even though it meant giving up the only time available for a little extra weekend sleep. He woke up fifteen minutes earlier every morning to say his daily prayers.

* * *

All of this meant less time spent with Rebecca and Jacob. He once perfunctorily asked the boy to join him for Sabbath services, but Jacob sullenly refused. He never asked again. Silence reigned in the household.

"Aaron, why don't you talk to Jacob?"

"I'll talk to him when he apologizes and treats me with respect."

"But you're his father, and he's only a child. Pulling away from him will just make things worse. What does it matter if you make the first move?"

"He must learn respect for his elders."

Frustrated and feeling caught in the middle, Rebecca stopped trying to intervene in the situation.

They're both so stubborn. I feel helpless. I can't think of anything else to make things better.

* * *

Because of the problems going on in her family, Rebecca unexpectedly welcomed her new job. After Jacob went off to school—he now knew the way and walked there by himself—she would serve the morning meal to Meir. Then, she would prepare Malka's unvarying breakfast of tea with cheese and bread, carry it up the stairs, and knock on her door. Most of the time, Malka would reluctantly open it and allow Rebecca to straighten up the room while she picked at her breakfast. Rebecca would collect any dirty laundry and dirty dishes and then leave the room. Usually, no conversation passed between them. She would pass lunch and dinner in when Malka cracked open the door and later picked up the dishes, which Malka would leave in the hallway. Rebecca often wondered what Malka could possibly be doing all day and night alone in her room.

The rest of Rebecca's day would be spent cleaning the house, going to the marketplace, and preparing dinner. She would feed Aaron at 5:00 p.m., Meir just after 6:00—when he came from work—and Jacob upon his return from school. Sometimes, Jacob would arrive with Meir, and the three of them would sit down for dinner together as if they were a real family. When that happened, it was somehow comforting to Rebecca.

Aaron would not get home from the tavern until after 11 p.m., and, by that time, Rebecca was tired and usually asleep. If she were awake, Aaron would have little to say. He would prepare for bed and immediately fall asleep.

* * *

One blustery Thursday evening in early January, Rebecca had put Jacob to bed and was stoking the fire, which was left burning during the night to warm the house. She heard Meir's distinctive footsteps coming down the stairs and wondered whether she had forgotten to leave a clean nightshirt in his bedroom.

"You're doing a good job. I'm very pleased with your work. Even Malka has few complaints, which, to me, is a blessing."

"Thank you. You've been good to us and I want you to know how much we appreciate it."

"Your efforts and appreciation are well noted."

Silence.

Hesitantly, Meir continued, "I noticed that you and Aaron haven't been spending much time together recently."

"No, he's busy with work and with the synagogue," she replied, not knowing where this conversation was leading.

"Tomorrow evening, I'm going into town to take care of some business. Would you and Jacob like to come with me? We could have dinner together at the inn by the river. And we wouldn't get home too late for Jacob's bedtime."

Rebecca was conflicted. She desperately wanted to go. She rarely had a chance to leave the house and have some fun, but she was afraid Aaron would be angry.

But Jacob will be with us. What harm can come of it?

The next night, the three of them went into town. Meir took care of his business with a local supplier, and afterward they went to an inn called The Golden Duck. They had a wonderful meal of caviar with chopped egg and onion, cabbage soup, and crispy duck served with fried eggplant. Meir ordered white wine to accompany the dinner. It was the first time that either Rebecca or Jacob had been to such a fancy place, and they loved every minute of it.

"Thank your Uncle Meir," said Rebecca when they returned home about 9 p.m., a bit late for Jacob's bedtime.

Jacob gave Meir a big hug and went up to bed with his mother.

Neither Jacob nor Rebecca mentioned their little outing to Aaron. Jacob didn't see much of him, and when they were together the atmosphere still was strained.

A week later, Rebecca was once more tending to the night fire when Meir came downstairs.

"Is there anything you need?" asked Rebecca.

"I have something for you," he said.

Meir reached into his pocket, took out a medium-sized box, and handed it to Rebecca.

"Open it."

Rebecca was surprised. The gift was unexpected. She slowly opened the box and took out a lustrous tortoise shell comb carved with a beautiful scroll and flower design.

"What is this for?"

"I'll show you."

Meir took the comb, moved behind her, untied the red hair ribbon, and began to gently run the comb through her thick, dark tresses.

With his other hand he began to gently rub the back of her neck. After a minute or so, he stopped the combing motion and used both hands to massage her neck. Then he gently kissed her hair, put down the comb, and ran both hands over the swell of her large breasts. He could feel her nipples harden. It had been over a year since she and Aaron had had any sexual relations.

* * *

Rebecca was in a quandary. She loved the feeling of a man initiating a sexual dance with her. It was the first time in her life any man seemed to really appreciate her womanliness. But she knew that it was wrong to give in to the temptation of a sexual relationship with a man who was not her husband.

But Meir is sad and lonely. His wife is like Aaron. She pays no attention to him, even when he does everything for her. And he is a good man despite his crippled legs. Neither Malka nor Aaron appreciates what they've got. They don't want to be with us. And Aaron isn't really my husband.

All of this ran through her mind in the few seconds that Meir massaged her from behind.

Meir is the first man who wants to give to me, make me important, think of my needs. Even think about my son. And that's a wonderful feeling.

Her body had made the crucial decision even before her conscious mind was aware of it. She watched as if from afar as it turned to face Meir and her hands gently moved around both sides of his head. She felt her lips pressing against his in a sustained kiss. As the long-repressed passion in each of them began to surface, caution was thrown to the wind. Disregarding the danger of Jacob waking up or Aaron coming home early, he pulled her long apron off and unbuttoned her dress, pulling it over her head. As he roughly and ineptly removed her undergarments, she expertly unbuttoned his shirt and trousers. She pulled them down exposing his undershorts—now tented by a large erection. Rebecca looked down at him.

He might have a short leg, but there's nothing wrong with his putz.

They spent an hour rapturously exploring each other's bodies on the carpet in front of the fire. It was the first time in their lives that either of them could be said to 'make love.' Meir's few attempts to engage sexually with Malka had never been successful; she would not permit penetration. And Rebecca's experiences with Aaron were mechanical at best. He always lay passively as she carried out the sexual act almost by herself.

Rebecca made love to Meir the way she had always wanted to make love to Aaron, stroking, tickling, and teasing him until he was worked into a frenzy of excitement. When she sensed him closing in on the point of climax, she used tricks she had learned from secretly watching her mother to delay and prolong the sexual tension until it slowly began to rise again, ultimately exploding in an unrestrained burst that was twice as powerful.

Meir, at first, was clumsy in his response because of his inexperience. Soon, though, he instinctively found his rhythm and, using his body parts in ways in which he only now realized they were meant to be used, began to seek ways of pleasuring Rebecca in return. Just the awareness of the attention that Meir paid to meeting her needs stimulated her more than any physical act. Both of them were surprised to find Meir hard and ready to begin again after a few moments of respite.

I never knew it could be like this, they were both thinking as they lounged in front of the fire, their passions finally spent.

"We'd better get back to our rooms, Meir. Aaron will be home soon."

And they both bounced up the steps and fell asleep, having wonderful dreams before Aaron opened the front door.

Chapter Nine

The political situation in the country continued to deteriorate. In the tavern, Aaron began to pick up whispers of plots and counterplots against the czar and his government. Unrest pervaded the land.

Having no one else with whom to converse, Aaron began to talk to Rebecca after he came home from work to let off steam.

"The czar is stirring up riots against the Jews again. There was a pogrom by the Cossacks in southern Ukraine last week. Jewish towns were burned down, and people were killed. They even raped our women. And they kidnapped young Jewish boys, who end up as cannon fodder in the army."

"What can we do about it?" asked Rebecca.

"Many Jews are leaving for Palestine," he replied.

"I couldn't live in that bug-infested, scorching hot country worrying about where our next meal was coming from."

"Jews there live on communal farms. We wouldn't starve. Things here are getting pretty bad and might get worse."

"Maybe the Bolsheviks will get rid of the czar."

"That will only mean more bloodshed."

Rebecca thought for a while. "Maybe we should go to America. Lots of Jews are leaving to go there."

Aaron drew back from that suggestion. "On second thought, I really couldn't leave my parents in this country. I'd never see them again."

"Then I guess we'll just have to watch and wait," answered Rebecca.

*　*　*

While Aaron did not sympathize with any of the Bolshevik groups, he had, over the months, become acquainted with many of their members. Conversely, these men had also become familiar with him. They knew that he kept his mouth shut and so had dropped their guard to some degree when discussing their plans and ideas.

One Monday night, he overheard Anschul, the bastard, talking to three friends in the back of the room.

"So we'll grab the Pole on his way home from church on Sunday and kill him. He has no children, so the land will be up for grabs. And, in the confusion that follows, we'll be able to divert most of the fruit and meat in his warehouses to our troops. That will be the end of the Polonski dynasty!"

Aaron's ears perked up when he heard the familiar name. He listened closer.

"We'll leave here on Wednesday morning. It will take two days for the coach to get to Jelzai. We'll take a room at the inn and scout out the place on Friday and Saturday. On Sunday morning, he usually goes to 7 o'clock mass. We can get him on his way to church. No one will be around that early to interfere."

"A good plan," said Avram, whom they called the Fat One. "We'll weaken the czar's stranglehold on eastern Poland if we get rid of Polonski."

"Too bad," said Anschul. "He's well-liked by the Jews of the town. He treats them well."

"We can't concern ourselves with that," said Avram. "Although his death may cause some pain in the short run, they'll thank us when they live in a free and equal country."

Aaron could not believe what he was hearing.

They would kill a kind and innocent man just to further their own revolutionary agenda? How can men be so cruel and callous? I can't let this happen. I don't know what I'll do, but I've got to do something.

Aaron couldn't think clearly while he was working in the noisy tavern.

I'll close early so I can go home and think in quiet. Maybe I'll even ask Rebecca and Meir what they think I should do.

In order to allay any suspicion, Aaron waited another hour and a half, until 9:30 p.m., to close the tavern. By that time, the topic of conversation had changed and the men were pretty drunk.

"I don't feel well tonight," he announced to his customers. "I'm sorry, but I'm going to have to close early."

No one protested.

"Too bad your pretty young wife isn't here to take over for you. I think you just want to go home to get a piece of ass," cackled Avram, and the whole room guffawed.

Aaron locked the door after they left. He did a quick, superficial clean-up and rushed home.

*   *   *

Aaron ran all the way, thinking about possible actions he could take.

If I report this to the police, I'll gain a reputation as a spy, and business at the tavern will dry up. They'll never trust me again. Besides, how would I know if some of the local authorities secretly sympathize with these rebels? They would find out who reported them and might even kill me. My only choice is to travel back to Jelzai myself and warn Count Polonski personally. I can't let such a wonderful man be murdered for no reason. I owe it to him after what he did for me. And, while, I'm there, I'll have a chance to see mama and papa.

Aaron burst through the door of the Kemelski house, eagerly anticipating sharing these recent developments with Rebecca and Meir. His bubble suddenly burst as he entered the living room.

Rebecca and Meir were tangled together, nude, on an oriental carpet in front of the fire. They were so focused on their lovemaking that it took several seconds for them to realize that Aaron was watching them.

Aaron was stunned. He couldn't believe what his eyes were witnessing. The woman for whom he had given up his hopes and dreams was shtupping the man for whom he had worked so hard. The righteous morality by which he had run his life had failed him. He felt triply betrayed.

"What are you doing?" he screamed at the top of his lungs. "How could you do this to me?" His accusatory words were directed at both of them. "I've given up my life for you! I've forsaken my parents. I've thrown away my chance for yeshiva. And this is how I get repaid?"

Meir and Rebecca had scrambled apart and tried to hide their nakedness by holding their clothes in front of them. The effort was not very successful. Their faces were red and frightened. They could think of nothing to say.

As Aaron continued to rant at the top of his lungs, none of them noticed Jacob standing on the staircase watching them. Behind Jacob, Malka Kemelski also appeared, finally roused from her bedroom by the ruckus downstairs.

When Aaron's voice became hoarse from screaming, he finally slowed down.

"I'm leaving and never coming back," he shouted hoarsely.

As he turned to go upstairs and pack his things, Jacob finally broke down.

"No, no, papa, please don't go! I'm sorry for disobeying you. I love you. I'll never disobey you again!"

Aaron ignored his son's pleas.

"Let him take care of you," he said, pointing at Meir, who was still hiding behind his pants.

Then Aaron stormed past Jacob and the silent Malka and charged up to the attic, taking the steps two at a time.

I mean it. I'll never return. They'll have to survive without me.

Mama was right. I should have sent her away when this first happened.

He brushed aside the guilt that was beginning to surface about abandoning his son.

This isn't his fault.

The rage and anger pushed those feelings back. Reason had disappeared.

Aaron packed his belongings, took whatever savings they had managed to collect, ran down the steps, and slammed the door.

The last voice he heard as he rushed down the street was that of his son sobbing, "Papa, papa don't go. I'm sorry! Take me with you. I love you!"

When Meir finally dressed and wearily went back to his room, his wife startled him as she burst through the door unannounced.

"You are a pig!" She spat out the words. "You've shamed me and the memory of my father who gave you everything you have. Get that woman out of my house immediately! I never want to see her or her little bastard again." Then she turned around and returned to her secluded den.

As his wife slammed the door behind her, Meir was shaken to the core by the events of the night. Nothing like this had ever happened to him before. He was not used to the role of a villain.

I can't think straight. I must try to get some sleep.

Rebecca had taken Jacob up to their attic room. He was still sobbing uncontrollably.

"Papa will be back. He was just angry and saying things he didn't mean," she tried to reassure him.

"It's all your fault," his quivering voice cried out. Jacob wasn't sure exactly what his mother had done to make his father so angry, but he knew that she shouldn't have done it. And he could see that his 'Uncle Meir' was involved as well.

Yet, despite his accusatory words to his mother, he was thinking, *It's really my fault. If I hadn't been so disobedient, papa would never have left.*

Chapter Ten

Aaron arrived in Jelzai on Thursday. He had been sure to catch the Tuesday coach because he didn't want to run into the conspirators, who, he knew, would be leaving on Wednesday. The two-day journey brought him to his old village early in the afternoon.

I really want to go home and see mama and papa, but first I've got to complete my mission.

Aaron thought of his journey as a mission sent to him by God to save a life.

Upon disembarking from the coach, Aaron headed to the town's common grazing pasture and crossed the bridge over the creek—the same bridge where the two young peasants had accosted him years ago. He proceeded down the road past his old school.

Amazing. So much has happened since the last time I was here. It seems like a lifetime ago.

Aaron had no desire to stop and visit his former teacher. He continued down the road until he reached the cutoff to the home of Count Polonski.

After walking the path for perhaps a half-mile, Aaron suddenly topped a small rise and, for the first time, gazed upon the imposing façade of the Polonski manor house. It looked to be at least a hundred-and-fifty years old and was three stories high. The structure was built of local granite by local masons and was clearly meant to last. With its high turrets and small windows, it looked like a fortress or even a castle. The stately building and wide, manicured lawn surrounding it intimidated Aaron. He even considered aborting his mission, but he had come too far for that.

Aaron was sure that the count would not recognize him. For one thing, he had cut his long hair and no longer dressed in the manner of an observant Jew. The time spent among unsavory characters had seen to that. For another, his adolescent frame had grown into a man's body during the six years that he had been away.

So far, Aaron hadn't met anyone as he approached the house. He walked up to the massive front door of heavy timber with forged iron hinges and hesitantly knocked.

Aaron expected a servant to open the door and was quite surprised when it swung silently open and Count Polonski stood before him.

"Yes?" asked the count. "Can I help you?"

"I know you don't remember me, but I have something of great importance you need to be aware of."

Count Polonski closely examined the young man standing before him. After looking him over for a few seconds a light seemed to come on in his brain. With a broad smile, the count said,

"Ah yes. You are the young Jew with the old silver coin in the embroidered pouch. I'm happy to see you. You've become a man. Have those ruffians been bothering you again?"

"No, sir. I've been living in Vilnius for the past six years." Aaron remembered that Christians referred to Vilna as Vilnius.

Without providing much detail into his own life, Aaron explained why he had come and the details of the planned murder.

The count was surprised and grateful for Aaron's efforts. He had no idea that the anti-czarist feelings were so strong. And he certainly was not aware that he was perceived as an ally of Czar Nicolas, a man whose policies he detested and whom he personally considered a greedy, dishonorable monarch with no consideration for the welfare of his subjects.

"Thank you for warning me. I'll take the necessary precautions to apprehend these murderers. I owe my life to you."

"No, sir. I'm only paying back the favor you did for me," replied Aaron modestly.

The count insisted that Aaron take some refreshment with him and then showed him around the manor house. The young man was impressed by the fine furnishings as well as the works of art that had been in the Polonski family for centuries.

As Aaron was leaving, the count looked him in the eye and gently said, "I do owe you my life, and if there is anything I can ever do for you, please let me know."

Aaron walked back to town whistling. The painful memories of Rebecca and Jacob were quickly receding. He moved with a spring in his step as he hurried to the bridge and broke into a run until he reached the front door of the Pechtrowicz bakery.

It was Thursday evening. Rivka and her husband would be closing the small shop, Aaron knew. They would be setting up supplies for the morning's work. The next day was Friday, when all of the pre-Sabbath baking had to be done.

Aaron silently entered the shop, tip-toed behind his mother, who was bending over as she swept the dirt floor, and hugged her. Startled, she turned around and let out a shriek of joy as she recognized the son whom she had not seen for six years. Alarmed at his wife's shriek, Yitzchak came running from the house behind the shop. It took him a few moments to recognize his son, who had changed so much. When Aaron's presence finally registered, Yitzchak began to cry. He had thought that he would not live to see his son's face again.

Tears began to stream down Aaron's cheeks, and the three of them stood crying and hugging each other so that their wet faces rubbed together mixing the tears of joy.

The family stayed up past midnight as Rivka and Yitzchak listened closely to Aaron's recounting of his experiences in Vilna. They had many questions, for most of which Aaron had no clear answer.

"How could you work such long hours?"

"Why didn't you come home sooner?"

"What will happen to them if you don't go back?"

"Will you be safe from those assassins?"

After most of the important history had been imparted and discussed, Rivka asked some questions to indulge her feminine curiosity.

"What is the manor house like?"

"Does the count live with anyone?"

"Is he as rich as they say?"

The family went to bed that night knowing that difficult decisions had to be made. Aaron's parents were unconcerned with Rebecca's fate but uncomfortable with the idea of him abandoning his son, their grandson, yet they could come up with no suitable solution. Rebecca could not return under any circumstances. The community already knew her as Rivka's sister. He couldn't bring the child back to Jelzai even if Rebecca stayed in Vilna; since he wasn't married, Jacob would be ostracized by the community as a bastard. This would also mean ostracism for Aaron, who would not be able to remain in town or proceed with his career. And they could not make up a story of a non-existent, out-of-town marriage with the wife dying because Jacob would eventually reveal the truth.

"We'll talk some more tomorrow," said Rivka, stretching and yawning sleepily. "I can't keep my eyes open."

After his parents went to sleep, Aaron sat before the fire in the common room. Memories of his first trysts with Rebecca flooded his mind.

How naïve I was, how innocent. How quickly one's life can change from one day to the next. I should be finishing my studies and finding a wife, but everything is wrong. Where will my life go from here?

As he sat weighing these heavy issues, he pulled out the velvet pouch from under his shirt. It was hanging around his neck and contained his treasured coin. He rubbed it between his thumb and fingers. This repetitive action seemed to calm his anxiety.

* * *

The next day was like old times. Aaron accompanied his father for the pre-Sabbath ritual bath. He greeted old friends heartily and with real pleasure. Most were polite enough not to ask too much about his six-year absence. They had put two and two together and figured out what must have happened. For those who were boorish enough to ask insensitive questions, the family had devised a cover story about going to Vilna to study in the yeshiva.

Aaron appreciated his father's presence more than ever. He knew that Yitzchak was getting old and his time was getting short. He felt the need to be with the old man as much as possible. Occasionally, thoughts of his own son growing up without a father would sneak into his consciousness, and he would be flooded with guilt momentarily but was somehow able to compartmentalize and repress the feeling. He couldn't let the connection surface, for it was too painful. As the comfortable days wore on, Aaron convinced himself that Rebecca and Jacob would make out all right without him. He even rationalized that they would be better off with him not around so that Rebecca could find a man to marry her and be a father to Jacob. Maybe even Meir would get rid of his wife and marry Rebecca.

He certainly seemed to like her well enough,

With a flash of jealousy, Aaron pictured their interlocking bodies nude on the floor in front of the fire.

Rumors reached the townspeople that Count Polonski had discovered an assassination plot against his life and that he and his men had caught and killed the plotters. The village was astonished at the news. Neither Aaron nor his parents divulged Aaron's part in preventing the plot from succeeding, though Rivka was tempted to brag about her son. They did not want to attract attention for fear of reprisals.

Two weeks went by. With each passing day, Aaron felt more and more at home and thought less and less about Rebecca and Jacob. He and his parents finally concluded that it was best to leave things as they were and that Rebecca and the child could get along on their own.

Chapter Eleven

The morning after 'the explosion'—as Rebecca would always think of it—Meir dragged himself up the stairs to the attic.

Rebecca had not had the heart to send Jacob to school that day. He was still very upset. His eyes were red from crying, he refused any food, and he would accept no comforting words from his mother.

As Jacob sat inconsolably in the corner, Meir sat down on the bed next to Rebecca and took her hands.

"Malka knows everything that's been going on between us. She knows how much I care for you. She insists that you and Jacob must leave the house. If you don't, she threatens to tell her brother everything, and he'll use his influence to ruin my business. I've taken out many loans to make investments, and he's guaranteed them for me. I'll be bankrupt if he carries out her threats, and I have no doubt that he would. I'm afraid I must ask you and Jacob to leave."

"But where will we go? We have no one else here."

"I don't know, but I'll give you six months' wages to tide you over until you find other employment and living arrangements. That should help out considerably."

* * *

Rebecca felt desperate as she packed their few belongings. She had no idea where Aaron was and whether he would return.

If he doesn't come back, what will I do? He's not an unfeeling person, He would never abandon us and leave his son to grow up alone without a father.

Meir did not emerge from his room to say goodbye. He left her money on the table in the parlor by the front door. She and Jacob left the house holding the handles of their large wicker suitcase between them. They began to walk aimlessly down the street, Rebecca trying to hide her tears from her silent son, who moved as if in a trance. He had withdrawn into himself and was oblivious to outside stimulation.

After walking a few blocks, they reached the little park across from the Orthodox church. The wicker trunk was heavy and, without speaking, they sat down to rest, the mother with red, tear-stained eyes, the son with a stone-like countenance. Both were silent, staring straight ahead.

Neither noticed Father Ignatius crossing the street for his midday walk.

"What's the matter, my children?" asked the kindly old man.

Rebecca burst into tears and could not talk for her sobbing. The priest waited patiently until her crying had diminished.

"My husband left, and we've been thrown out of our lodgings. We have nowhere to go." She started sobbing again.

"Come, come my child. Things are never as bad as they seem. Tell me what's been happening."

Disregarding Jacob's presence, Rebecca began to spew out the story of her life. She was surprised that she felt so comfortable relating such intimate details to a relative stranger. This was the first time in her life she had spoken to anyone so openly. The priest listened intently.

"You certainly have had a difficult time," said Father Ignatius when she had finished her sad tale. "Why don't you and the boy come stay with us at St. Basil's until you can figure out where to go from here? We have plenty of room there, and feeding you won't be a problem. We'll keep a lookout for your husband in case he comes searching for you."

Rebecca was grateful for the offer. She had no idea what she would have done if the good father hadn't appeared.

Rebecca and Jacob were given a sparsely furnished but adequate room in the church rectory. There were two single beds with a small nightstand in between. An old, unpainted wooden dresser with three drawers stood against the almost bare walls, and a small, square desk and chair occupied the far corner of the room. Two thin, rectangular woven mats lay on the floor on either side of the bed. Above each bed was a wooden crucifix showing Jesus on the cross. The only other decoration in the room was provided by two framed gilded icons showing different aspects of the Holy Mother and Child.

The current mother and child occupants ate in the rectory kitchen with Maria the housekeeper and Stanislav the gardener.

Father Ignatius generally took his meals alone in the large bedroom on the second floor, though occasionally he would join them for breakfast.

During one such breakfast a few days later, the priest said to his guests, "And what will we do about Jacob's education?"

Rebecca wasn't sure what to say. She knew from inquiries made by the priest that Aaron hadn't been seen since 'the explosion' and that Jacob would not be welcome in his former classroom.

"I don't know," she replied. "I haven't given it much thought."

"The nuns of the order of St. Stephan run a school for young boys. It's just a few blocks away. There, Jacob can learn to read and write the language of the land, a skill that will serve him well in the future."

Not knowing what else to say, Rebecca answered, "That sounds like a good idea. What do you think, Jacob?"

Jacob's stony face did not react to her question. He sat staring off into the distance.

"I'm sure he'll like it once he starts," said Father Ignatius. "I'll make the necessary arrangements and accompany you to school next Monday."

* * *

The following Monday, the priest, with Jacob and Rebecca in tow, led the way to Jacob's new school. Jacob carried a small bag with some bread and cheese for lunch. It was, as Father Ignatius had said, about three blocks away, on the other side of the small park, a squat, two-story, red brick building with narrow windows and a large crucifix over the front door.

"Wait here," he said and went inside to fetch someone.

He emerged a few minutes later with a tall, stern-looking woman dressed in a long, black gown and a black headpiece covering her hair.

"This is Reverend Mother Anietka," explained the priest. "She's in charge of the school. She'll see to it that Jacob gets a good education."

The Reverend Mother took Jacob's hand and pulled him away from his mother. Jacob began to scream, "No, mama! I don't want to go. I want to stay with you!"

"Never mind," said the Reverend Mother, "he'll be just fine. We're used to dealing with situations like this."

"Come, Rebecca," coaxed Father Ignatius, "they'll take good care of him, and you can pick him up this afternoon."

Rebecca allowed herself to be led away gently by the priest. She could hear Jacob screaming as she walked down the block.

* * *

Jacob stopped crying after about twenty minutes.

"Now then, that's better", said the Reverend Mother. "I'll take you to your classroom to meet your new teacher and the other students."

Jacob said nothing. He stared straight ahead.

He was taken to a classroom where fifteen or so boys were sitting at small wooden tables. Another nun with a shorter habit sat at a larger desk at the front of the room.

"Jacob, this is Sister Annemarie," she said curtly. Without

waiting for a reply from either Jacob or the teacher, she turned and marched out of the classroom to take care of the many other items that clamored for her attention.

"Hello Jacob," said the teacher. "We're happy to have you join us. This will be your seat." She pointed to a desk in the front row directly opposite her own. "You may sit here until you are more familiar with the school and get to know some of your classmates."

As Jacob took his seat without resistance, he heard laughing and whispers behind his back. Some of the boys had occasionally seen him enter the Jewish cheder not far away.

"Look at the dirty Jew," one said. "He wants to be like us."

"We don't want him," said another. "Send him back to where he came from."

Jacob turned around to see where the remarks were coming from. He saw a blond boy about a year older than himself laughing and pointing at him. Disregarding the older boy's large size, Jacob walked over and gave him an unexpected hard push that toppled the perpetrator out of his chair. Another stood up to defend his friend, and a classroom brawl began.

Sister Annemarie was a young woman of nineteen just out of the novitiate. She had no experience dealing with children in a classroom setting. She tried to break up the fight but quickly realized that her efforts were useless and ran down the hall to get help.

"Stop this immediately!" boomed the voice of Reverend Mother Anietka when she returned to the classroom. "What is going on here?"

The boys slowly disengaged and pointed their fingers at Jacob.

* * *

"He started it!"

"What happened?" she asked Jacob as she turned him around and looked him in the eye.

Jacob did not answer. He stood mutely glaring at the other boys, his right eye was beginning to swell, and blood was running from his nostrils. His trousers were torn and bloodied.

"Answer me, or you'll be punished. What happened?"

Jacob continued to stand and glare mutely.

The Reverend Mother picked up the paddle lying on the teacher's desk for just such an occasion.

"Pull down your pants and bend over."

When Jacob did not respond, she jerked his pants and underwear down, exposing his bare buttocks. His genitals were likewise exposed. The other children had never before seen a circumcised penis.

As the other boys giggled, the Reverend Mother paddled him five times, showing no restraint.

"This should teach you a lesson. We permit no misbehavior or fighting in this school. If it happens again, you will receive more paddles."

When the Reverend Mother left the room, she pulled Sister Annemarie with her to give her some advice.

"Keep the Jew separated in the corner. Make a special effort to teach him Bible stories about our Lord. It will be our mission to bring this black sheep into the fold."

While the nuns were outside, the boys began a sing-song chant, "Jacob has no pri-ick, Jacob has no pri-ick."

Instinctively placing his hands over his genitals, Jacob looked straight ahead and tried to ignore the taunting. His buttocks were red and sore so that it was painful to sit.

Tolerating the pain and refusing to cry, he remained in the corner for the rest of the day—and for most of the following year.

Chapter Twelve

Aaron had been at home for three months. His days had become routine, helping his aging father and overworked mother run the family bakery. He would wake up at 6 a.m., dress, say his morning prayers, and milk the cow and feed the chickens while his slow-moving parents took their time waking and had their breakfast.

It's the least I can do to make things up to them.

Aaron did not consider his activities to be hard work. He knew what hard work was. It was getting up at dawn and working through the day until midnight, holding down two jobs, and taking care of a baby. Now that was hard work.

Sometimes, he wondered what had become of Rebecca and Jacob, but, once again, he would not allow himself to think about it. Doing so caused him to feel too conflicted.

He rather liked the monotonous routine that he had fallen into. He enjoyed being close to his parents and slowly taking over the running of the family business.

While his parents were happy to have him home again, they

worried about his future and talked about it every night in their bedroom before sleeping.

"He has no future here," his mother would say. "He should get married and find some way to make a better living."

"What's wrong with staying here and running the bakery?" Yitzchak would reply.

But he said it only half-heartedly. He knew that Aaron would not be happy doing this for the rest of his life, and his aspirations for his son had not disappeared.

"Maybe he'll meet a rich girl, and her father will take him into his business." Rivka would usually continue.

"That would be nice," Yitzchak would sigh as he turned over and went to sleep.

* * *

Aaron himself was confused about his future.

I don't want to stay in the bakery the rest of my life. But what else can I do here? Everyone knows what happened to me, even if they never say it to my face. They laugh behind my back. No one would want to marry me. I'm damaged goods. I could go to America and join my brothers, but who would take care of mama and papa?

* * *

As Indian summer turned into late autumn, rumors reached the little village of a severe flu epidemic sweeping Eastern Europe. It was a brutal epidemic killing great numbers of people, although it was not as destructive as the pandemic that arrived over a decade later.

The townspeople grew nervous and stayed away from any stranger who entered the town. Sabbath dinner invitations were discontinued. Garlic was hung around necks to ward off evil spirits. But the devastating killer moved relentlessly through Russia, the Ukraine, Poland, and Lithuania. Hundreds of thousands developed a high fever and cough. There was no treatment for the disease. Half of those stricken died, with the very young and the elderly especially affected.

One morning, Aaron noticed that his father was having difficulty breathing.

"Papa, what's wrong?"

"Nothing, son. I'll be fine."

Aaron had a sinking feeling in his stomach. He knew that his father's health was failing and that he would have little strength to resist a serious illness. Yitzchak could hardly sit up in bed. His body was burning hot. Aaron yelled for his mother to apply cold compresses to his father's forehead and ran to fetch Kenchek the medicine man.

Kenchek himself was exhausted. He had visited twelve townspeople already that day. He looked at Yitzchak and shook his head helplessly. There was little he could do.

"Your father's life is in the hands of God," he whispered softly.

Yitzchak held on for three more days. He knew that he was dying. On the third day, he called Aaron to him. Aaron knelt by his father's side, tears streaming down his face.

Thank God I came home in time to see him before he died.

Yitzchak had great difficulty getting out his words.

"My son, I have always loved you," he whispered, his breathing labored. "Take care of your mother and make the best life you can for yourself. You are smart. I have great confidence in you."

He made a supreme effort to place his right hand on Aaron's head.

"You have been a dutiful son, and I bless you forever."

And with those words, his hand fell to his side, and Yitzchak passed into the sleep of eternity.

*   *   *

Aaron and his mother, dressed in the black clothing of mourners, stood in the old Jewish cemetery watching the coffin descend into the grave. There were no others present. So many people had died that the aging rabbi was having a hard time keeping up with the funerals. People were too wrapped up in their own problems to attend the funerals of friends or neighbors. The bearded old man had to rush to get to the next funeral service. Aaron could see the other family waiting as he looked through the headstones across the cemetery. Some of the markers were tilted and crumbling from the effects of age and weather.

"Look, mama. This stone is three hundred years old. Our people have been here a long time."

Reb Rosnowski and Aaron together recited the Kaddish, the Jewish prayer for the dead that never mentions death but simply praises the Lord. Aaron had to speak the words more quickly than usual to keep up with the rabbi, who was obviously feeling pressured by the situation.

"Rabbi, why are you doing that?" Aaron asked as Reb Rosnowski then took out his pen knife and slashed halfway through the black ribbons that he had pinned on the mourners.

"It is a sign of active mourning for thirty days after the death of a close relative," replied the rabbi. Then he shook Aaron and his mother by the hand as he expressed his condolences before scurrying across the cemetery to the next service while trying to avoid stepping on any of the graves. The graves, however, were packed so closely together that the rabbi's efforts were in vain, and, each time he accidentally stepped off the narrow path onto a mound, he would stop, bow, and utter a short prayer of apology to its occupant.

"He'd do better to walk slowly and take his time," Aaron smilingly said to his mother. He marveled that he was able to appreciate a humorous situation at such a time of grief.

*　*　*

Aaron and Rivka closed the bakery and prepared to sit shiva. For the seven-day mourning period, they sat on a low bench and walked around the house with no shoes in a show of respect for God and the deceased. They also covered the mirrors so they could not see their own reflection; the superstition was that the departing soul might see a person's image and take him or her with it.

Ordinarily, neighbors and extended family would have prepared their meals, but this, too, was not practical given the circumstances. Aaron and his mother stayed in the house alone, with no visitors coming to call. Often, they sat in silence, wrapped in their own thoughts.

This is a terribly depressing atmosphere. I wish the neighbors could visit.

On the fifth day of shiva, Rivka developed a hacking cough. She pooh-poohed the symptoms.

"I'm too young to die," she told her son.

However, her symptoms got worse. By the seventh day of shiva, Rivka had developed a high fever and was becoming dehydrated, weak, and listless.

Aaron once again left his mother's side to fetch the medicine man. He found Kenchek himself in bed with a high fever.

Is this God's way of punishing His people? What have we done, Lord, to deserve such a horrible scourge? What kind of God would kill so many innocents?

God didn't answer.

Aaron dragged himself back to his mother's bedside. He bathed her face in cold water and prepared nourishing soup for her to eat, but Rivka had no appetite and could not keep anything down. He tried giving her any remedy that he heard about. He even scoured the woods for herbs that were rumored to soothe the body and reduce fever. But nothing worked.

This can't be happening to me. Is God singling me out to punish me above others by taking both parents at the same time? Have my transgressions been so great?

Rivka held out a little longer than her husband. She died on the eighth day of her illness.

* * *

Aaron stood with Reb Rosnowski again intoning the Kaddish prayer, this time over the grave of his mother as her coffin was lowered to rest next to that of his father.

At least they'll be together again. I'm the one left alone. I'm an orphan now.

The thought was sobering. He hadn't thought of it that way before.

I'm alone in the world.

The old rabbi patted him on the shoulder as if echoing his thoughts.

"Good luck. You're on your own now," the touch seemed to say.

The old man had aged noticeably in the past two weeks. His skin was ashen, his body bent, and his eyes tired. Aaron wondered how much longer he could keep up the pace before he himself became a victim. From here, he was on his way to a wedding in the cemetery. It was believed that, if two orphans were married in that place of the dead at community expense, the plague would end. Aaron, though, didn't see how this could be possible.

If they believe it will work, maybe it will.

Aaron spent the next week in solitude, too distraught to think clearly about his next move. He went through the days in a trance, praying, making small meals for himself, trying to eat to keep his strength up. When the shiva period was complete, he looked around the old shop and the little house connected to it.

My family has been here for hundreds of years, but I know I can't stay in Jelzai any longer. There's nothing here for me.

The possibility of rejoining Rebecca and Jacob crossed Aaron's mind, but he associated them with the sinful behavior for which God was punishing him and dismissed the thought as soon as it appeared.

Maybe I'll go to Kovno and see what opportunities are there.

"Aaron Pechtrowicz?"

A squeaky feminine voice issued from the front door of the shop as Aaron was figuring out what he could salvage from the bakery. He needed to raise some cash. His parents had nothing left but a few rubles. He had decided to leave the town, though he had no idea where he would go.

"Who's there?" he asked as he turned toward the front of the shop.

"It's me, Yetta Tabachnikoff."

Aaron recognized Yetta as the town matchmaker. If he hadn't become involved with Rebecca, his father would have contacted her to arrange the best possible marriage for him.

What could she possibly want with me?

"I bring my condolences. Your parents were lovely people. It seems like half the good people in the village have been taken by this terrible illness. Thank God you have been spared. Tzu, tzu, tzu." She spat on the floor three times to ward off the evil eye.

"Thank you," Aaron replied politely. He knew that offering condolences was not the real purpose of her visit.

"It has come to the attention of a certain respected citizen of our town that you are a good man, a scholar, and available for marriage," she went on. "He would like you to consider marrying his daughter, a wonderful girl; not too pretty, perhaps, but she comes with a large dowry."

Aaron was floored.

What woman in her right mind would want me?

"Who is this 'certain respected citizen'?" countered Aaron.

"His name is Asher Rozin."

Aaron knew of Asher Rozin. He was a wealthy merchant who managed the agricultural holdings of several local landlords, overseeing the planting, picking, sale, and transport of their fruit and vegetables. He remembered seeing his daughter on occasion, a homely, obese girl with few prospects of marriage. He thought her name was Sadie.

Yetta continued.

"He is planning to sell his holdings and move his family to the New World. He thought you might be willing to go with them since you no longer have family here to worry about."

Aaron's head was swimming with questions.

"Why me? He knows nothing about me."

"He knows all about you, young man. He has looked into this matter very closely."

Then he must know why I left. And still he wants me? Is this a message from God? Do I want to go to America? What is there to keep me here?

Yetta explained that, if Aaron agreed, Asher Rozin would pay all of the moving and travel expenses. Aaron would receive five thousand rubles in cash and a new house when they arrived in America. Additionally, Asher would provide the funds to set his son-in-law up in business. Or, Aaron could join Asher in whatever endeavor the latter might develop. Was there anything else Aaron might want?

Aaron realized that Asher wanted to be sure that his daughter would have an appropriate husband from the old country before they left. He didn't trust what might happen in the New World with its unfamiliar ways, and he didn't want his daughter to be alone, in case anything should happen to him.

Aaron told Yetta that she would have his answer in two days. He needed some time to think it over.

* * *

Six weeks later, Aaron married Sadie Rozin. It was a small wedding, attended only by the bride's family and friends. Aaron had no one to invite. The village had been decimated by the flu epidemic. No family was untouched. The affluent father sensitively chose to keep the celebration modest in recognition of the many deaths the villagers had suffered.

The wedding was held in the large living room of Asher Rozin's house. Sadie was dressed in a white gown of pleated silk that fell to the floor from her large bosom. It had been designed with no waist in order to create a slimming effect.

* * *

Reb Rosnowski performed the ceremony. He had managed to survive the epidemic with few ill effects. "I feel fine, dank

Gott," he told Aaron. Perhaps the marriage of orphans in the cemetery had been effective, for the epidemic seemed to have burned itself out.

Again, in recognition of the recent losses, there was no dancing, but Asher Rozin provided mountains of food to please his guests. Many of the dishes Aaron had never tasted before. They included honeyed lamb with currants, brisket of beef with bow ties and groats, and veal cutlets breaded and fried to a delicious golden brown. Exotic fruits, such as pomegranates and bananas, were served with light phyllo pastries for dessert. A single fiddler playing in the background provided a soothing ambience. Aaron had never seen such a bountiful spread before. He was impressed with the munificence of his new father-in-law and thought it boded well for his future.

When the celebration was over, the newly married couple retired to a private, upstairs bedroom. Aaron was apprehensive about his ability to perform his marital duties. Unlike his experience with Rebecca, he felt no sexual attraction whatsoever for his new wife. He was relieved to find that she seemed eager to participate in this new exploration, and he felt somewhat smug about his superior knowledge of the art of love-making. The fact that he had gone almost two years with no sexual release (except when he overcame his guilt and allowed himself some self stimulation on a few occasions) contributed to his easy arousability, and he had no difficulty maintaining an erection. He even made an effort to give his new wife some pleasure, as Rebecca had tried to get him to do for her.

Aaron smiled in self-satisfaction.

All in all, I did pretty well. I wonder what other men do on their wedding night when they've had no previous experiences and no Rebecca to show them what to do.

He moved into his father-in-law's house as the family began to make preparations for closing out their businesses in Jelzai. Much time was spent planning the exciting journey to America. Asher Rozin was planning to settle in Philadelphia, where he had numerous relatives. This was a pleasant surprise to Aaron, who now looked forward to meeting the brothers he had only heard about. They had carried on the family tradition by setting up a bakery in a neighborhood Yitzchak had referred to as Strawberry Mansion.

Strawberry Mansion, thought Aaron, *such a name is enough to make your mouth water. It sounds good enough to eat. With all these mansions, it must be a very rich neighborhood.*

Prior to the wedding, Aaron had sold off his parents' meager possessions. In total, they garnered a mere fifty rubles.

Fifty rubles is fifty rubles; but, living amidst the luxurious surroundings of Asher's Rozin's house, this seemed like a paltry sum indeed.

Aaron busied himself getting to know his new wife and family while they made their elaborate preparations to leave.

Chapter Thirteen

Nearly a year had gone by since Rebecca and Jacob moved into the rectory. Every day, Rebecca hoped to learn some news of Aaron's whereabouts, but no one heard anything about him.

A few weeks after 'the explosion,' there had been rumors about the death of two of the tavern's customers in a failed assassination attempt near Jelzai. Rebecca wondered whether Aaron had anything to do with it, but no one seemed to have any detailed information.

The young mother felt that she was in limbo. She spent her days helping the housekeeper do chores around the church. Sometimes, she would scrub the floors and dust the pews of the house of worship. At such times, she felt at peace, surrounded by burning candles and the silence of the nave.

Each Sunday, the priest invited her to join the congregation at worship services. He tried talking to her about the Savior and the importance of saving her soul and the soul of her son. He frightened her when he thundered,

"Unless you and Jacob accept baptism, you will never get to heaven and will go straight to hell!"

Rebecca was uncomfortable with these attempts to convert her. She knew he was well-meaning but, while she felt grateful for the kindness extended by the church, remained quite uncomfortable in the presence of the many crucifixes and renderings of Jesus on the cross, bleeding and tortured. To give up the religion of her birth seemed a betrayal of her identity, of the essence of herself.

I can't keep saying no to them and continue to accept their generosity at the same time. We can't stay here much longer, but where are we going to go?

Jacob continued to be a problem for his teachers. He refused to cooperate in almost any activity. When Sister Annemarie tried to work with him on a one-to-one basis teaching him Bible stories and the catechism, he would throw the books on the floor and refuse to listen.

"I don't want to learn about Jesus Christ," he would shout. "I'm Jewish!"

The teacher was about at the end of her rope.

Almost every day, it seemed, the other boys in the class would find something to taunt Jacob with and Jacob would respond with violence.

"The Jews are Christ-killers," they would whisper to him so Sister Annemarie couldn't hear.

Around Easter, they taunted him, "Stay away from Jacob! He needs some Christian blood for Passover." One of the boys squeezed a handful of cherry juice on his clean white shirt. "Here is some blood, use this!"

"Go to hell," he snapped at his tormentors, not attempting to modulate his voice. Then Jacob would get out of his seat and punch whichever boy happened to be the torturer of the day. The result was more paddling, and Jacob's buttocks began to develop chronic blisters that often became infected. Still, he persisted in his behavior.

* * *

One day at lunchtime, a group of six boys tried to pin Jacob down and stuff pork into his mouth. He spat out the non-kosher meat, wriggled free, and slammed into the six classmates standing around him. This was one of the few times when Sister Annemarie witnessed most of the action. That day it was the other boys who were paddled, much to Jacob's pleasure.

At least she can be fair sometimes.

However, the pattern remained unchanged. The nuns told Rebecca that her son was incorrigible in class.

"Why do you get in such trouble?"

"Because they call me names and say I'm a dirty Jew."

"Ignore them!"

Jacob did not want to argue with his mother, but he knew, at some very deep level, that, if he ignored them, he would be giving up his personal dignity, of which he had precious little.

I can't give them the satisfaction.

Jacob did, however, manage to master the reading and writing of the Cyrillic alphabet. He seemed to have a gift for languages and was a quick learner.

* * *

One Friday afternoon, Rebecca and Jacob were sitting in the park across from the church when they ran into Nafty the brothel owner on his way home for the Sabbath.

Jacob ran to him and gave him a big hug.

"It's so good to see you!" cried Rebecca, kissing him on the cheek. "We've missed all of you so much."

Nafty was pleased with this reception.

"I'm happy to see you too," he grinned. "What are you doing now?"

Rebecca explained her situation.

"I don't like where I am, and I know I've got to find another place to live and work. But I've been waiting for Aaron to return. I just know he'll be back soon."

Nafty's eyes shifted to the ground and he seemed to shrivel up some.

Rebecca saw the change in his demeanor.

"What's wrong, Nafty. Tell me. What do you know about Aaron that we don't?"

Nafty lifted his face to look directly into Rebecca's clear green eyes.

"Aaron won't be coming home, Rebecca. We heard from friends in Jelzai that he's recently gotten married and is preparing to leave for America with his new wife."

"No, that can't be," sobbed Rebecca. "He already has a wife and a son. He wouldn't leave us here alone."

Jacob said nothing, but tears formed in the corners of his eyes.

* * *

Rebecca knew what she had to do. That night at dinner, she asked to see Father Ignatius.

"Thank you, father, for all you've done. I know we've been a real problem for you, and I appreciate all the chances you've given us."

She recounted her news to the priest and informed him of her plan.

"Jacob and I will be leaving tomorrow. We'll be taking the morning coach to Jelzai to bring back Aaron. I'm sure this whole marriage business is some kind of mistake."

Father Ignatius smiled.

"I hope you're right, Rebecca. You're a strong-minded young woman who knows what she wants."

The priest placed his hands on the heads of the mother and son.

"May you travel with God," he intoned.

* * *

Rebecca and Jacob arrived in Jelzai three days later. She had used the salary that Meir had given her to pay for their fares and food. She had just enough left over for three coach fares back to Vilna.

Jacob had never been out of Vilna. To him, the trip took on the characteristics of an adventure. His mother had told him that he would see his grandmother and grandfather. He was impatiently looking forward to this because all his classmates had family, and he wanted to be able to say, "My grandparents live in Jelzai. We just came from a visit."

Rebecca alighted from the coach, took her son's hand, and headed toward the old Pechtrowicz bakery. She was stunned to find it boarded up and empty.

The mother and son walked next door to the butcher shop.

"Where are Yitzchak and Rivka?" she asked Chaim the butcher, a note of desperation in her voice.

"They died in the flu epidemic," Chaim replied. I give you my condolences." He knew that Rebecca was Rivka's sister but wondered about the young boy.

Jacob's face fell.

"And where's Aaron?"

"He's living with his new wife in the house of her father, Asher Rozin. They're leaving for America in two days."

* * *

Rebecca felt like a bullet had just pierced her heart. She had to sit down on the bare ground to keep from fainting.

"I can see your sister's death is a shock. Can I get you a drink?" asked the solicitous butcher.

Rebecca accepted a glass of water from her former neighbor.

"Can you give me directions to the house of Asher Rozin?"

* * *

The distraught mother and son found their way to the house. With trepidation, Rebecca lifted the heavy brass knocker and rapped three times.

The door was opened by the housekeeper. "Yes?"

"May I please see Aaron Pechtrowicz?"

"Who shall I say is calling?"

"His wife and son," replied Rebecca with a defiant wave of her head.

The puzzled housekeeper thought the woman was crazy, but she called Aaron to the door.

Aaron was dumbstruck to find them waiting on the steps.

"Papa!" cried Jacob, as he ran up to his father and wrapped his arms around his legs, the only part of his body he could reach.

"What are you doing here?" Aaron screamed at Rebecca as he pushed Jacob away and stepped backward." I told you I was never coming back. Get out of here!"

Rage was building in his voice. He herded Rebecca and Jacob away from the house so as not to be noticed by his wife or her parents.

"But Aaron, how can you abandon us? How can you let Jacob grow up without a father? We have nothing, no money. What are we to do? Where are we to go?"

By this time, Aaron's rage was out of control. He pushed Rebecca away.

"I'm leaving for America, and I never want to see you again. Do whatever you must do. I don't want to hear about it."

Aaron stuck his hand into his pocket and pulled out the money that he had on him.

"Take this," he said and threw the bills and coins on the ground in front of Rebecca.

Turning to go, he stuck his hand under his shirt and pulled

out the pouch containing the coin. His visage softening a bit, he yanked it from his neck. Turning to face Jacob, he hesitated and then tossed the pouch to his son, as if the sacrifice of his treasure would ease the burden of guilt on his heart.

Jacob picked up the pouch as Aaron turned away.

"You'll never see me again," he declared. "Don't try to contact me."

* * *

Then he marched back toward the house where his new wife, in the early months of pregnancy, had been watching, eagle-eyed, from the top of the stoop. She slipped back into the house before he noticed her there.

At the top of his lungs, Jacob screamed, "Papa! Papa! Don't leave me! Take me with you! Please!"

Jacob fell into a sobbing heap as Aaron entered the house and slammed the door behind him.

Chapter Fourteen

"**H**appy birthday, Jacob," they said in unison when the twelve-year old entered the house in the late afternoon.

They had been waiting for him to arrive. Three of the four girls had prepared a small gift wrapped in colorful paper and ribbon. They had already changed into their working attire for the night. Three wore dresses of filmy gossamer material through which were visible their dark areolas and nipples. The skirts barely reached past the top of their thighs and didn't try very hard to cover the triangular dark patch between their well-shaped legs. They wore no underwear.

The fourth young woman wore nothing but a short silky robe, which parted to her belly button whenever she moved her legs.

Rebecca stood off to the side smiling at the scene. She looked around at the red velvet furniture and gold damask draperies that decorated the living room.

This is my family. These are my sisters.

She watched as her son opened his gifts.

There was a silver key ring from Elka and an embroidered white linen shirt from Alisha. Brigit gave him a shaving cup, brush, soap, and straight razor. "You need it now," she laughed as she ran her hand over the downy but thick tufts of hair on his face and chin.

Jacob was no longer a boy. Though not yet in his teens, he had the tall, well-proportioned, muscular body of a sixteen-year-old. The young man had the striking good looks of his mother—intense green eyes flecked with brown, a straight aquiline nose, and curly dark hair.

Anna, the girl in the robe, came over and kissed his ear.

"I have a very special gift for you," she whispered so no one else could hear. "Come to my room tonight after we close, and you'll find out what it is."

Tonight will be the night. I'll finally get to know what really goes on behind those doors.

He was glad it would be Anna who initiated him. She was his favorite, always buying him special little treats and comforting him through the years when he had arguments with his mother.

Jacob had grown up quickly. Abandoned by his father, he had realized that he was 'the man of the family' at the age of six. His mother treated him in ways that were confusing. Sometimes, she wanted him to be her dependent little boy, overprotecting him and demanding that he obey her every command, while, at other times, she acted as if he were her father or husband, asking him for advice and wanting him to protect and take care of her. Nevertheless, Jacob understood what she had gone through and had eventually learned to handle her moods without getting into constant fights with her. He simply listened to her words and then went out and did whatever he pleased. It wasn't that he wanted to disobey her, it was just that she usually could not think straight and gave him mixed messages. If he had listened to her, he would have ended up either crazy or being kicked around by the world.

* * *

Jacob was a survivor. He had become adept at reading people and situations because he knew that his advantage was anticipating what another would want or do. He had learned the tactics of street fighting because, since he had fought for his dignity at St. Basil's, other bands of boys and men had been trying to take it away from him. Gangs of Christian schoolboys roaming the streets would try to beat him up, but Jacob had learned to run when the odds were stacked too heavily against him and to use every dirty trick at his command when a fight was unavoidable. He had become known as a formidable opponent, and now most of the neighborhood hooligans left him alone, much to his relief.

Jacob had not returned to the Jewish school. The teachers didn't want him, and he refused to return to the classroom where his father had spent so much time.

The work that he did for 'Uncle Nafty' the bordello owner—Jacob didn't like the term 'whoremaster' considering it demeaning—took him to the roughest parts of town. Jacob had worked for Nafty ever since he and Rebecca had returned from Jelzai, where Aaron had rejected them. In desperation, his mother had turned to Nafty, who brought them to his 'house,' gave them room and board, and added Rebecca to his stable of high-class prostitutes. Nafty was kind to his girls. He allowed them to keep forty percent of their earnings, and the girls usually stayed with him for four or five years until they had saved enough to go back to their little villages and start a new life.

Nafty's bordello was designed to make its clients feel that they were being entertained in the lap of luxury. The sitting room had red velvet couches, floors with thick carpeting, and fancy wallpaper decorated with figures of nude men and women. There were six bedrooms with mirrored ceilings and a toilet facility at the end of the hallway. Nafty maintained a second dwelling next door to the bordello where the girls slept and had their own bedrooms. This was where Jacob would find Anna waiting for him later that night. Nafty had given the boy his own tiny room to sleep in. It was little more than a closet, but Nafty understood the privacy that a growing boy needs from his mother.

The whorehouse wasn't Nafty's only business operation. He ran a series of floating crap games around the city and took bets on various sporting events. Every week, Nafty would collect the cash from these various endeavors. Sometimes, if he deemed a collection not to be too dangerous, he would send Jacob for the money. Nafty would then pack it into three envelopes and place them in a leather suitcase, and Jacob would go on his weekly bank rounds. His first stop would be at the Jewish Landschaft Bank, where he would hand the bank president, Reuven Langweber, the first envelope. Jacob would proceed to the two other Jewish banking establishments in Vilna and repeat the procedure with their presidents.

Nafty knew that a young boy walking with a small leather satchel would not garner too much attention. "Never store all your potatoes in the same hole," he would tell his young protégé, "or let any one person know too much about your business." Jacob would receive twenty kopecks for each run.

Sometimes, if one of the girls left the house during the day, Nafty would motion for Jacob to follow her without being seen. "I just want to be sure that she's not doin' a little business on the side," he would explain a bit apologetically.

Jacob did not like this part of the job. He loved all of the girls and felt that he was betraying their trust by spying on their activities. Luckily, he never caught any of them doing anything suspicious. If he had, he really didn't know whether or not he would have said anything to Nafty, whom he also loved and thought of as a surrogate father.

* * *

Jacob was looking forward to his birthday present from Anna. He knew, of course, what the girls were doing with their 'customers' behind the bedroom doors. He was much too bright and had been around far too long not to know. What he didn't know and wanted to find out was what it felt like. He had heard the noises, the moans and groans and squeaking of the beds, for many years.

Tonight, I'll experience it firsthand.

He looked down and noticed that his pants were tightening in his groin. His body was already anticipating tonight's event. His hand, automatically it seemed, began playing with the silver coin that he had hung in its pouch on a silk cord around his neck and never took off. Rubbing the coin calmed him, though he felt no overt anxiety. His trust of the girls was such that it never crossed his mind to question their handling of him.

Jacob slipped into Anna's bedroom after everyone else had fallen asleep. The house was dark, but his eyes had adapted. Besides, he knew each nook and cranny by heart. He had lived there for almost six years.

Anna took his hand and closed the door softly behind him. Without a word, she pulled him close to her and pressed her body against his, kissing him deeply. This felt good to Jacob, and, when she momentarily paused, he surprised her by firmly returning the kiss. Pleased, she ran her hands over his skin under his shirt, sending a chill up and down his spine and giving him goose bumps. Pulling her face away, she lifted his shirt over his head and, slipping out of her robe, unbuttoned his pants and continued to undress him. She chuckled to herself as she realized that he had deliberately not worn underwear in anticipation of the moment. Gently pushing him back against the wall for support, she helped him step out of his trousers. Then, after tracing her tongue over his chest and abdomen, she guided him onto her bed.

As Anna moved up and down his body, seeking and finding every crevice of erotic sensitivity, she could feel Jacob working up to a fevered pitch. Several times he tried to mount her but she adroitly shifted position and delayed his climactic moment as long as possible. Finally, she straddled him and moved into the rhythm of the motion using no more delaying tactics. She was surprised to find herself becoming extremely aroused as Jacob prolonged the dance on his own, intuitively sensing her response to his activity. Finally they exploded together, each surprised at the intensity of their reaction.

Jacob knew her response was genuine.

I can really do that. She's responding to me.

Anna was astounded. She had had sex with many men almost every night of the past few years. With everyone else it had been a mechanical action and she had feigned any sexual response on her own part. But this time it was different.

I can't believe that a young boy having sex for the first time can make me feel this way. He will be some lover!

Jacob did not want to leave. Each time Anna felt exhausted and ready for sleep, he would begin to stimulate her again. She could feel him ascending a steep learning curve in what seemed like no time at all. Each time she again became aroused and was brought to climax. Each time she was surprised by her unexpected response.

How can he do this to me? What power does he have?

Finally, as light began to filter through the windowpane, Anna pushed him off firmly.

"I need some sleep, and so do you."

"It was a wonderful birthday present," said Jacob softly. "The best I've ever received."

It was better than I ever thought it could be.

He slipped on his clothing and walked out of the room with a swagger and new confidence—all remaining vestiges of his childhood gone with the rising sun.

Chapter Fifteen

A few weeks after Jacob's twelfth birthday, a letter stamped with the imperial crest of Russia was delivered to Rebecca Pechtrowicz. Rebecca had never before received any mail, let alone mail from the imperial government. She opened it with trembling hands.

Dear Mrs. Pechtrowicz,

This letter is to inform you that your son, Jacob Pechtrowicz, is hereby instructed to report for duty in the Czar's army on August 15, 1912, at the Central Vilna Armory. He will be inducted for a service period of five years.

If he fails to report, he will be subject to arrest and imprisonment for failure to perform his required military obligation.

Colonel I.M. Petrikoff

Commander

Third Army

Sobbing uncontrollably, Rebecca took the letter to Nafty.

"What can we do? He'll die if he goes into the army."

"Calm down. I'll have to look into this."

"How did they get my son's name?" She could barely form the words between gasps.

"Rebecca," Nafty gently explained, "the Jewish Council has been forced to provide a census of all Jewish citizens to the Russian government. Even the children and their ages are included. With the Reds getting stronger, the czar is getting desperate. He's trying to build up the army to fight them."

"But we haven't had any trouble around here."

"That's true. So far, most of the fighting has been in the Ukraine. But the troubles are rapidly spreading here."

"But Jacob is only twelve years old."

"Do you think the damned czar cares about sending Jewish children to their deaths? They're just cannon fodder to him. Thirty years ago, they were kidnapping little Jewish boys eight years old and sending them to the army. These people are heartless beasts."

"Can't we bribe the police to take Jacob's name off the list? I remember that Aaron's father used to give the police chief money every year to keep Aaron out of the army."

"That was then; this is now. It used to be easy to bribe the officials, especially in the little villages where everyone was on a first-name basis. I don't know what it's like there now, but, here in Vilna, the officials are afraid. They know that, if they're caught taking a bribe, they themselves will be arrested and thrown in prison.

"Oh, God. Nafty, what will we do? I'll die if Jacob is sent away!"

"Let me see what I can find out."

* * *

The next day, Nafty paid a visit to Eliyahu Yarkanski, the head of the Vilna Jewish Council.

"Who can I talk to?" he asked, after explaining the situation.

"It's getting very tough. Ivan Ivanovich, the deputy police chief, has been altering the lists for years. He used to charge five hundred rubles. Now that the situation is more dangerous for him, he has upped his fee to two thousand rubles, and even then there's no guarantee he'll be successful. He's being watched very closely."

"Two thousand rubles? That's impossible. Who can afford two thousand rubles?"

"That's the only suggestion I can give you. And, like I said, there's no guarantee."

Eliezer shook his head sadly. "I wish I had better news for you."

* * *

Nafty brought Rebecca the bad news.

"There is nothing that can be done. Where are you going to get two thousand rubles?"

"Thank you, Nafty. I've got to try."

Rebecca rushed to her room, locked the door, and pulled a locked box from under her bed. She had never trusted banks. Inside the box was her life savings. Making sure that no one was around to interrupt, Rebecca emptied the metal container onto the floor. Out poured a pile of gold and silver coins mixed with paper currency. Carefully, she began counting her secret nest egg.

* * *

"Nafty!" Rebecca called out when he arrived at the bordello that evening, "I must talk to you." She pulled him into the small room that served as his office.

"I've managed to save up twelve hundred rubles over the past six years. If you'll lend me the extra eight hundred, you can take it out of my salary until you have all your money back."

Nafty was at a loss for words. He had made a practice of never getting involved in the private life of his girls, but Rebecca was a special case. And he truly cared about Jacob, whom he often felt was like the son he had never had.

The next afternoon, Rebecca walked to the office of the police department with two thousand rubles hidden in her purse. "Would you please direct me to the office of the deputy police chief?" she asked.

The young officer looked at the beautiful young woman in front of him and smiled.

"His office is on the second floor at the top of the stairs. But you may have a bit of trouble finding him."

Rebecca wasn't sure what to make of the policeman's reply. Not wanting to call too much attention to herself, she ascended the staircase and found a door with a glass panel on which was painted IVAN IVANOVICH—DEPUTY CHIEF. The door was ajar. Two men were emptying out the desk in the center of the room.

"Pardon me," Rebecca said. "Is Deputy Chief Ivan Ivanovich here?"

The men laughed. "And what would a pretty thing like you want with our deputy director?"

"I just wanted to ask him a question."

"Well, you'll have to go to Treblinka Prison if you want to ask him anything. He was just arrested for taking bribes to alter the conscription lists."

Rebecca nearly fainted.

* * *

The next morning, Rebecca pulled Jacob aside.

"Jacob, you must do something. You just can't let them take you away."

"Don't worry, mother. Let them come after me. They'll never find me. I'll move around from place to place. This is a big city."

"Oh, Jacob! You can't live the rest of your life in hiding. Sooner or later, they'll catch you."

"What do you think I should do?"

Rebecca had thought about this for quite a while. She had heard that several boys scheduled for recruitment had cut off the ends of their second and third fingers, which prevented them from being able to fire a gun, so the boys were rejected for service.

"We'll chop off your fingertips and then they won't want you," Rebecca announced triumphantly.

Jacob recoiled in horror. "Are you crazy? I would never do anything like that."

Rebecca's face fell dejectedly.

"Jacob, you must do it. I'd die if they took you away."

"I can handle myself, mother. They'll never catch me."

Over the next few days, Rebecca persisted in her attempts to convince Jacob to mutilate himself.

"For God's sake, leave me alone, mother. Having to stay here with you is getting to be just as bad as having to run and hide."

Unsatisfied and terrified, Rebecca determined her plan of action.

* * *

In the meantime, Jacob was forming his own plan.

Mother is right. If I hang around here trying to hide, sooner or later, they'll catch me. And, even if they don't, what kind of life can I have? It's bad enough to be a Jew here, but a Jew on the run will be treated with no mercy. I could go to America, but that would leave my mother here alone. Maybe that wouldn't be so bad, though. Nafty and the girls will take care of her.

Jacob was aware that Nafty and his mother had a special relationship. Sometimes he would come home a little early and hear Nafty's voice coming from his mother's bedroom accompanying the noises of lovemaking. He knew that sex was a part of their friendship and felt good that the two people whom he loved most enjoyed each other on many levels. He was certain that, if he left for America, Nafty would take care of his mother. But she would take his leaving as a difficult loss.

I'll bring her to America when I've saved enough money for her passage. She'll like it there. But I can't tell her I'm going or she'll make a big scene, and then I might not be able to leave.

The night before he was due to report for military duty, Jacob surreptitiously packed a few items of clothing into a small cloth sack and hid it under his bed so that Rebecca would not notice.

He stuffed the fifty rubles that he had managed to save from his work in his pants pocket. He made sure his father's pouch and coin were under his shirt on the silk cord around his neck— where he had carried them for the past four years. His father had told him the story of that coin many times when he was little. He knew that he would never sell it under any circumstances. It was all that he had left of his father.

Earlier that day he had written Rebecca a short note, which he placed under his pillow.

Dear Mother,

I'm going to America. When I get there I'll write and tell you where I am. I'll save my money so that you can join me there. Don't worry about me. I'll be fine.

Jacob

The one good thing about going to St. Basil's is that I learned how to read and write.

Jacob slid under the sheets completely dressed, waiting for the house to fall asleep.

* * *

In the quiet of the early morning hours, he was about to get out of bed when he heard the squeak of his door opening. Smelling his mother's perfume, he pretended to be asleep. Suddenly he felt his wrist being grabbed and, opening his eyes, saw the glint of a blade.

"What the hell are you doing?" he shouted as he pulled away and snatched a butcher knife from her hand.

At the top of her voice, Rebecca began to scream. "I can't let them take you! You'll die. Let me cut them off! Let me cut them off." Then, she broke down sobbing at the foot of his bed.

"I can't believe you would do this to me!" Jacob raged. "My own mother, trying to cut off my fingers!"

"It's because I love you," she whimpered between sobs.

Angry beyond words, Jacob stood up and pulled his sack from under the bed. Then he grabbed the letter from under his pillow and threw it at his mother. Without a goodbye to the girls who had heard the ruckus and stuck their heads out of their rooms, Jacob stomped down the steps and left the house.

"Jacob, come back! The voices of his mother and the women he loved followed him as he stormed down the empty street.

Jacob never looked back.

Chapter Sixteen

It took Rebecca about an hour to regain some semblance of control. As she lifted her wet face from her son's pillow, she noticed a piece of paper drift to the floor.

"Oh my God! No!" she screamed as she grasped the import of the note Jacob had left.

"He can't do this. I'll be alone. I'll never see him again!"

In her nightgown, Rebecca ran out of the house and down the street looking for her son. Aimlessly, she dragged herself from street to street, hair blowing and eyes wildly glazed, like a madwoman. The city was deserted at that time of night. The few people whom she passed steered away from her, frightened by her behavior and concerned that she might be dangerous.

"Jacob! Where are you? Come back!"

Two hours later, Rebecca, exhausted and by now oblivious to the world, slumped semi-conscious under a street lamp, her nightgown drawn up over her thighs and her breasts hanging loosely inside her flimsy bodice.

"What have we here?" Rebecca barely heard a far-off voice.

Three soldiers with uniforms disheveled and caps askew had come upon her on their way back to the barracks after a night of drinking.

"I do believe I see a woman of the night. She's been waiting for us to come by. What do you think, boys?"

Oh, no, she tried to say, I'm searching for my son. But no words came from her lips. Her voice was gone.

"I think she wants to come with us," laughed another of the soldiers.

Picking Rebecca up like a rag doll, the three men drunkenly carried her to a small, deserted park nearby and threw her on the ground.

"Let's see what she looks like," said the first soldier as he tore her nightgown from her breast with a yank. Her feeble scream stuck in her throat.

Mercifully, Rebecca sank into unconsciousness as the men had their way with her. When Nafty found her dead body sprawled on the grass under a tree the next morning, he sank to the ground and wept.

Chapter Seventeen

Angry but relieved that he now had a reason to justify leaving, Jacob headed instinctively in the direction of the central market. He ambled along deep in thought, trying to formulate a plan of action.

The city was beginning to awake. He suddenly realized that it was market day when he found himself in the midst of farmers hauling their produce and other wares to the market where they set up their stalls. There were plums, cherries, apples, and a vast array of fresh vegetables for sale. People were rushing back and forth, old friends were greeting one another, and he could make out bits and pieces of conversations.

"It won't be long now. The Reds are getting stronger. Pretty soon they'll take over."

"Naw, it'll never happen. The czar is too powerful. He has all the guns."

"Don't be too sure. Many of the officers are just waiting 'til the time is right to join the rebels."

"Be careful. Many of those officers and policemen are

starazniks. They pretend to be rebels, but they really are informants for the czar. Just last week, the Reds killed a policeman when it was discovered that he was spying."

War is going to break out. This is a good time to leave.

Thinking about the significance of the chatter that he was hearing, Jacob wandered through the noisy market. He smelled the tantalizing odors of roasting nuts and fish frying with onions. He realized that he was very hungry, not having eaten the night before, and used a bit of his money to buy breakfast.

I need to save money for my passage to America—if I ever get out of here.

Jacob spent a few kopecks on some pickled herring, onions, and a large wedge of pumpernickel along with a glass of hot tea to wash it down.

The boy sat on the grass behind one of the stalls and ate his breakfast, keeping his small sack of belongings within arm's reach. Every time a policeman or soldier passed by, Jacob clutched his sack and try to blend into the background. However, nobody paid much attention to him, and he finished his meal in peace.

The young man tried to focus on developing a specific plan to get to America. First, he needed to gather some information.

Many people who are leaving will be going by train. That's probably a good place to start. I'll go to the railroad station and see what I can find out.

The large railway terminal was located in the central business district. It covered three city blocks and was constructed of locally quarried stone. There were large Ionic columns at the front entrance, between which hordes of people rushed in and out of the building. Smartly-dressed business types mixed with travelers carrying large wicker trunks, smaller leather satchels, and tapestry rucksacks. Peddlers hawked cakes, cookies, bagels, and fruit. Coachmen dressed in livery roamed the floor holding their horsewhips, looking for business.

* * *

Jacob was awed by the bustling station. He had never seen so many people together at the same time. Looking for a source of information, he scanned the terminal and spied a family of four people carrying six large pieces of luggage. They seemed to be a father, mother, and two daughters aged about ten and twelve. Jacob squeezed through the crowd and sat down on the floor within hearing range of their conversation.

"Papa, where do we go after we get to Kovno?"

"We must then find the boatman, who'll take us down the Niemen River."

"How will we find him?"

"He's to meet us at the inn where we'll stay tonight. Don't worry, Gittele, everything will be all right."

The father is talking to his youngest daughter. He's trying to reassure her, but I can tell that he himself is worried.

"How far is it to Kovno?"

"About six hours by train," answered the well-dressed woman sitting with them.

That must be the mother. She is worried, too. I can hear it in her voice.

"I, for one, am looking forward to the trip," said the other girl. "I think it is a great adventure."

"That's a good way to look at it, Saraleh. I'm sure we'll get there without a problem. Many of our people have paved the way for us."

Ahh! That older girl is a brave one! She isn't afraid of taking risks.

Jacob continued to take in their conversation. Once they nodded off to sleep, he moved around the terminal, plopping himself near anyone who he thought might be a source of the information that he was seeking. He listened to their conversations and deduced most of the details that weren't stated explicitly.

In a short time, Jacob built up a significant store of information. He learned that there were several possible routes out of Vilna to the New World. The shortest and, theoretically, quickest was to travel to Libau on the Baltic coast, take a ship to England, and there transfer to a U.S.-bound transatlantic liner. Libau, however, was under Russian control, and, while no passport was necessary to enter another country, Russia insisted that every emigrating citizen must carry one in order to leave Russia. Of course, the Russian officials used this procedure as a way to bilk departing citizens of money. They would ask for unexpected 'fees' and hold up issuance if they weren't paid, or they would find other reasons to withhold approval if the citizens did not bribe them sufficiently.

Most Jews, not trusting the Russian government, preferred to take a land route out of Russian territory to Germany and bribe officials to turn their backs as they crossed the border.

Once in Germany, they would travel by train or coach to Bremen or Hamburg, where a fleet of German liners waited to take them to America—steerage class, of course. Most emigrants could not afford the price of a first- or second-class ticket. A smaller number of emigrants would travel to England or Holland to board transatlantic liners. The choice often depended on which shipping company relatives in America chose when purchasing the tickets for them.

The shipping companies were hungry for the emigrants' business and sent agents to all of the cities and towns with a large Eastern European Jewish population. These agents would hire sub-agents to operate in the villages. They not only sold tickets but also often made the arrangements for their clients to be smuggled across the various borders.

After digesting all of this new information, Jacob formulated his plan.

First, I have to get to Kovno. That's where everybody seems to start off because it's closer to the German border. Then I'll worry about what to do next.

The boy did not want to spend any more of his carefully hoarded cash to pay for a train ticket. Wandering around the terminal, walking the tracks, and observing the operations, he soon determined that several freight cars loaded with animals, produce, and manufactured goods were attached to each passenger train. He then watched and easily discovered which train the emigrants boarded whom he knew to be on their way to Kovno.

I'd better bring along some food. Who knows when I'll eat again?

He fortified himself with a loaf of bread and cheese. Then, he found an attached unlocked freight car and, holding tightly to his rucksack, pulled himself up into it, remaining as inconspicuous as possible. The car was dank and moist and smelled as if it had recently transported cattle. Piles of hay and cow manure were scattered on the floor.

Who cares? I'll make a little pallet of hay for myself, and I'll be OK.

To his amazement and relief, no one bothered to check the empty car. He ate his meal and soon fell into a deep sleep. When he woke, it was six hours later. Night had fallen and the train was pulling into Kovno.

Chapter Eighteen

J acob slipped down from the freight car onto the tracks. The night was dark and chilly. He took a sweater from his sack.

Anna gave me this sweater for my birthday last year.

He smiled at the memory of the gift that she had given him this year.

He picked his way among the multiple sets of tracks, trying to step only on the wooden ties, heading for an area of light that he assumed to be the terminal building.

"Stop! Who is that?' growled a deep voice from somewhere behind him.

Jacob took off, scampering across the yard like a scared rabbit. He tried to keep in the shadows of the cars but had to cross areas of light. He ran parallel to the building that had been his goal and, when he reached it, ducked into its shadow. Seeing that he was no longer being pursued, Jacob looked into the window.

The terminal was surprisingly crowded for the lateness of the hour. The members of families unable to afford overnight lodgings sat or lay on the benches and floors with their blankets and wicker baskets, readying themselves for the night. Awaiting connections that would not arrive until the next morning, they munched on the provisions that they had brought with them, while the ever-present pushcarts were also doing a brisk business selling herring, cheese, bread, and fruit.

Jacob spied the family of four that he had observed earlier. They had collected their belongings and were following a coachman to the front of the terminal, the girls trailing behind their parents. Saraleh, the older one, kept a close eye on her sister, who stopped repeatedly to investigate anything that happened to catch her eye. At one point, she noticed a small dog that had found his way into the building and was looking for something to eat.

"Can I give him a piece of cheese, Sara?" she asked her sister.

"No, Gittel. We have to go. Father is taking us to an inn for the night. Tomorrow will be a long day. We take the boat down the river. We should see lots of interesting sights."

Jacob watched as they stepped into a four-passenger coach pulled by two chocolate-brown horses. The driver loaded the luggage onto the open ledge in the rear.

Without thinking about it, Jacob sprinted across the central square to the loaded coach and jumped unseen onto the luggage rack.

They seem to know what they're doing.

After a relatively short ride, the coach entered a small courtyard with stucco walls. There was a gas light over the door of the building within. Jacob made out a painted sign hanging over the door with the picture of a bed. Underneath was painted a knife and fork.

As the coach slowed to a stop, Jacob jumped off and started to run toward the stables. He wasn't fast enough, though, for the driver leaped down, grabbed him by one arm, and tore his rucksack from his grasp.

* * *

"Trying to steal from these good people?" the driver asked.

"Oh no, sir. This is mine. I was only trying to find my way to the German border, and I knew these people were going there."

"Some story," the driver said to the girls' father, whose name was Abba Zuckerman.

Sara, who had descended from the coach, eyed Jacob carefully.

"Papa, this boy was at the train station in Vilna. I remember him because he was sitting not far from us and listening to what we were saying."

Abba examined the rucksack and satisfied himself that it was not one of theirs.

"Tell me, boy. Why are you here?"

"Oh, sir! I am on my way to America. The Russians were coming after me to join the army, so I ran away. I overheard you speaking about leaving the country, so I thought that, if I followed you, I would know where to go."

"Do your parents know where you are?"

"My parents are dead," lied Jacob. He had no idea that, in fact, his mother had been murdered.

Abba was impressed with the boy's courage. He fully understood the situation in which Jacob found himself and sympathized with it.

"Well, son. It's true that we're leaving the country, but we're going to South Africa, not America. However, we still have to cross the German border. We'll be going to Bremen to catch a ship to England and from there to South Africa. But there are many ships in Bremen that travel to America. If you make it across the border, that's where you should head."

Without quite knowing how it happened, Abba found himself giving Jacob permission to tag along with them to the German border. When he had a moment to think about it, he wasn't sure that he had done the right thing, but by then it was too late.

Oh well, it will only be for a few days. And he can help out with the luggage. Another pair of strong hands is always good to have around, especially if we run into trouble.

That night, Jacob slept in the stable with the horses.

The next morning, Abba invited him to join the family for breakfast. Jacob did his best to freshen up at the water pump in the courtyard. He didn't want to look dirty and disheveled to his benefactors, but it was really Sara whom he wanted to impress.

After breakfast, he helped the coachman load the cart and sat with the luggage as they were driven through the lovely countryside. The trees were just beginning to lose their summer leaves, and many had begun changing to the reds and oranges of autumn. Jacob began to feel unaccustomed pangs of homesickness.

I may never see this country again. He shrugged off the feeling.

The coach made its way over the rutted dirt road, bumping and shaking all the way. After an hour's ride, the passengers could see the reflection of a quiet river flowing slowly ahead of them. They stopped at a makeshift dock where a barge with a covered canvas shelter was waiting.

Abba observed the boat with narrow eyes.

I hope it can make the trip. It doesn't look very sturdy. Too late now to do anything about it.

After paying the coachman, including a little extra to keep quiet, the party boarded the vessel with their luggage. The boat settled rather deep in the water but had no major problems taking them down the river.

The sun was strong and the day warm—a lazy day in late August. The family huddled beneath the canvas to escape the withering heat. Jacob remained in the uncovered bow with the boatman, not wanting to crowd the shaded area.

"Jacob, come here," called Sara.

Blushing and uncertain, the boy did as he was bidden.

"Tell me about your life."

Jacob thought about being abandoned by his father, living with his mother in a church, and being raised in a bordello.

If I tell her the truth, she'll hate me. They'll kick me off the boat.

"My mother and father died in the flu epidemic. I was raised in the town orphanage and hated every minute of it. And then the army wanted me, so I decided to try and change my luck."

He suddenly thought about his father's half-brothers, the bakers, and added, "I have two uncles in America—in Philadelphia. I thought I'd go there."

"Oh, you poor thing."

Sara didn't press for more personal history. They spent the next few hours talking about her school outside of Vilna, her piano lessons, and what she hoped to find when her family reached South Africa.

"My father's brothers are there. They've already started a mill like my father had here. He'll join them. I want to go to school and study music."

Jacob was surprised. He didn't know any girls who were permitted to go to school. The men whom he knew would laugh at such an idea.

But why should only men learn about important things? I think it's a good idea.

When Sara asked him what he hoped to accomplish in America, he didn't know how to answer her. He had never even thought about it.

"I just want to be free to do what I want," he replied, "without worrying about the czar and being conscripted for the army."

And having a lot of money wouldn't hurt either.

After more desultory conversation, the boat grew quiet. The passengers sank into their own thoughts or fell asleep in their chairs. Sara's mother distributed cold meat and bread with pickles for dinner. The boat continued its progress down the river until well after dark.

With the stars shining overhead, the vessel made its way to a small dock on the west bank of the river. An open horse-drawn wagon was there to transport the passengers to a wayside inn where they would spend the following day. At nightfall, they would board a ten-passenger van that would take them the twenty miles to the German frontier, where he would negotiate with the guards to let them cross.

This must be costing Mr. Zuckerman a fortune. I hope these guys can be trusted.

* * *

Jacob didn't like the looks of the driver. He had long, unkempt hair, a scraggly beard, and shifty eyes that moved independently of each other. It was hard talking to him because one couldn't figure out which eye to look at while speaking. He must have come from Hungary or Romania because he spoke Russian with a thick accent. His coarse voice and gruff manner also made his speech difficult to understand.

"Come! Get in vagon!" he growled, jerking his thumb in the general direction of the horses.

Spying Jacob, he counted the number of people using his fingers to count with.

"Too many. Only supposed to be four." He put up four fingers.

Eager to move his family to safety quickly, Abba said, "He's our luggage man. He'll help you. I'll give you an extra five rubles to bring him to the rest house."

Grudgingly nodding assent, the driver took the five-ruble coin and motioned for Jacob to lift the heaviest wicker trunk onto the wagon. Jacob complied.

The thirty-minute drive to the rest house was uneventful. Upon arrival, the innkeeper explained that the house was full, so Jacob would have to sleep once again in the stable with the horses. He didn't mind. The night was warm and fragrant.

The innkeeper served a poorly cooked dinner of meat pie with potatoes. Joining them at the table was another emigrant family consisting of a giant blacksmith, his wife, and their two muscular teen-aged sons. They would all be traveling together to the border. Their presence made Jacob feel more secure.

After dinner, the families retired to their rooms, and Jacob made his way to the stable. The stalls were only a few feet across from the back door of the kitchen. As he lay on a bed of hay under the window looking up at the stars, he could clearly hear the clatter of dishes and the conversation of the two kitchen maids as they cleaned up from the day.

"Them two young men looked pretty good."

"Tickled your fancy did they?" laughed the other one. "The bulge in their crotch looked pretty big."

"Do you think a Jewish prick feels any different?"

"Nah. Once inside they all feel the same."

"Did you see the dresses on those girls? They cost a fortune. They must be stinkin' rich."

"Yeah. And they take it from poor people like us."

"Don't worry. Those Jews won't have nuthin' left after our boys get through with them tomorrow night."

"Yeah," cackled the first one, " they think they're so smart. But they won't even know what happened. We'll see who's smarter."

As Jacob listened to this conversation, his heart was beating so loud that he imagined it to be audible all the way in the kitchen. After the girls left, he tried to figure out what they could possibly have been talking about.

Jacob lay scrunched up against the wall below the stable window for several hours trying to figure out the problem. Unable to do so, he dozed off sitting up.

Shortly after midnight, he was awakened by the soft clopping sound of horses being tied up nearby. Then he heard two sets of footsteps approach the kitchen door. He tried to make himself even smaller as he heard a third person whisper from inside the pantry.

"You dere?"

It was their driver.

"Yeah. It's us."

"Vee got some rich vuns dis time. Should haff lots of good stuff."

"Where will you do it? Don't do it where there's lots of high grass. Last time, it took us forever to find the small bags with the good stuff. By the time we found the last bag, you were almost back with them to look. If we had gotten caught, we'd be in big trouble."

"Aw, dunt verry. Dere too 'fraid ta call de police. But I try ta do it vehr it's clear, jest past de big curve after de crick."

"OK. We'll be there at nine."

Jacob stayed up all night trying to figure out what to expect.

The next evening, Jacob helped the driver load up the coach. The large open van had two long side benches for the passengers. The luggage was placed in the middle. The driver sat up front alone, though the seat could accommodate two.

The passengers climbed in. Zishka, the blacksmith, sat just behind the driver. Next to him sat his oldest son. Abba sat across from the smith and next to the second son. The girls and ladies came next, and Jacob sat at the back of the wagon next to Sara.

The party started out as darkness set in. There wasn't much talking. They held their own counsel. Jacob looked to the well-being of the ladies, solicitous of anything that he could do for them.

"Would you like a pillow?" he asked the smith's wife, who looked uncomfortable. She shook her head.

* * *

Deep darkness set in. The moon provided the only light. As the wagon rounded a large curve, the driver spoke.

"Vee must be werry quiet 'round here. Sometimes dere is soldiers. Vee dunt vant dem to hear us."

Just as he finished speaking, there was a crack and rush of air as the bottom of the wagon opened and most of the luggage fell to the ground.

"Stop the wagon," commanded Abba Zuckerman into the driver's ear."

"Kviet. Vee kent stop here. De soldiers vill hear us."

Suddenly the driver felt his head jerked back and felt a sharp blade at his throat.

"You'll stop here or else your throat will be cut," said the blacksmith, as his oldest son jumped next to the driver and took over the reins.

As the wagon slowed, the second son, along with Jacob—both armed with knives—jumped out of the wagon and ran the short distance back to where the bags had fallen. They reached the spot before the driver's confederates had a chance to appear. Guided by the blacksmith's oldest son, the wagon turned around. They closed the trap door and reloaded the bags while the knife remained at the driver's throat.

As Jacob had figured out, these conniving thieves had designed a wagon with a trap door made to look like loose planks. The driver would unobtrusively open it from his seat at a prearranged location, and most of the luggage would fall out; he would blame the mishap on the bad roads. Then, finding some reason not to stop immediately, he would turn the wagon around a few minutes later and return to search for the lost luggage. By this time, however, it would be gone, picked up by his confederates.

Neat trick, thought Jacob. *The maids were right: we'd never have known what happened.*

Abba spoke to the driver. "Empty your pockets. Give me all the money you've got, including what we paid you earlier." With no options, the driver complied, turning over a large wad of cash as well as a nasty-looking dagger. Zishka searched him for any other hidden weapons.

"When we get to the frontier, you'll negotiate with the guards as we agreed. We'll give you the necessary money at that time. You'll accompany us until we safely step into Germany. At that time, we'll return everything we've taken and pay you the balance of what we owe. Zishka will remain at your side with the knife. He speaks fluent German. If you try to get us in trouble, you will have a knife in your back before you can get the words out. The guards will get their money anyway, so they won't care."

Knowing that he had been outfoxed, the driver nodded.

When they reached the frontier, the driver did as he was told. He saw this as only a temporary defeat.

"Damned Jews! How did they figure it out? Never mind. I'll make up for tonight with the next group that comes through. They won't be as smart."

There was no fencing or other marking of the frontier. Abba hoped that the driver and the Russian guards were telling the truth about the location of the border. The group moved in the direction indicated by the guards. They paid off the driver who, in turn, paid the soldiers, and then they began to walk. After about half a mile, they stopped. Abba led them in a prayer of thanksgiving, though they weren't sure exactly where they were.

Chapter Nineteen

A s they paused to figure out their next move, they spoke in whispers, afraid that German border patrols might be roaming the area who could arrest them for illegal entry.

They found themselves in what seemed like a medieval forest, with towering trees on all sides, thick scrub on the ground, and no light by which to navigate. They had brought candles, but the wind blew them out each time they were lit.

"I think we should remain here until morning," Abba whispered loudly so that all could hear. "It's too dangerous to travel in the dark without knowing where we're going."

"But what if we're picked up by the border patrol?" asked his wife.

"We're more likely to draw attention if we're moving around," chimed in Zishka. "Besides, it's very possible we might wander back into Russia since we can't see where we're going."

They all shuddered at the thought.

With the heads of both families agreed on a course of action, the decision was made. They found a small clearing and prepared to stay for the night. Beside their luggage, they made themselves as comfortable as possible with the blankets and pillows that they had brought. Jacob had no such luxuries, so Sara let him borrow one of her blankets. He lay down on the grass next to her.

As the members of the party dropped off to sleep one by one, Sara wiggled a little closer to him so that their blankets were touching.

"It was a very brave thing that you did. You know you saved us from being robbed and maybe even saved our lives."

"All I did was tell your father what I overheard."

"No. You heard only bits and pieces. You put the puzzle together and figured it out."

Jacob said nothing. Silence.

I wonder why I always try to help people if I can. I guess it just makes me feel good inside

"Aren't you afraid to be traveling all alone in strange places?"

Jacob was beginning to feel uncomfortable. The questions were getting too personal.

I would give anything to have a mother and father who took care of me and protected me. You don't know how lucky you are.

"I've learned to take care of myself."

Jacob was aware of a melange of feelings within him. Other than his mother and the girls at the brothel, Sara was the first person to show concern for him and what he was about. That made her the first friend he had ever had. More than that, she was the first girl his own age to whom he had ever related. He was apprehensive, excited, grateful, and confused at the same time.

As he lay next to Sara, their blankets—and now legs—

touching, he felt the stirrings of sexual desire. He had to break contact with her and shift position so that the blanket covering his crotch did not betray his increasing state of arousal. He recognized that any physical contact with her was inadvisable. She was very young and innocent. Her father would be very angry about any such activity. Jacob was grateful to Abba and wouldn't chance any action that might jeopardize that relationship. But he was having a difficult time controlling his raging adolescent hormones.

Sara was persistent.

"But what do you do for companionship and someone to talk to?"

"I talk to myself. It's too dangerous to talk to other people."

Sara was irritated that her efforts were rejected. She hadn't before run into a boy who was so independent, worldly, and good-looking. Most of the boys with whom she had come into contact were meek, mild-mannered, and interested only in studying. They had no experience with the real world. They were blindly obedient to their parents and the rules of their religion.

I would never marry one of them.

However, she felt oddly attracted to Jacob. Sara had reached puberty at the age of ten and begun to have sexual fantasies by the time she was eleven-and-a-half—though there was no one she knew with whom she could discuss any of this. She dreamed about what her first kiss would be like. She didn't know very much about the details of sex, but she was determined to find out.

Abba knew that Sara would not be docile and fall easily into the role of a typical Jewish housewife. She had an independent streak that made her extremely irritating and endearing at the same time. She questioned everything, especially the traditional Eastern European Jewish attitudes about not educating females or allowing them to participate in religious life. While he respected her for her intelligence and questioning manner, he worried that these characteristics would get her into trouble.

Abba liked Jacob. He was especially grateful that Jacob had saved them from being victimized by their driver. He realized that Sara had never been exposed to a boy like Jacob and knew that she would find him attractive and engaging. Both physically and emotionally, she was older than her years. He worried that those powerful hormonal drives might push them into a potentially disastrous situation. So, as the group rested for the night, Abba placed himself in a position to monitor and observe the couple.

Feeling annoyed and rejected by Jacob's non-receptivity to her emotional advances, Sara stood up and took her blanket to lie down next to her little sister. Abba felt relieved and closed his eyes.

* * *

The next morning, as the members of the group ate their small breakfast of fruit and cheese, Zishka pulled out a map of the area that he had brought.

"If we walk due west, we should run into the road to Tilsit," he said, looking at the sun rising in the east and pointing in the opposite direction.

"I hope you're right," said Abba. "I'd hate to walk back into

Russia."

Gathering their belongings, they started off. Jacob carried Sara's wicker basket in addition to his rucksack. She walked ahead, still smoldering from last night's rejection.

"Hallo! Welcome to Germany," boomed a voice in Yiddish as the straggling cluster made its way onto a dirt road. "You've made it to Tilsit."

Startled at first by the unexpected intrusion, the group paused and pulled closer together. When they realized that a Jewish face was greeting them in Yiddish, they broke into a loud cheer.

"Danken Gott, we are here," Abba whispered loudly as he dropped his tearful face to the ground in thanksgiving.

"Who are you?" shouted Zishka in a friendly tone.

"My name is Menachem Zundel. I'm part of the Jewish Aid Society. We're here to guide you into town and protect you from the many goniffs who will try to take advantage of you. Every morning, I make my rounds along this road to find those who have crossed during the night. I see you managed to get across with your luggage. You're lucky. Most have already lost theirs by the time they get here."

"Yes. Thanks to Jacob here," replied Abba pointing to the young hero.

"Come, you must be tired. I'll take you to one of our lodging houses."

* * *

Menachem led the nine exhausted travelers into town, a

walk of about an hour. He dropped them off at a modest wooden house with a gabled roof at 90 Bergstrasse—a cobblestone street near the central marketplace. The house had four bedrooms, none of which happened to be occupied, so each family had the luxury of two bedrooms at their disposal. This time, Jacob did not have to sleep in the stable. He roomed with Zishka's two sons, who were happy to have him, for they, too, were grateful for his gallant action.

Jacob didn't quite know how to handle his newfound reputation as a hero. No one in his life so far had treated him in this way. Even to the girls at the brothel, he was more of a mascot—a child—than a man to be respected. He gloried in the attention he was receiving but tried not to let it show.

I hope I can live up to my reputation. I don't want them to be disappointed in me.

The group remained in Tilsit for two days. During that time, they were fed by the Jewish Aid Organization. The local Jewish community taxed themselves in order to support these efforts on behalf of the emigrants in transit.

On one or two occasions, the families wandered through town to do some sightseeing. Abba insisted on buying Jacob some new clothes and shoes as a way of thanking him.

Sara's anger at Jacob seemed to dissolve, and she walked by his side holding his arm through the town.

* * *

The most significant help provided to them came in the

form of warnings. Menachem and his friends described in detail some of the scams that were being perpetrated against the unsuspecting Jews.

"When you reach Bremen," he explained, "the authorities will place you in a 'control station' until your ship sails. These are really just large sheds with bunk beds. The food is terrible, and the prices are exorbitant. They do everything to take advantage of people who have no other choice but to buy from there. It is best to bring your own food if you can. Also, don't allow your money to be seen by others. One of their biggest scams is to ask you to remove your clothes for de-bugging. They tell you to hold your money in your hands so it won't get ruined by chemicals. Then they target the more affluent families for victimization."

Abba and his family were wide-eyed upon hearing these admonitions. They couldn't believe that those officials designated to help them could be so malevolent. They were even more upset at Menachem's next warning.

"Also, be careful about buying tickets from agents who claim to represent the large steamship companies. Many of these are bogus, and, when people try to board their ship, they find out that they have thrown away their precious funds on worthless paper. Often, they are forced to return home in ruin. If you need to buy a passage from the ship companies, they usually have offices somewhere in the dock area where valid tickets can be purchased."

To help them understand better what they were dealing with, Menachem painted a broader picture.

"Germany set up these control stations for a dual purpose.

The first is to drive all business to the German steamship companies. Therefore, if a traveler arrives possessing a ticket for an English steamship company, like Cunard, the government makes it difficult for them. They're forced to pay all kinds of fees and taxes to get to where they want to go."

"What goniffs," said Zishka. "I'd like to get my hands on those thieves who take such advantage of helpless travelers."

Menachem continued. "The other function of the control station is to keep 'undesirable' immigrants from settling in Germany. They don't want any more Jews, or any other poor people, remaining in their country. These control stations are a brilliant way of solving both problems."

Abba and Zishka were extremely grateful for this information, but Jacob especially took the warnings to heart.

How lucky I am to get ahold of this information. I'd be in big trouble if I hadn't met these people.

"Forewarned is forearmed," said Abba.

* * *

The party took leave of their hosts two days later. They were taken to the local train station, where they embarked on the long, rough ride to Bremen. Before stepping onto the railroad car, Abba handed Menachem a wad of cash.

"Thank you. I'll place this into the coffers of the Jewish Aid Organization."

The ride to Bremen took a day and a half. Consistent with the usual German efficiency, the trains ran on schedule and were well-maintained. By Russian standards, the rail cars were luxurious. The seats were made of leather, and the compartments had benches that transformed into beds at night. In addition to the usual men hawking fruit and rolls, the train had a dining car that served meals rather formally, with tablecloths, fine dinnerware, and crystal glassware. Abba treated the group to supper there. Jacob drank in every detail of the luxurious surroundings.

Someday, I'll have enough money to live like this. I won't be poor forever.

During the day, Sara sat with Jacob, again trying to pierce his defensive emotional armor.

"Would you consider coming with us to South Africa? You have no real ties to America."

Jacob considered this.

It's true. No one would care if I went to South Africa instead. Why shouldn't I? At least I would have these friends and I wouldn't be alone.

At that moment, Jacob's body bolted upright as a thought bubbled up from the depths of his soul—a thought that he had never consciously acknowledged: *But then I would never find my father.*

Jacob was so taken aback by this realization that he forgot where he was.

"Are you all right?" cried Sara, frightened by Jacob's sudden change in demeanor.

Forcing himself to come back to his senses, he said, "I'm okay. I was thinking about your question and just realized how important it was for me to find my uncles. They're the only family I have. I'm sorry for frightening you."

Sara hid her disappointment. Her fantasies of an ongoing relationship, maybe even marriage, with this very special young man were dashed, yet she could understand how he felt. She couldn't imagine being all by herself in the world and knew that, under similar circumstances, she would do the same thing.

"Well, we still have a few more days together. Let's make the most of them."

* * *

The train pulled into Bremen and, just as Menachem had outlined, the emigrants headed for the port area were herded into large wagons and transported to the control centers. Because Abba and his family would be traveling first class on a German ship to England, they were permitted to travel into the city on their own. Abba insisted that Jacob remain with them for the three days until their ship sailed. He even paid for Jacob to have his own hotel room.

Once again, Jacob was impressed by the luxury of the hotel. His room had sturdy wooden furniture with carved arms and legs. The chairs and cushions were upholstered in heavy gold brocade. The mattress was thick and bouncy. Each morning, a housekeeper would clean up the room and replace the bed sheets.

They're not even dirty.

The hotel provided a large breakfast of eggs, fruit, croissants, and breads. Jacob saw platters of what looked like meats that he didn't recognize. There were crinkled strips of something, and pink slices of something else. Sara told him that these were pork products, bacon and ham. He noticed with incredulity that Abba ate large portions of them without hesitation.

A Jew eating pork? Jacob could hardly believe his eyes.

Abba took his family for walks in the bustling city. There was the filthy dock area, with its complement of foul-mouthed seamen, but there were also beautiful parks. The second night that they were there, the Bremen Symphony Orchestra gave a magnificent performance in the outdoor stadium near the park. Jacob had never heard such sound. It transported him to a different place of peace and contentment. When the concert was over, Jacob wished it would start all over again.

Abba was happy that he had been able to repay Jacob to some degree. He knew that Jacob's world had expanded immeasurably in the past three days.

"Are you sure you won't come with us to South Africa?" Abba asked, echoing Sara's sentiment.

"Yes sir. I appreciate everything you've done for me, but I really want to find my family."

"All right, son. Take care of yourself. There are many people who will try to take advantage of you."

"I will sir."

"Do you have enough money for your passage?"

Jacob still had most of the fifty rubles that he had brought with him. He assumed that such a munificent sum would cover the cost of a steerage ticket.

"Yes, sir. I've been able to save all my money because you've paid for everything else."

"If you ever change your mind, contact us at this address," said Abba, handing Jacob a piece of hotel stationery with an address in South Africa.

"Thank you, sir."

Abba gave Jacob a big bear hug. It brought tears to Jacob's eyes.

If only my father would treat me like this.

Just before they left to board the ship, Sara pulled Jacob aside behind a corner in the hotel hallway. Before he had time to react, she put her arms around his neck, pulled him close, and gave him a long, firm, drawn-out kiss. Their tongues did not touch, but the kiss was sensual and stimulating. All of Sara's pent-up fantasies and dreams went into that kiss.

"Sara, where are you?" called her father from down the hall.

As she reluctantly pulled away, she smiled and said, "I'll never forget you, Jacob. A girl never forgets her first kiss."

And she was gone. Once again, Jacob was on his own.

Chapter Twenty

Feeling depressed and lonely, the boy-man wandered for a few hours along the cobblestone streets thinking about Sara and Abba and not paying much attention to where he was going.

Did I make a big mistake? It's the only real family I've ever known. Maybe I should have gone with them.

He became aware of the velvet pouch pressing against his chest under his shirt. Rubbing it gently, he allowed himself to fantasize about all the ways in which he would exact revenge on his father across the sea in the New World. His focus seemed to return with the anger that he allowed to bubble up against his father.

I'll find him. I'll make him pay for what he did to my mother and me. He told me never to contact him again. He'll be plenty sorry when he sees me.

Jacob found his way down to the port area. A greasy-looking man wearing a dirty shirt and stained slacks noticed this young man wearing new fashionable clothing. He tapped Jacob on the shoulder.

"Hey, kid. Do you want to buy a ticket on the *SS Niederlander?* My friend had to cancel his trip and asked me to get rid of this ticket. I can give it to you at a large discount, just thirty-five rubles."

Remembering that Menachem had warned them about counterfeit tickets, Jacob ignored the man and went looking for the office of the Kirsten steamship Line, which he found on American Quay. Kirsten was one of the larger German companies making transatlantic crossings.

Jacob took a deep breath and entered the small waterfront office of the steamship company.

"Can I help you?" asked an angry-looking, tight-lipped clerk in German, jealously observing the fine clothes that Abba had bought for Jacob.

"I speak Russian," Jacob answered.

These damned Jews, the clerk thought, *stealing money off of the rest of us.* However, he answered somewhat disdainfully in Russian. "What do you want?"

"I'd like to buy a steerage passage to America."

"That will be seventy-five rubles."

"What? How can it be so expensive? I've only got fifty rubles."

"Sorry," said the man brushing him off as if he were not worth the effort of their conversation. "Come back when you have the money."

As the unpleasant clerk turned his back on Jacob to work in the adjoining file room, the latter spied a pile of blank ticket forms on his desk. As he impulsively moved to steal one from the top of the pile, the clerk turned around.

* * *

"Stop and get out of here this minute, you dirty Jew thief!"

Jacob fled as fast as his feet would carry him, looking back to see whether he was being chased.

He was devastated. "How will I ever get to America?" he sobbed as he roamed aimlessly through the docks. "I wish I'd known this before. Abba would have given me the difference." Abba was gone, though, and now he would have to develop a new plan.

Jacob wandered around the waterfront trying to decide what to do. He passed enormous fenced-in yards with boxes of cargo piled up waiting to be loaded onto large freighters. He walked down streets with sleazy bars smelling of stale beer and women hanging out windows beckoning to him.

"C'mon little boy. Let's see what a real man you are."

This area reminds me of home.

It was the tough part of town where you had to be aware of everything going on around you and not let your guard down for a minute. Otherwise, you would end up robbed, beaten, and lying in the gutter—if you were lucky.

Night fell. The streets were dark but brightened here and there by a shaft of light from a bar or filthy restaurant. Jacob could hear loud laughter and music drifting from some of the noisier establishments. Occasionally, one or two grubby seamen would pass arm in arm with prostitutes dressed in short skirts, boots, and skimpy tops.

Jacob was hungry, but he didn't want to spend any of his precious money on food.

I can't afford to eat. I need every penny of it for my ticket.

Tired and hungry, Jacob came upon a small, deserted, park-like area with a bench partially hidden under the branches of a tree. He lay down on the bench face up with his arms crossed over his chest and quickly fell asleep.

* * *

Jacob was awakened by the point of cold steel against his throat.

"Ah, young man. I see you are a visitor to our lovely city." Jacob heard a gravelly man's voice speaking to him in German.

"Nicht verstehen," Jacob said, using one of the few German phrases that he had picked up.

"Oh, you're one of those Russian Jews," replied the man in broken Russian. He stank of alcohol and tobacco and looked as if he hadn't had a bath in a year.

"Give me your money!"

Jacob understood exactly what he had said.

"Nein! Ich gehe Amerika."

The man scowled and pushed the knifepoint harder against Jacob's throat.

"Your money! Now!"

Slowly, Jacob sat up and took his wallet out of his pocket. He withdrew the fifty rubles and gave the money to the drifter.

Noticing the silk cord around the boy's neck, he pointed and said, "Whatcha got there?"

"Nothing."

The man yanked the cord away from Jacob's neck. It broke, cutting into Jacob's skin painfully as the velvet pouch came into view.

Still keeping the knife at Jacob's throat, the man rubbed the pouch between his fingers.

"Ah! You were hiding this from me."

Jacob panicked. He tried to tell the robber, "Take the money! The pouch and the coin are all I have left of my father," but, of course, the man did not understand, and it would have made no difference if he had.

He put Jacob's money and pouch into his pants pocket and continued to stare at Jacob. A gleam of desire appeared in his eyes.

"Ah! You are a nice-looking boy."

Holding the knife a few inches from Jacob's throat, he began to run his free hand sensually through Jacob's tousled hair.

"Be nice to me, and maybe I'll let you go," he whispered softly.

Keeping the knife pointed at Jacob, he unbuttoned his fly with his free hand. As he fumbled to pull out his organ, the stench of unwashed flesh mixed with stale urine and alcohol overwhelmed Jacob. Unable to accomplish his goal with one hand, the thief lowered his other hand to better manipulate himself.

Jacob knew that this was his chance. If he didn't do something now, he might end up with his throat slashed. From his sitting, position he jumped up and plowed headfirst into the chest of the man standing in front of him. The knife dropped to the ground, and the two of them went after it. The man was surprisingly strong for one so marinated in alcohol. Jacob got hold of the knife, but the man was squeezing his wrist hard while he resisted. They struggled for what seemed to Jacob like an eternity when the man's arm suddenly gave way. With the resistance gone, the knife in Jacob's hand plunged deep into the other's chest. Blood began to stain his shirt. He fell back and was still. His partially naked body lay lifeless on the grass.

For a few moments, Jacob was stunned into paralysis. As his head began to clear, he realized that he had to flee the scene. He fumbled through the dead man's pockets and retrieved his pouch and his money. He was half hoping that he would find more money, but there was only a small flask of cheap whiskey.

Jacob picked up the knife and sprinted away as fast as he could. He didn't want to leave the bloody weapon lying around in case it might somehow lead the authorities to him. When he had run so far that his chest seemed ready to explode, he slowed and paused at the water's edge. Making sure that no one was watching, he threw the knife as far as he could and watched it sink into the deep water. Then he walked a little further before allowing himself to rest.

* * *

He sat, panting, on a large boulder by the harbor.

That was a close call. Serves me right for letting my guard down.

Suddenly the significance of what had just happened dawned on him.

I'm a murderer and a near-thief. And I'm only twelve years old.

Experiencing an odd and unexpected feeling of pride, he smiled guiltily.

I handled myself pretty well. I'm a pretty good fighter. But I need some food and a place to sleep. I can't take a chance on sleeping outdoors again. I'll have to spend some of my money and worry about it later.

* * *

Jacob wandered until dawn, when he spied a seedy-looking hotel with a tired old cafeteria attached. Stepping inside, he ordered some rolls and cheese from a grandmotherly woman behind the counter.

Recognizing him as a foreigner, she asked in Russian, "Where are you headed?"

"I'm going to America."

"Are you a Jew?"

Why is she asking? Am I in some sort of danger?

The old woman saw him stiffen, and her voice softened. "You're all right here. I'm Jewish myself. It's just that it's unusual to see emigrants permitted to go outside the control stations."

Jacob relaxed somewhat. He explained his situation but didn't mention anything about his run-in with the drunk.

Nita, who turned out to be the owner of the cafeteria, pondered his state of affairs as she prepared the rolls and cheese.

"You know, the steamship company needs help to handle all the passengers in the steerage section. They require strong young men to clean the filthy latrines, help serve meals, and protect the single ladies from the advances of lecherous men. They might be willing to give you a reduced fare in return for your taking on some of these duties."

"Thank you," Jacob answered gratefully.

After finishing his meal, he ascended the steps to a tiny room that he rented for fifty pfennigs. He tossed and turned for hours on the hard cot, and, when sleep finally came, it brought nightmares of daggers, blood, and death.

Bleary-eyed and edgy, Jacob walked to the office of the Kirsten Steamship company at nine o'clock the next morning. Every time he passed a policeman, he tried to fade into the shadows. He kept imagining himself being arrested and executed for murder.

Who would believe I did it in self-defense?

* * *

He kept his ears open for any news relating to the crime but heard nothing.

Jacob prayed that the clerk whom he had run into earlier would not be around. He spent an hour watching people going into and out of the office and did not see any sign of the nasty clerk who had dealt with him before.

Instead, that day, a pleasant and attractive young woman was serving as the clerk. Jacob turned on his most charming personality and once again, almost flirtatiously, explained his situation, this time asking about a possible fare reduction in return for work.

His effort was rewarded.

"You're in luck," she smiled. "As it happens, one of the men we had hired just quit. We're in need of another assistant. The minimum age, however, is sixteen. How old are you?"

"I'll be seventeen on my next birthday." He lied slickly and easily without a moment's hesitation.

A skeptical look passed over her face, but it left quickly.

"Your passage will cost twenty-five rubles. You'll receive a bunk and the same food as everyone else. In return, it will be your responsibility to see that things run smoothly in your section of the steerage accommodations."

She outlined the duties involved. They were much as Nita had explained at the cafeteria.

"The ship is the SS Dusseldorf. It leaves in two days. Report here tomorrow morning at 10 for your medical examination."

Jacob was elated. There would even be twenty-five rubles to tide him over until he reached America.

He returned to the hotel cafeteria, skulking along the side streets so as not to be noticed. Back at the cafeteria, he walked behind the counter and gave Nita a big hug and kiss.

"Thank you, thank you. You've saved my life."

Embarrassed and blushing, she kissed him back.

Jacob reported as directed for his physical. Because he was a last-minute hire, the exam took place at the company's office. Jacob was relieved because he would otherwise have been examined with the rest of the passengers out in the shed.

Dr. Reichmann was an obese, scowling man with a gruff manner. His breathing was labored, the air making musical sounds as it entered and left his lungs. He spoke minimally.

Every word seemed like an enormous effort.

"Open your eyes wide."

The doctor shone a light into the center of each eye and turned each eyelid inside out, searching for signs of any eye infection. Apparently finding none, he moved on.

"Take off your shirt."

He placed the head of the stethoscope against Jacob's chest. Jacob jumped. The coldness of the metal startled him. He had never before been examined by a true physician.

"Breathe deeply."

He wondered what the doctor was doing, but complied.

"Drop your pants."

Jacob's heart was pounding. He didn't know what to do. His mind had flipped back to the scene of the drifter in the park.

"I said to drop your pants." The doctor's wheezy voice had an insistent edge.

Jacob tried to reason it out.

I'm here at the steamship company. They want me to do this. The clerk is in the other room. I guess nothing bad will happen.

He trembled as the doctor pushed at his genitals looking for a hernia or signs of venereal disease. He breathed a sigh of relief when that portion of the exam was finished.

The next part of the procedure involved answering a set of questions. Jacob was caught off-guard and had to think quickly. He knew that his answers would be checked again at Ellis Island and that, if he gave the wrong answers, he could be refused admission to America.

I must be very careful.

"What is your name?" asked the doctor.

"Jacob Pechtrowicz."

"Where are you from?"

"Vilna."

"How old are you?"

"Seventeen."

"What year were you born?"

Jacob hadn't expected a question like that. He hemmed and hawed trying to figure out an answer to match his lie.

It took him a few seconds to make some hasty mental calculations. Finally, hoping he wasn't tripping himself up, he said, "1896."

The doctor smiled. He had a hunch that the boy was lying, but was glad that he had managed to come up with the right answer.

"How much money do you have?"

"After paying for my passage, I'll have twenty-five rubles." Jacob knew that America required a minimum of twenty dollars for admission into the country. His twenty-five rubles would more than cover the requirement.

"Whom will you be staying with?"

"My uncles in Philadelphia."

After a few more questions, the doctor grunted, apparently indicating that Jacob's answers were satisfactory.

As Jacob turned to leave the room, his examiner grabbed his shoulder.

"Not so fast. Pull up your sleeve."

Without a word of explanation, the doctor brought forth what looked like a small glass needle. Jacob began to panic as the doctor proceeded to scratch his right shoulder multiple times with the sharp point.

"This is called a vaccination", the doctor finally wheezed. "It will keep you from getting smallpox. Without it, they'll send you back." Jacob was relieved that the needle didn't hurt.

He dismissed Jacob with a nod of his head. Outside, in the main office, the pretty clerk took the paperwork and called him over.

"You passed with flying colors. The ship leaves tomorrow at noon. Report to the ship's purser by 7:00 a.m."

* * *

Jacob rushed back to his hotel, still checking over his shoulder for any sign of the police. He decided to isolate himself in his room for the rest of the day just to be on the safe side. If they were looking for a murderer, he wouldn't be obvious. That evening, he felt safe enough to treat Nita to dinner at a nearby inexpensive café. He even bought some cheap wine to celebrate with.

They won't be looking for a boy with an old woman.

Also, he felt deeply indebted to Nita.

I have plenty of money to get me to New York. I can afford to spend a little on her.

The wine helped Jacob sleep restfully through his last night in Europe.

The old woman had never had children of her own. She felt

as if she were sending off her own son and provisioned Jacob with a mountain of food, stuffing his rucksack with oranges, apples, cheese, rolls, and even cold chicken.

"Gehe gesunt! Go in good health," Nita cried as she waved goodbye at 6 a.m. after cooking him a substantial breakfast of hot cereal, eggs, and rolls. Jacob tried to pay her. She refused. He hugged her tightly.

"Write me when you get there," she said. "Tell me what it's like. I never got a letter from America. That will be my payment."

Jacob whistled all the way to the dock. The bad memories were already receding. He was ready to begin the rest of his life.

Chapter Twenty-One

The SS *Dusseldorf* was twenty years old and still operating at full capacity. It was not as large as some of the other ocean liners, which could hold over one thousand passengers in their steerage areas. The Dusseldorf's less expensive accommodations had a capacity of only four hundred and fifty.

The two levels of steerage compartments began at the ship's bow below the main deck and ran its entire length and width. Located below the waterline, the compartments had no direct opening to the outside. The only circulation of air came through vents that passed through the upper decks first. On rainy days, water came down through the hatchways and leaks in the ceiling, soaking the passengers below.

Each steerage deck was separated into three compartments by wooden dividers. On the upper steerage section, the forward compartment was reserved for families. The middle room was meant to be the dining area and general lounge, but, when the ship was full, part of it was also used for sleeping. The aft section was reserved for single women.

On the lower steerage level, the area was similarly divided. The middle lounge area, however, was packed mostly with bunks, leaving only a small area with a few wooden tables on which food could be eaten. Both the middle and aft sections were packed with men since there were considerably more single men than women making the journey. The forward section was again reserved for families.

Each section was filled with small iron bunks three tiers high. There was no room for the storage of personal baggage; every item of luggage had to be kept somewhere on the bed. Each steerage passenger was issued a thin mattress, a small, understuffed pillow, two paper-thin gray blankets, and a life preserver.

To say that the quarters were inadequate, crowded, and allowed no privacy would be a considerable understatement.

The latrines were four steps above the upper steerage level. For four hundred and fifty people, there were eight toilets and sinks for the women and the same number for the men. There were no bathing facilities of any kind. Here, too, privacy was non-existent. Most of the time, the toilets didn't flush properly and human excrement would overflow creating the vilest of odors. The sinks had only cold seawater. Between the leaking toilets and overflowing urine, the floors and seats were constantly wet. It was impossible for the passengers to use the facilities without soaking their feet or the bottoms of their clothing. The most heroic efforts to keep clean were doomed to failure.

In order to reach an outside deck, steerage passengers had

to climb one or two decks above their quarters. Hardy sea-goers could accomplish this, but passengers who became seasick had neither the will nor the energy to climb the stairs. They lay in their bunks as if in a stupor, without spirit or volition, vomiting on themselves and everything nearby. Their neighbors were glad when they could no longer eat because it meant that their vomiting would diminish. The stench in the sleeping areas was almost as horrific as that in the latrines.

Jacob was assigned to serve as the steward in charge of the single women's compartment and latrines. He woke every morning at five, when the latrines would be least crowded, and did his best to swab the floor and pour buckets of seawater into the toilets to flush the excrement into the holding tanks.

"These toilets are a disgrace!" the women would rail at him. "You should be ashamed of yourself."

"Madame, these are not my toilets," Jacob would answer patiently. "I have to use them the same as you. I'm doing my best to keep them as clean as possible."

I'll never travel this way again. I'll make enough money to travel in luxury. This steerage is disgusting.

The dishes and silverware were stored in one corner under a table, and it was Jacob's job to see that they were washed in a tub of soapy water after each meal. There were not enough dishes and silverware for everyone. When the first clatter of dishes rang through the dismal compartments, there was a rush of people who grabbed whatever they could and descended on the food. They ate wherever they could sit or stand. The ship made some effort to provide decent food. There were coffee, rolls, and cheese for breakfast, and, sometimes, they would send down boiled beef and potatoes for lunch or dinner. However, the food was tasteless, the quality was poor, and there was never enough to go around.

Some of the other stewards, who knew the ropes, would produce a private stash of fruit, bread, cheese, and herring that they had brought on board with them. They would sell the food at exorbitant prices and, often, desperate parents would spend their last few pennies trying to nourish their hungry children.

I hate the way these so-called stewards are taking advantage of the poor, distressed passengers. They deserve better.

Feeling protective of his temporary wards, Jacob gave away much of his own food supply whenever he could to people who he thought needed it more.

The single female passengers quickly grew to like and trust their protector. One of them approached him the second day out and said, "Jacob, let us help you with some of your work."

At 7:00 a.m., it was Jacob's job to go up to the steerage kitchen area on the main deck and bring down trays of food. It took a long time to complete the circuit. The women organized a brigade to pass the food trays down the line until they reached the dining area. Then they would place the food on the few tables available for eating.

Thereafter, when Jacob washed the dishes after each meal, he was joined by a few of these women. They would collect the utensils and sit with him at the washtub cleaning them.

Whenever Jacob went up to the kitchen to collect the food and caught a glimpse of the first-class dining room, the same thought would flood his mind: *Someday, that will be me.*

After lunch, Jacob was assigned to swab the floors of the women's cabin area. He used a mop and strong disinfectant that covered the foul odors temporarily with a stronger, irritating chemical odor. The passengers would hold their noses and try to nap.

Jacob's bunk was strategically positioned at the entrance to the woman's section by the stairway that ran up to the main deck and down to the men's level. Often, some of the young men would stand outside of the women's section trying to kibitz with them. Most of the women ignored their advances. Occasionally, one of the men who had drunk a little too much (many brought liquor on board, for it was easy enough to carry) would grab a woman and try to squeeze her breasts or buttocks. Jacob had to protect these girls from unwanted advances.

"Get off of her, you pig!" Jacob would shout.

He would pull these tipsy men off the girls and send them downstairs to bed. The boy had heard stories about women being molested while lying in bed by the very stewards who were there to protect them. He thought that detestable and unworthy.

What kind of man would dishonor himself so?

Of course, there was the occasional woman who went out of her way to encourage the men's attentions. To try and control this type of situation, the captain had posted a sign at the entrance to the women's section.

ALL COUPLES MAKING LOVE TOO WARMLY WILL BE MARRIED COMPULSORILY AT NEW YORK IF THE AUTHORITIES DEEM IT FIT, OR WILL BE FINED OR IMPRISONED.

Jacob didn't think the sign would do much to discourage any couple intent on having a sexual relationship aboard ship.

On the fourth night of the journey, Jacob was sleeping in his bunk. It was a little after midnight. Suddenly he was awakened by a woman's piercing scream coming from somewhere near the top of the stairs.

"Help!"

He rushed up the iron steps and found one of the ship's crew in the ladies' latrine attempting to strip Rose, one of his charges, of her nightgown. The crewman was much larger and heavier than Jacob, but the boy jumped onto his back and squeezed his throat until he let the woman go. As the sailor turned to deal with Jacob, Rose escaped down the stairs into the woman's quarters.

"Who the hell do you think you are, you little piece of shit? I'll teach you to cross paths with me."

He punched Jacob in the face and then in the stomach. Jacob fell, the back of his head slamming against the wet tile floor. As he was losing consciousness, he dimly heard voices rushing into the area.

He woke a few minutes later lying in his bunk. He was

surrounded by a group of women tending his wounds. One had placed a towel soaked in cold water on the back of his head. Rose was gently cleaning the blood from his eye and nose where the sailor's fist had landed. The eye was swelling. A third girl ran to get another towel soaked in cold water. Jacob was disoriented for several hours. The next day, the grateful women took turns carrying out Jacob's usual chores, and one was assigned to remain with him to meet any needs he might have.

Jacob observed the activity going on around him and grinned. *The fight was no fun, but I sure like the service.*

* * *

By the sixth day of the crossing, Jacob was feeling better. He resumed most of his duties, though the women (he had begun to think about them as his women) checked regularly to make sure that he didn't overtax himself. Rose stood by most of the day to help him out.

"If it wasn't for you I would have been raped. I'm going to New York to marry my Gershon. I don't know what he would have done if anything happened to me. You have my everlasting gratitude, and Gershon's too."

The day before the ship would be docking in New York, the doctor strolled through the steerage compartment to take a last look for anyone who was obviously too sick to be admitted to the United States. Any who he found would be prevented from disembarking and returned to Europe on the same ship.

The doctor noticed Jacob's black and very swollen eye. He came over to take a closer look.

"It's just the result of a fight onboard ship," he told the doctor. "It's already healing." All the girls clustered around to back up Jacob's story.

"All right, but you'd better be able to explain it to the doctors at Ellis Island."

* * *

The next morning, the entire steerage population walked up to the main deck to watch the ship pass the Statue of Liberty in New York harbor.

"The New World!" cried one older woman as tears sprung from her eyes. "At last."

"Don't celebrate until you get past Ellis Island," said another. "I heard they can be very tough."

Jacob felt a sense of exhilaration as the famous lady holding her torch came into view.

> GIVE ME YOUR TIRED, YOUR POOR
> YOUR HUDDLED MASSES YEARNING TO BREATHE FREE

Jacob couldn't read the words inscribed on the base of Lady Liberty, but they were written for him, and he was thinking when he saw the statue, *I did it. I'm here. I'm free.*

He was so excited that he spontaneously hugged an elderly woman standing next to him. She hugged him back.

Jacob walked back down to his bunk to pack his belongings. When he reached his bed he pulled back in horror. Someone had dumped all his things on the bed and had taken the wallet with his money.

It was that sailor I tangled with. I'm sure of it. But I can't prove it. What am I going to do for money? Without at least twenty dollars, they won't let me enter the country. Thank God my pouch was around my neck, or he'd have gotten that too. But even that isn't worth twenty dollars—and I wouldn't spend it anyway.

Jacob's joyful mood turned black.

They'll send me back. Everything will be wasted.

As much as he tried to control them, tears arose in the corners of his eyes and rolled down his cheeks. He was, after all, only twelve—almost thirteen—years old. The girls saw him crying and felt terrible, but none of them could afford to replace Jacob's lost money.

The ship finally slid into its berth at New York Harbor. The cabin passengers were taken to shore first. When the last one had left the ship, the four hundred and fifty steerage passengers were herded onto a large barge and towed to Ellis Island. They were a motley-looking collection, with their tickets pinned to their caps or clothing. Most were silent. It was as if God himself were about to sit in judgment upon them. Jacob shuffled off the barge, eyes downcast, a dejected figure in a sea of expectant faces. Many of his fellow passengers were on their knees kissing the ground beneath them. In a daze, Jacob joylessly followed the herd as they headed into the cavernous reception area.

Chapter Twenty-Two

E llis Island was a complex of buildings constructed in the late 1880s on three small islands in New York Harbor connected by causeways to replace the old Castle Garden, which had become inadequate to handle the surge of immigrants coming to the United States. The immigration officials were underpaid and overworked, often having to deal with as many as five thousand newly arrived immigrants in one day. The complex operated seven days a week and holidays. Any major backup could cause the system to break down entirely.

The officials were generally hard-working and conscientious. They were forced to witness heart-breaking situations every day and fought to avoid becoming callous and insensitive, as naturally happens. They had to operate within the set of rules developed by Congress and the Department of Immigration but attempted to grant as much leeway as possible in complex situations. Of course, some inspectors were more rigid than others. It was often the luck of the draw that determined whether an immigrant with a borderline situation was turned away or allowed admission.

As the immigrants left the barge, they were formed into three long lines. These lines passed into the expansive first floor of the reception hall, which was called the baggage room but was really a massive waiting area.

The three lines were separated by rows of piping. They moved slowly up a large staircase to the reception area proper. There, two doctors were assigned to deal with each line.

Because of the large numbers involved, each doctor had about two minutes per person to decide a prospective immigrant's fate. The doctors would observe each person ascending the steps and walking toward him. He looked for signs of any obvious disability, starting with the feet and moving up the legs, body, hands, arms, face, and head. He checked to ensure vaccination against smallpox. Any deformity, even a crooked finger, was noted. Whenever there was the least suspicion of disease, the doctor would place a chalk mark on the immigrant's coat lapel. Various colors of chalk corresponded to various possible health problems.

As the line advanced, the immigrants were witness to several anxiety-producing interactions.

"Let me see your arm," an official said to one incoming passenger and, after a close examination, "I don't see your vaccination scar."

"I swear I had it done in Bremen," pleaded the passenger in Yiddish as his wife and two children looked on.

"Sorry," the immigration official steeled himself to reply,

"but I cannot allow you to enter this country."

"But I have a family. What will they do?" asked the devastated father as his wife broke into loud sobs and the children echoing her distress.

Looking down to hide the tear in his eye, the official again carefully examined the man's arm. "Oh, I do see a blurry scar. I must have missed it the first time," and gave each family member a gentle shove to indicate that they were approved to advance to the next examining station.

"Dank you, dank you!" they cried in the only words of English that they knew and in Yiddish added, "May you be blessed with a long and happy life."

* * *

At the next checkpoint, the potential admittees encountered another physician, who examined their eyes. He would roll back each eyelid with a round stick resembling a pencil, looking for signs of trachoma, a highly infectious eye disease that could cause blindness or even death. Any positive finding meant immediate rejection.

The line then moved on to the legal inspectors and teams of interpreters. There, the immigrants were asked the same questions that they had been asked prior to boarding, and the answers were checked against each other. Any suspicious discrepancies meant a chalk mark and further questions.

The question-and-answer process tripped up many of the immigrants.

"Have you been promised a job?" one man was asked.

"Yes," he replied, not really understanding the situation he was in.

"Then you are not allowed to enter the United States," said the immigration officer curtly as he chalked a large red X on the coat of the poor Irishman, who was trying to join his brother in New York City. "You'll have to return on the boat which brought you here."

"But what did I do wrong?" Wailed the burly blond man in a Gaelic accent. The officer ignored his cries and pushed him on to another official who pulled him out of sight into another room where deportable passengers were being held temporarily.

Everyone within hearing distance looked down at their feet and wondered what unknown regulation was about to block their own entry.

Jacob knew what the problem was; he had overheard one of the passengers saying that her brother had been refused entry for this very reason the previous year She had explained that U.S. contract labor law prohibited laborers who had been "induced, assisted, encouraged, or solicited" to migrate. Those who said that they had been promised a job were technically in violation of this law. Many of the inspectors at Ellis Island understood that some men had been given vague promises of employment by relatives or friends and did not use this information to bar them, but others were not as compassionate. The men, and sometimes the families that accompanied them, were refused admission and sent back to Europe.

The screening process was designed to prevent the admission of any foreigner who might become dependent on public welfare. Because of difficulties in the communication process, some immigrants were unable to understand what was being asked of them and were classified as 'feeble-minded,' another category of those who were automatically rejected.

About half of the immigrants ended up being marked with chalk for one reason or another. Families were separated without knowing why. Mothers were frantic, thinking that their children were lost forever.

"Where are you taking my child?" screamed one mother as her little girl was taken by a female officer to be examined at a pediatric station. "You can't have her. Leave her alone! I'll bring her back to Russia!" The woman had to be taken out of line and reassured by a Yiddish-speaking official that the child was simply being examined and would be returned shortly.

After the last round of inspectors, those who had passed muster were allowed to walk through an iron gate to the 'stairway of separation.' Depending on their destination, they were sent either to board a ferry bound for New York City or to immigration officials who accompanied them to the railroad station to help them to buy their tickets and find their trains.

Friends and relatives of immigrants headed for New York were permitted to meet them in the ferry waiting room, known as the 'New York room.' There were joyous reunions full of laughter, tears, and loud chatter as young men greeted their brides-to-be, husbands met their wives and children—sometimes seeing a youngest-born son or daughter for the first time. The officials liked to visit this room. It lifted their spirits and made them feel that their hard work had a positive impact. They competed for duties that brought them to this room on a regular basis.

Those with chalk marks on their lapels were sent to special detention rooms for further examination. Some passed and went through the gates to freedom. Any who were temporarily ill were sent to the hospital. Immigrants classified as deportable were given further examinations by special inquiry boards. those who didn't pass the final examination had the right to a further appeal, but reversals were rare.

As Jacob reached the first of the examiners, he noticed the doctor looking at his very swollen, black-and-blue eye. The examiner said nothing about it since the next inspector would look at it. Knowing that his eye would be examined, Jacob had made sure that 'his girls' were moving along with him so they would be in a position to back up his story of how his eye was injured. However, the lapel of Jacob's coat was marked with a large blue X. His heart sank.

I'm in trouble. And they don't even know yet that I have no money.

Jacob was passed on to the next set of examiners.

"What happened to your eye, boy?" asked the eye examiner. The translator repeated the question in Yiddish.

"I was beaten up on the ship," replied Jacob.

Hearing what was going on, Rose and several of the other girls who were in line behind Jacob all began speaking at once, vigorously confirming his story.

"You have quite a cheering section here," smiled the eye doctor. "But, because your eye is so swollen, I can't properly examine it. We'll have to detain you for a while until it heals. Meanwhile, go on to the next inspectors."

Once they discover I have no money, I know they'll send me back.

Jacob's mind raced as he tried to figure some way out of the hole he was about to step into.

He approached the next inspector and the companion translator.

"What's your name?"

"Jacob Pechtrowicz, sir"

Of course, his name came out as a guttural 'Ya-ah-kovh Pe-ecchh-troh-veece' since that was the native pronunciation.

"That's a pretty hard name to pronounce. How old are you?"

"Seventeen, sir." It rolled off of Jacob's tongue.

"Where are your parents?"

"They're dead, sir."

"Whom will you be staying with?"

"My uncles in Philadelphia, sir." An idea began to germinate in Jacob's brain.

"How much money do you have?"

"My money was stolen on the ship sir, by the person who beat me up."

Jacob briefly explained what had happened. The inspector noticed that the girls behind him were listening closely and nodding their heads enthusiastically.

"You mean you have no money?"

Jacob took a deep breath.

"Not now, sir. But if I can telegraph one of my uncles, he'll come to meet me here in New York and bring the money."

The wheels turned in the head of the inspector, who found Jacob to be a likable and somewhat heroic character. He thought that the boy would make a fine U.S. citizen, indeed, better than many of the individuals who passed through his station on a daily basis.

"Well," said the inspector. "You're going to be in the hospital for a while until your eye heals enough to examine it properly. Have one of the telegraph agents contact your uncle collect and instruct him to be here one week from today. By that time, we'll know if your eyes are all right. If you pass the eye exam and you have the money, you'll be cleared to enter the country. And, by the way," he added, as Jacob was slowly led away to one of the large detention rooms, "find yourself a new American name."

Jacob didn't know whether to be happy or upset with the way his examination had unfolded. On the one hand, the eye created a problem for him. In another way, though, it had given him time to stall and try to find a solution.

There's no way I'm going to telegraph my uncles. They don't even know that I exist. My father would certainly never tell them. I can't contact my father—even if I knew his address. That son of a bitch told me never to bother him again. I hate him. I wouldn't get in touch with him if he were the last man on earth. But what am I going to do?

Jacob decided not to talk to the telegraph agent. He and a group of about thirty other chalk-marked immigrants were led from the detention room through a maze of hallways to another wing of the complex. The hallways were gray and shadowy, lit only by an occasional bare electric bulb. Depression hung in the stale air.

After about ten minutes of shuffling down seemingly endless corridors, they came to a dead end. The large sign on the wall read:

United States Department of Immigration

Ellis Island Immigrant Hospital

A smaller sign underneath read:

◄— General Hospital

Contagious Diseases —►

There, they were divided into two roughly equal groups. Jacob was taken to the General Hospital. Most of those taken to the Contagious Disease ward were children suffering from measles, scarlet fever, or diphtheria.

Jacob walked into a large room more brightly lit than the hallways. There were small, narrow windows high on the wall, though they didn't admit much light because they were set too high to reach from the floor to prevent escape attempts.

Off the main area, two sets of doors led to the infirmaries proper. There was a ward for women and children and one for men. Each was designed to handle no more than three hundred and fifty occupants, but there were usually more than five hundred in the rooms at any given time.

The white metal beds were packed close together, giving no privacy whatsoever to the occupants. When the doctors made their rounds, any necessary exams were carried out in front of the entire ward—a very humiliating experience, especially when one's private parts were casually and insensitively put on display by the examiner.

Though the doctors were interested in examining only Jacob's bruised eye, he felt his anxiety rise each time they entered the ward. He noticed that they pulled down other patients' bedcovers and pulled up their hospital gown, and he was worried that they might try to examine him with his private parts exposed as well.

"Vy dey dunt covvir ya ven dey eggsemin ya?" Jacob asked one of the nurses in broken English. He was already starting to pick up some of the language as he heard it spoken around him.

"Sometimes, doctors are very insensitive about their patient's feelings," the nurse replied. But Jacob still wasn't sure how he would react if the doctors tried to examine him 'down there.'

One section of the all-white room was set up with long, wooden picnic-type tables and benches, each of which seated eight. As on the ship, meals were served 'family style.' A plate of food would be placed on each table, and whoever arrived first had the most to eat. The quality of the food was poor. When Jacob asked one of the friendly Yiddish speaking nurses about the poor food she explained, "I can understand why you're wondering about that. You see, even though this is a hospital, contracts for suppliers are given to the lowest bidder. After a cut off the top for the government officials, the suppliers find the cheapest food they can." Embarrassed at her own words she looked around to make sure no one was listening. Then she continued in Yiddish, "those contractors figure that no one cares about you immigrants – you don't vote. Even when we doctors and nurses complain about the situation, nothing ever comes of it."

* * *

Jacob spent his days in the infirmary helping out with the sicker patients. Many of the older immigrants were suffering from heart- and lung-related diseases. Jacob would help them sit up in bed so that they could breathe more easily. Sometimes, he would bring them a bedpan and even empty it for them. There were only two nurses for each infirmary, and they were always very busy handling acute issues. The seriously ill patients would be deported on the ships on which they had arrived if they lived long enough for them to be readied for the return journey.

Other patients, like Jacob, were being observed for conditions that were not immediately life-threatening but had to be watched to determine whether an eye or skin disease would render them deportable.

* * *

The nurses in the ward appreciated Jacob's efforts. Soon, they began to ask him to help them with tasks that didn't require extensive medical knowledge. He would take temperatures, apply ice packs to injuries, give alcohol rub-downs to fever patients, and serve as a general errand-boy. Jacob continued to expand his natural talent for languages. He was picking up more English phrases and able to understand much of what the nurses were saying.

The nurses, who couldn't or wouldn't pronounce Ya-ah-kovh, began to call him Jack. Jacob liked his new name. It was short and sounded very American. After a few days, he asked Olivia, his favorite nurse, "Vhat nemm vood sond Merikan?"

Olivia, a second-generation American Jew, reflected for a few moments. "Why don't you take the name Perle? Perle was my mother's maiden name. 'Jack Perle' has a nice ring to it. It's short. It rolls off the tongue easily. And it keeps the first two letters of your original name."

Jacob had no qualms about making the switch. He was anxious to rid himself of any trace of his family background and European origins.

* * *

Every other day, one of the doctors came to make rounds, but none had been able to examine Jacob's—Jack's—swollen eye adequately. It wasn't until the sixth day of his hospital stay that the examining physician was able to roll his eyelid back and verify that there was no evidence of trachoma.

Jack's relief was tempered by the fact he had not yet figured a way to obtain the necessary twenty dollars. He knew that he would be brought in front of a board of inquiry the next day for review. If he didn't have the money, he would be deported.

* * *

When the next morning rolled around, Jack had resigned himself to his fate. He knew by now that coming to America was absolutely the right decision for him. He liked the energy and the intensity of the people, even though he hadn't yet left Ellis Island.

Well, I made a valiant effort. Next time, I'll know what to do.

When he heard his name called by the official in the main room, he made his good-byes to patients who had become his grateful friends. It was harder to say goodbye to the nurses who had taken such a kind interest in him. They would have helped him if they could but were forbidden to give money or other valuables to needy immigrants, which would have created too many problems.

"Don't worry, Jack. You'll be back. We have confidence in you."

Jack followed the official through the maze of dark hallways back to the large reception area. When he passed a window, he could see the Statue of Liberty with her torch raised in the distance. He worked hard to stem the tears of disappointment rising within.

I wonder where they're taking me for my hearing.

He was a little puzzled when he was taken past the long lines of today's arrivals. They took him to the 'iron gates of freedom,' then to the 'steps of separation,' and, finally, to the 'New York room.'

"Your uncle is waiting out there," said the official, handing Jack his entry papers.

* * *

Stunned and at a loss for words, Jack saw Rose and her new husband waiting for him. She ran over and hugged him. Placing her mouth close to his ear so that the immigration official would not hear, she whispered, "Gershon was so grateful for what you did, that he insisted on giving you the twenty dollars you needed."

Jack was overwhelmed. He couldn't believe that he was about to start a new life and put his past behind him.

The official shook the boy's hand. "Good luck to you, Jacob Pechtrowicz."

"My name is Jack Perle," said the beaming young man as tears ran down his face.

Chapter Twenty-Three

Gershon Needleman had a terrible temper and was a violent man. Even his widowed, invalid mother was the target of his anger.

"Gershon, please get me a glass of water," she would say.

"Get it yourself, you fucking bitch!" he would answer, leaving the house and slamming the door after him.

He had been in America for two years. He hailed from the Ukrainian city of Kishinev, where his father had been killed in a Cossack pogrom. At the time, Gershon was fifteen and already an angry, wayward young man.

* * *

After his mother's death, the rebellious and anti-social Gershon made his way with two young friends to the big city of Kiev, where they joined a ring of pickpockets and petty thieves. Within a year, they had broken off to form their own gang. Gershon was the brains, and his friends provided the brawn. When the rumblings of the approaching revolution began to grow loud, the three of them decided that they would have better pickings and fewer hassles in the New World.

Gershon had met Rose the year before he left for America. Despite coming from a traditionally observant Jewish family, Rose was a fun-loving young woman who loved to dance and could match most men in putting away large amounts of vodka and slivovitz. It wasn't unusual for the two of them to stay out until dawn dancing, drinking, and carousing in one of the many small cafes in the central district of the city.

Rose intrigued Gershon. He had had his fair share of sexual encounters, but, no matter how much alcohol she imbibed, Rose would never permit him to cross the definitive line that she had drawn regarding sexual intercourse. Gershon had tried many times in many ways to get her drunk enough to let down her guard, but she always managed to maintain her virginity while not making him angry. This was quite a feat, since Gershon had a violent temper that triggered easily. But not with Rose. She had a magic touch that could simultaneously build up his ego and allow him to feel in complete control. His macho self-image was never damaged by the limits that she set.

As boorish and crude as Gershon was, he recognized and valued that rare quality. Rose was not only beautiful—she had dark blond hair and clear blue eyes—but she possessed great common sense. He could talk to her as if she were a man. Her advice was sound, and Gershon usually acted on it. He knew that he had a propensity for behaving impulsively and came to rely on Rose's gentle counsel.

When Gershon made the decision to emigrate, he had feared that Rose would be angry, but she surprised him. She not only wasn't upset but even encouraged him to make the move. She knew that conditions were getting worse in Russia and that America offered opportunities for a better life. Rose was also betting that Gershon would miss her enough to send for her once he had established himself.

"I think you should go, my love. This place has gotten dangerous for Jews. And I will be here waiting to hear from you if you want me," she would say.

Her bet paid off. The night before he left, Gershon took her out for a quiet dinner. Seated at a rear table behind a heavy velvet drape, he whispered, "You're the only girl I've ever loved. Will you marry me?"

"Of course I will, my love. I will wait forever to hear from you whenever you want me to join you.»

However, Rose still gently refused to go to bed with him, even on that last night. She knew that, if she did, it would diminish her aura of mystery and intrigue. Feeling that he had finally won the game, he could easily allow her to slip into oblivion when he was faced with the temptations of his new life. He promised to send for her when he had saved enough money to allow them to live decently. Gershon kept his promise—much to Jack Perle's good fortune.

When Gershon arrived in America, he and his friends continued where they had left off in Russia. After getting the lay of the land, they decided to begin by taking the least risks possible. They would threaten the poor Jewish peddlers on the street with violence should they refuse to pay protection money. Once they had staked out their turf—a few very crowded blocks in the Jewish ghetto on the Lower East Side—they expanded to extorting money from established shopkeepers. If they met resistance, they would beat the defenseless shopkeeper into submission. The frightened victims were afraid to call the police. Their painful experiences with police in the old country made them wary of trusting any officials, even American ones. Recently, Gershon and his thuggish friends had added gambling to their repertoire of activities. They would spend each morning on their established streetcorner taking bets on the horse races and numbers.

Gershon Needleman and his gang had become dreaded figures in the neighborhood. His friends had nicknamed him 'Needles' in the tradition of hoodlums such as 'Kid Twist' Zweibach or 'Dopey' Benny Fein. Needles Needleman liked his nickname. It made him feel big and powerful and like a real American.

Needles was not a modest man. His clothes were expensive, though in poor taste. He wore loud colored suits and print silk ties that didn't match. A large diamond ring set in heavy gold graced his right pinkie. He didn't realize that the diamond was really glass set in gold-plated metal, having bought it at significant cost from an unscrupulous con artist who claimed that it had previously been owned by a Russian nobleman who came upon hard times.

True to his nature, Needles rented a large, two-bedroom

flat in one of the newer tenements on Hester Street. It was considered a premium apartment because it was one of only three on the second floor of the walk-up and next door to the bathroom. Needles wanted his new bride to be duly impressed with his success.

Needles' offer to rescue Jacob was less a show of gratefulness for protecting the girl whom he loved than a way of showing off that he could afford to throw away twenty dollars. He also knew that Rose would be pleased and even more in his debt. He wanted to bring her independent spirit under his control.

When Needles suggested that Jack stay in their extra bedroom until he was able to establish himself, Rose was delighted. Having nowhere else to go, Jack jumped at the chance.

Needles liked having Jack around. He was getting ready to expand his sphere of activities and needed someone who would carry out his orders with no questions asked. He liked the fact that Jack was tall and physically strong for his age. Needles sensed that Jack was loyal and thought that he could take advantage of this characteristic. He especially liked the fact that Jack had no family or friends and could be made dependent on whatever favors Needles chose to grant.

* * *

For two weeks after their arrival, Needles took Rose and Jack sightseeing in their new land. He showed them the skyscrapers of downtown Manhattan and took them by subway to the rides at Coney Island. They took the train to visit the beautiful suburban areas of Yonkers and Queens.

Needles loved showing off his recently acquired skills in navigating his new environment. He spoke passable English with a heavy Russian accent and managed to make himself understood.

"Vell, vhat chew tink aff your new kaantry?" he asked.

"I can't believe I'm here. I've never seen anything so big and beautiful," Jack answered in Yiddish. He was still unsure of using his new English language skills.

Jack understood Gershon quite well. He had been listening carefully to those around him in an effort to learn the language. Rose, on the other hand, found English intimidating and made little effort to learn.

"I don't need to learn English," she would say to Needles. "Everybody in the neighborhood speaks Russian or Yiddish. Why do I need English?"

"Because you are now an American and should speak the language!" he would respond. "You're not always going to be around here. If you go out of the neighborhood, you won't be able to talk to anybody."

"So you'll do the talking!"

This was the first contentious issue that had come between Rose and her husband. Needles felt somewhat smug in his position because it was usually Rose who encouraged him to expand his horizons by learning new things. This time, he claimed the higher moral ground.

"Do you want everyone to call you a greenhorn all your life?"

"Who cares if I'm a greenhorn? Do their insults bother me? No!"

In truth, Rose's refusal to learn English did bother Needles. He saw himself climbing the social ladder of assimilation and didn't want to be held back by a wife unable to meet the demands of his increasing aspirations.

She's a smart girl. I know she'll change her mind after a while.

Jack had made up his mind to speak his new language flawlessly.

I want to speak so well no one will ever know I wasn't born here.

"Where can I go to school to learn English?" he asked Needles shortly after his arrival.

"There's a settlement house nearby that gives classes at night."

Jack began classes the very next week. Needles was pleased. He suggested to Rose that she go with Jack, but she refused.

"Have you decided what you'd like to do?" Needles asked Jack about three weeks after his arrival.

* * *

"Not really. I don't want to work in a sweatshop, but I have no real skills."

"How'd you like to work for me?"

Jack didn't really know what kind of work his host was involved in.

"What would I have to do?"

"Run errands, collect money, do odd jobs. I need somebody I can trust."

That's not so hard. I did the same thing for Nafty. I could do it here too. Maybe I could learn enough to go into business for myself someday.

"Sure, I'll do it. How much will I get paid?"

"Five dollars a week plus room and board. When you've saved enough to move into your own place, I'll raise it to seven dollars a week."

Seven dollars a week! That's a fortune.

"You've got yourself a man."

* * *

Needles started Jack off slowly. The first week on the job, he assigned him to observe and familiarize himself with the corner bookies and their customers. If any strangers were getting too interested in their activities, he was to report it. Needles was concerned about both police intervention and any 'new kids on the block' who might try to muscle in on his territory. Shortly after lunchtime, the 'betting offices' were closed. Jack took the money and paperwork to Needles, who would record the bets in a large ledger. Needles then took out the amount of cash that he would need to pay off the previous day's bets and prepared the balance to be deposited into a bank account under a fictitious name. Jack would carry the briefcase full of cash to the local branch of the Manhattan Bank and Trust Company, where it was duly deposited.

Jack monitored the operation for a few days.

"Why don't you split the cash into three different accounts? That way, no one person will be able to know how much money you have, and your business will be safer," he suggested to Needles. "Never store all your potatoes in one hole." He was, of course, repeating Nafty's rule.

Needles thought about what Jack had suggested.

This boychik is smart. I'm going to have to watch him.

* * *

Two weeks into Jack's new job, Needles was pleased with his performance.

It's time to increase the pressure.

"Today, Jack, I'm going to give you a new responsibility. You're to visit some of the shopkeepers on Hester Street and collect money that they owe me."

Why would shopkeepers owe him money? Maybe they're gambling debts.

* * *

Jack began his rounds that morning at Goldberg's Kosher Butcher Shop. The distinctive smell of freshly butchered meat mixed with the aroma of sawdust strewn across the floor reminded him of the old country. He could hear the chickens cackling in the back. He knew that, come Friday, most of them would have their necks slit and the blood drained out of them in preparation for the Sabbath holiday. His thoughts went back to childhood Sabbaths at the Kemelski home when his mother, father, and Uncle Meir sat around the table eating Annabel's wonderful food.

"Can I help you?"

Jack's thoughts were interrupted by the appearance of Isaac Goldberg.

"My name is Jack Perle. I've been sent by Mr. Gershon Needleman to collect the money you owe him."

A look of terror crossed the butcher's face.

"Tell him I don't have the money. It's been a bad week, and my wife's been sick. It cost me two dollars to take her to the doctor. Please, don't hurt me. I'll pay him next week."

Jack was taken aback.

Why was he so frightened? Why did he think he would get hurt?

"Of course I'll tell him. I hope your wife is feeling better."

* * *

Jack visited four other shopkeepers that day. All had the same look of terror on their faces when he told them why he had come. Three of them had given him fifty cents each, but the fourth, like the butcher, asked for an extension.

That evening, Jack turned over the money to Needles and reported the day's events. He watched carefully for Needles' reaction. Something didn't feel right.

"Those bastards. That butcher always gives me excuses. It's about time he learned his lesson. I want you to go back tomorrow and ask for the money again. If he doesn't give it to you I want you to 'rough him up' a little."

"What do you mean, 'rough him up'"?

* * *

"I mean a couple of punches in the face and belly. Enough to scare him."

"But he's already scared."

"Not scared enough to give me the money. He needs a little push."

"Why does he owe you money?"

"I protect him from anyone who might want to destroy his business."

"Who wants to destroy his business?"

Needles was getting angry with Jack. He didn't want questions, just obedience.

"Look, I told you what you need to do. Just do it!"

That night, Jack couldn't sleep. He could hear Needles in the next room yelling savagely at Rose. Needles's temper was showing itself much more often. It seemed that Rose's magic had lost its effectiveness. Jack even thought that he heard a slap and then Rose starting to cry. He was worried about her because she had confided to him that she was several weeks late for her period and might be pregnant. This was no way to treat a woman in such a delicate condition.

Jack thought about Needles's protection' scheme—he recognized it for what it was, extortion of defenseless victims—and his blood started to boil as recalled the many ways in which Jews had been taken advantage of in the old country even as they tried to escape the horrible conditions.

This man is taking advantage of his own people in the same way. He is detestable. I can't do what he asks. Jack's brain went into high gear. *But what am I going to do? He has me by the balls. I have nowhere to go and no one to turn to.*

* * *

By morning Jack had come up with a plan.

"Mr. Needleman," Jack began, wanting to bolster his employer's ego by carefully showing respect, "I have a proposition for you. I just can't do what you asked. I'm not a violent person, and those people haven't done anything to hurt me. But I like the other aspects of your business, and feel I can be very helpful to you there. I'll move out of your house and take a salary reduction to four dollars a week. That will save you a lot of money. And I'll work hard to build up your gambling network. What do you say?"

Needles thought it over.

He is a very smart kid. He has good ideas. I could use somebody like him to help me run the operation. I'll have to watch him like a hawk, though. If he knows too much, he could easily cheat me. I'd save money on his food and wouldn't have to worry about him hearing what goes on between me and Rose. They're getting too thick anyhow.

"Okay, kid, you got yourself a deal. And your salary will stay at five dollars. You'll save me enough money by not having to feed you or pay you the extra two dollars for living expenses. We'll see how it goes."

* * *

Jack rented a small, one-room flat on the fourth floor of an old walk-up building. There was enough room for a single bed and small, chipped wooden dresser that he purchased second-hand from the previous tenant. It had an almost non-existent kitchen, just a small sink and a hotplate, but Jack didn't care. He rarely ate at home anyway. The toilet and bath facilities were down the hall.

Jack loved his new home.

This is the first time I've ever had a place of my own, he thought as he paraded around the room naked while observing himself in the mirror in every kind of contorted position he could think of. *This is real freedom. I haven't done badly for a thirteen-year-old kid with no close family in this strange country. I missed having a bar mitzvah but I know that I'm a real man now.*

Within six months of his arrival, Jack was speaking almost fluent English. Within the following two years, he would fulfill his promise to himself that his English would be so flawless that no one would suspect him to be an immigrant.

* * *

Rose was unhappy that Jack was moving out, which left her pregnant and with no one to talk to at home. The loving relationship that she and Gershon once shared had deteriorated further. He abused her verbally almost daily and, when he had had a few drinks, would sometimes slap her around despite her growing belly. Nevertheless, she continued to refuse to make the slightest effort to learn English. At first, she had felt that doing so would somehow mean giving up part of her core identity. As time went on, though, the issue became part of a power struggle between her and her husband, with each staking out a stubborn position.

"I can't take you anywhere," Needles would complain. "What good is it to have a wife if I always have to leave her at home?"

"I don't want to go anywhere with your friends, anyhow. They're just a bunch of crude, dishonest thieves."

"You didn't seem to care about that back in Russia," Needles spat back. "All of a sudden, you've become a model of virtue."

Whatever the reason, Needles lost all sexual interest in his pregnant wife and began to stay out all night with any girl who happened to catch his fancy. However, he would not give the time of day to those who didn't speak English. Indeed, this seemed to be his main criterion for assessing any potential relationship. If there were dinner meetings to which his colleagues brought their wives, Needles went alone, ashamed of Rose's inability to speak the language and her unwillingness to adapt to the styles and manners of the New World.

Sometimes, he would have meetings with the bosses of other gambling rings to work out issues of turf. He often brought Jack along to those meetings, where the young man met such characters as Monk Eastman and Big Jack Zelig. He even was introduced to Melvin Meyers, known as the Moses of Jewish gangsters. As the leader of the 'Jewish mafia,' he was involved in directing most of the Jewish organized crime in the city.

* * *

Rose gave birth to a healthy baby boy about a year after her arrival in the United States. Needles was not at the hospital when the baby was born, but Jack was waiting outside the labor room.

Needles insisted that his son have an American name, so the child was called Richard Stephen Needleman after his father, Reuven Shlomo.

* * *

By the fourth anniversary of his arrival in America, Jack had built up a small gambling empire for his boss. He had hired twenty more young men to cover Needles's expanding territory.

On every street corner within ten square blocks of Needles's base of operations, a representative of his organization took bets until 1 p.m. For special sporting events, they would stay until 5. Jack oversaw the collection of monies and the lists of bets that went with it. After Needles totaled it up and prepared the paperwork, Jack would deposit the money, just before closing, in the four banks where the accounts had been set up. Needles was pleased with Jack's performance. He never found any money missing. Jack was now earning a hundred dollars a week, a large amount for a seventeen-year-old boy—now a man—living alone.

Over time, Jack had become acquainted with most of the people in his neighborhood. His good looks and considerate manner had endeared him to many. He often gave money from his own pocket to mothers whose children needed medical treatment or to destitute elderly immigrants whose children had moved from New York to other parts of the country.

Jack had a special place in his heart for the prostitutes who lived in the neighborhood and became good friends with many of them, offering tips about how to handle their tricks and increase their business. Often, prostitution was their only alternative to working in a sweatshop for pennies in order to support themselves. Sometimes, they were wives who had followed their husbands to the United States and then been abandoned. Unlike those back in Europe who operated in an isolated section of the ghetto, these women openly plied their trade. They were subject to community ostracism and often endured public displays of verbal abuse; people sometimes even threw objects thrown at them as they passed.

Jack had also kept his promises to those in the old country. He wrote to both Nita in Bremen and to his mother in Vilna. He learned of his mother's death from Nafty, who, even as the winds of World War I enveloped Vilna, intercepted his letter to Rebecca. He felt terribly guilty for leaving and was filled with increasingly vengeful thoughts toward the father who had abandoned them so carelessly. This was one of the first times he had given any thought to Aaron since arriving in America.

One of these days, I'll track him down and make him pay for this.

However, his life was interesting and very busy. Tracking down his father would have to wait.

* * *

One day, a group of the working women invited him to dinner. He was a bit surprised at the invitation, but curious to know what it was all about.

Sophie, who had come up with the idea and had the largest apartment, hosted the dinner. Each of the six girls who attended had cooked a special dish. One even brought several bottles of wine. The dinner was fun, replete with dirty jokes, tales of the trade, and much laughter.

After they had eaten, the girls grew quiet and seemed embarrassed. Jack sensed it.

"What have you girls brought me up here for?" he said with a smile. "Do you want to get me drunk and steal my virginity?"

They smiled demurely because they all knew that Jack had a reputation for being a great lover. He had had sexual relationships with many women, though never anything serious.

"Actually," began Sophie, "we have a business proposition for you."

"What's that?"

"Jack, we all love you and trust you. You have never hurt or cheated any of us. You always listen to us and gave us good advice, which really helps. We know we can do better business and take less risks if you help us. We want you to organize us and set us up in a real honest-to-God business. You can keep all the profits after expenses. We'll be your investment."

Jack was floored and flattered. He blushed, and the girls laughed. Each came over and gave him a kiss.

"Please," they pleaded.

"Let me think about it."

* * *

"Mr. Needleman, I want you to know that I've been asked by several prostitutes to help them organize their business and set up a bordello. I've agreed to do it. I'll do it on my own time and won't let it interfere with my work for you. If you have a problem with it, I'll be happy to quit my job and let you find someone else to take it over."

Jack knew it would be foolhardy to try and do it behind Needles' back. He'd find out sooner or later and be very angry.

"Why don't we do it together?"

"No, sir. I want to have something of my own, and this would be a good way to start."

Needles considered the situation.

I need him to run the operation. If he leaves, I'd have to start all over training someone new. I know I can trust him. He's never stolen a dime. I always knew that he'd want to go off on his own someday. This way, I can keep him a few years longer. What the hell; the few extra bucks he might bring in for himself won't bother me.

"All right, Jack. Go ahead and do it. But if it interferes with my operation, something will have to change."

"Thank you, sir. I promise you this won't take anything away from my work with you."

* * *

On his own time, Jack scoured the neighborhood for an appropriate set of rooms that could be converted into a bordello. He found an entire first floor available in an older tenement a little off the beaten track on the fringe of the ghetto. It was a rough neighborhood, home to few women and children who might create problems.

Jack had saved up several thousand dollars. He invested a good portion of it in the bordello, leasing the space and converting it into a luxurious suite of rooms suitable for his purpose. There was a large reception area with a bar and small kitchen where the girls could greet their customers and feed them sandwiches and liquor. Jack thought about watering down the alcohol but decided that it would be better to maintain the quality and increase the prices. Off the main room were six small bedrooms with mirrored walls, double beds, and silk sheets. Each contained a sink where the clients could wash up with thick terry towels before leaving. At the end of the hallway was a bathroom with erotic wallpaper and a marble toilet.

Because the girls were often asked by their tricks about their sexual health, they were required to get a medical examination for venereal disease every three months. The written results were framed and hung on the wall where they could be viewed by the clientele.

The couches in the reception area were covered with soft red velvet and had deep cushions. There were no single chairs, thus ensuring that no man would sit alone. Sophie, the leader of the prostitutes, took on the role of madame and watched over the place like a hawk. It was her job to recruit the talent and to manage the operation on a day-to-day basis. She consulted with Jack regularly. He would stop in for a few minutes almost every night to see how things were going.

The customers paid a minimum of ten dollars for an hour of a girl's time. If a customer wanted a specific girl, the fee was twelve dollars. Extra time was charged at the same rate, and the establishment charged fifty cents for one alcoholic drink. Sandwiches and soft drinks were on the house.

* * *

Like Nafty's establishment, the girls were permitted to keep forty percent of their earnings. Sophie got ten percent of the overall take. After expenses, Jack kept the rest.

For Jack, this was a big risk. If the business failed, he would lose most of the nest egg that he had so carefully built up. Because he could not openly advertise the existence of the new facility, Jack had his girls spread the word to their current clients, who then told their friends and business acquaintances. He needn't have worried. On opening night, the bordello was crowded beyond capacity. Despite the unfavorable economic conditions in the ghetto, many entrepreneurs had managed to make a great deal of money. Some had already moved their families to the better neighborhoods in Brooklyn and Queens but still patronized the establishments on the Lower East Side. They not only were able to afford Jack's prices but also vied with their colleagues to be seen at his establishment.

Within a year, Jack had made back his initial investment and was earning enormous profits as well. He was fast becoming a wealthy man. During the same period he had increased Needles' profits by twenty-five percent.

* * *

Meanwhile, the world was in a state of increasing turmoil as the United States declared war on Germany in April 1917. Jack worried that, after all of his efforts to leave Europe, he would be sent back again as a soldier in the U.S. Army.

I don't want to go back, escaping conscription into the czar's army only to risk my life again. What would happen to everything I've built up here?

Jack was relieved when he missed the first selective service draft in June 1917, which called up men between the ages of 21 and 31. He was 18 at the time, but an impending second round brought daily anxiety; when it came the following June, though it turned out that young men under the age of 21 were spared.

In September, though, Jack's luck ran out when the draft

was extended to include men down to the age of 18. All through October 1918, he anxiously prepared for the notice that he knew was coming.

"Boss," Jack told Needles, "you'll have to find somebody to replace me."

"What if we can get to somebody in the draft office and get your name off that list?"

Jack became thoughtful. He reflected on all that his new country had allowed him to accomplish. Finally, he replied, "No, boss. I feel like I have to go. I'm obligated to pay America back for all she has done for me." Needles wasn't happy about it, but he respected Jack's decision.

At last, Jack was ordered to report to the Amy Induction Center in the city on Tuesday, November 12, 1918. With sadness, he packed his bags and began saying his goodbyes to his friends. On the Sunday before his induction date, the girls at the bordello held a special goodbye party for him, and he had to be helped home by one of the girls at 4:00 a.m.

Around noon, Jack was awakened from a deep sleep by someone pounding on his apartment door. Groggy and disoriented, he opened his eyes.

I must have slept through my induction time. I hope I don't get in trouble.

Then he became aware of shouting in the streets and church bells chiming. Sophie was still pounding at the door, and he realized that she was yelling, "THE WAR IS OVER!" Later that day, the Army sent Jack a telegram canceling his induction.

Thank you, God. I'm a lucky man.

The U.S Selective Service Act ended shortly thereafter.

Chapter Twenty-Four

O nce a month, Jack would receive a note from Rose. He knew that she and Needles were continuing to experience marital problems. Needles had moved out of the flat a couple of years after their son was born, leaving Rose alone to deal with the child. Jack had visited periodically for a while but stopped doing so because their relationship made Needles furious. As long as Needles was his boss, he would have to be circumspect in his interactions with Rose, as she well understood.

In the spring of 1919, a few months after his brush with military service, Jack received a desperate note from her written in Yiddish.

PLEASE COME IMMEDIATELY AS I HAVE NO MONEY AND THE LANDLORD IS GOING TO KICK ME OUT.

ROSE

That night, Jack made his way to her flat on Hester Street. Rose looked like she belonged in a hospital, with both eyes swollen and black and blue and her nose bent as though it was broken. Her lips were so swollen that she could hardly talk.

"What happened?"

Rose began to cry.

"Ever since the baby was born, Gershon has not wanted me, as you know. He would stay out all night and come home drunk. When I tried to talk to him, he would beat me up. He never paid any attention to Richard and sometimes scared the little one to death by screaming at him for nothing. Sometimes, he even slapped him. But, until six months ago, he would at least show up and spend some time here.

"Then he told me that, if I didn't learn English in the next two months, he would leave. I said, 'Okay, I'll try.' I went to the Settlement House classes, but, no matter how hard I tried, I couldn't do it. Gershon said I didn't really try. He said he didn't want me anymore and I should go back to Russia. He said I must leave Richard here with him. I said 'absolutely not,' and he punched me. Then he said 'I'll show you.' Next thing I knew, he had stopped paying the rent on the flat and refused to give me any money for food. He was trying to get me to go back to Russia without the boy."

Rose took a deep breath and sighed.

"What would he do with the boy? Get married again and let a stepmother raise him? Never! I've been able to manage until now on the household money I stuffed away for emergency."

She paused again and wiped away tears.

"So, I figured I'd embarrass him into paying. I wrote a letter to the Jewish <u>Daily Forward</u>—you know, the Yiddish newspaper. They have a section called Bintel Briefs where they publish letters from abandoned wives and print a picture of the missing husband."

Rose picked up a newspaper clipping from yesterday's <u>Daily Forward</u> and handed it to Jack. Next to a picture of Needles was printed Rose's letter:

```
Gershon Needleman,
    Your son and I plead with you. Why have you
abandoned us and left us with no money and no
place to live? You are a rich man. Where is your
conscience? You have made money off of other people
and now you do not even take care of your own
family.
    For six years I have loved you faithfully and
taken care of you like a loyal servant. Yet I have
not had a happy day with you since I came. I was a
young, decent, educated girl when you brought me
here. Look what you have done to me.
    I bore you a beautiful son and then you left me.
You have made him a living orphan. And now you want
me to go back to Russia and leave him here with you.
What will you do with him? You haven't spent any
time with him for years. You just want to punish
me.
    Have pity on us. If you won't come back, then pay
for us to return to my family in Russia. Consider
what you are doing to us. My tears choke me and I
cannot write any more.
        Rose
```

"When Gershon saw my letter he was furious. He came here and beat me up worse than ever before. He told me that now more than ever he would not let the boy return to the Ukraine with me. Richard heard it all. He's so frightened he's hiding under the bed and won't come out."

Jack was appalled. He knew that Needles had a bad temper but never thought that he would injure his wife and son to that extent.

I can't let him do that to them. What kind of life would the boy have? I always thought that any father was better than no father at all, but I see I was wrong. When Needles finds out I'm helping them, he'll want to kill me. I won't be able to stay in New York. But I can't let this go on.

"Rose, you need to leave New York with Richard, but you know there's an armed revolution going on back home. How can you go back at this time?"

"Listen Jack! I'll have to take that chance. I can't stay here and I'm not going anywhere else where I can't speak the language!"

Jack acknowledged she was right.

Jack laid his plans carefully. He gave Rose some money to tide her over. He didn't want Needles to get wind of what he was doing, so he traveled downtown to arrange for a second class cabin to Bremen on the first available ship. He also purchased second class railway tickets to Kiev.

Rose deserves to travel in comfort and safety. If not for her, I wouldn't be here.

Jack didn't want to be around when Needles discovered what he had done. He put his boss's books in top-notch order and made sure they were up to date. He also took care of winding up his own business affairs. Sophie would continue to run the bordello. Jack trusted her completely.

* * *

Rose and Richard were due to sail on a Saturday morning in June 1919. On Friday afternoon, Jack closed his New York bank accounts and stowed the cash in a locked black briefcase. It amounted to a very considerable sum. With the briefcase attached to his wrist he took a taxicab to Rose's apartment scanning the street and apartment entrance to be sure that Gershon wasn't around. He spent Friday night helping Rose pack last minute items and comforting her anxiety about leaving America and returning to Russia. This shared feeling of impending loss of each other's friendship unexpectedly led to the first and only awkward love making occurrence between them. They both immediately regretted their actions. Neither wanted to blemish their longtime relationship and both were frightened about what might happen if Gershon found out. Afterwards, both pretended it never happened.

On Saturday morning Jack accompanied the mother and son to the Port of New York and watched them board the *SS Deutchland*. As the ship weighed anchor, he took a taxi to Pennsylvania Station, bought his three- dollar ticket, and stepped aboard the one o'clock train to Philadelphia. He decided that it was time for him to move on and explore the unanswered questions of his life.

Chapter Twenty-Five

Jack arrived at 30th Street Station in the late afternoon. He headed to the downtown area and checked into the St. James Hotel at 13th and Walnut. Because he was carrying such a large amount of cash, he decided to spend the weekend in his room until he could open a bank account on Monday morning. It was the first time that he had spent any time in his adopted country outside New York City, and he was eager to see what Philly and the rest of the country were like.

His meals were brought to his room along with copies of the Philadelphia newspapers the Record and Inquirer. He also asked for a copy of the local telephone directory and a map of the city. While most businesses now had telephones, only twenty-five percent of residences did. The directory listed only business numbers.

Jack ate his dinner staring at the telephone directory on the table in front of him. He paused after every few bites and unconsciously fingered the frayed and threadbare velvet pouch that never left its home around his neck.

What will I do if I find him? I'm not ready to face him.

Jack finally found the strength to open the phone book.

I know that my uncles have a bakery somewhere in the city. But who knows what name they go under now or what the name of their bakery might be?

He turned to the 'B' section and looked for bakeries.

BOGASLAVSKY

CARDINO

GOLD SEAL

HOROWITZ

As he approached the 'P' listings, his heart started to beat faster.

PAULS

PACIELLO

PECKS

For a moment, Jack couldn't breathe.

PECKS. It's got to be them. They probably shortened their name, too.

He stood up and began pacing the floor. His palms were sweaty and his hands cold.

What the hell is wrong with me? Why am I so nervous?

Jack took a few deep breaths and felt himself calming down. He opened the desk drawer, took out a sheet of hotel stationery, and jotted down the address and phone number.

PECKS BAKERY—1900 N. 31ST STREET ....Fremont 0139

Clearing the dishes from the room service table, he spread

out the city map. The address was in the north-central part of the city called Strawberry Mansion, just east of the Schuylkill River and not far from the Philadelphia Zoo.

On Monday morning, briefcase in hand, Jack walked to the Philadelphia Savings Fund Society and deposited half of his cash in a new account. From there, he walked to the Girard Trust Bank near City Hall and opened another account, where he deposited the remainder.

Relieved of his cash burden, Jack asked a policeman for directions to Strawberry Mansion. The officer pointed him to the Number 9 trolley, which dropped him off at 31st and Berks.

There, on the corner next to Weinstein's Delicatessen, stood Pecks Bakery.

Jack paused there for a few minutes trying to get up the nerve to enter the store.

I've been in a lot more dangerous situations, yet I've never been as scared as I am now.

He moved closer to the entrance. The aroma of freshly baked bread and pastries filled the air. In the window were trays of bagels, rye bread, kaiser rolls, pumpernickel, danish, and schnecken. His mouth began to water.

The reflection of the sun on the glass window made it difficult for Jack to see into the store, but he could make out the two middle-aged men behind the counter.

Could they be my uncles? I never had a real relative.

Jack walked into the store and waited until the men had finished with their customers.

"Can I help you?"

"Yes. I'm new in the city, and I'm trying to figure out where I want to live. I was walking by and smelled the wonderful aromas coming from your shop. My mouth started to water. I'd like a half-dozen bagels and a dozen schnecken."

"Where you from?" asked Lemel—for it was he, one of Aaron's half-brothers - in a heavy Russian accent.

"I just got here from New York. How long have you been here?"

"We came about twenty years ago from Lithuania," chimed in the other half-brother, Simeon, who had been listening to the conversation. "We're almost natives," he laughed.

"My father had some relatives in Vilna," said Jack. "Where in Lithuania are you from?"

"Aw, you never heard of it, a little shtetl called Jelzai."

Jack's heart jumped.

"Oh. You're right. I never heard of it. Did you have relatives here who brought you over?"

"No. We came alone. But our little brother Aaron, he came over about a dozen years ago."

"Does he work with you?"

"Oh no," Lemel laughed. "He's got a rich father-in-law. He works for him."

"What does he do?"

"They run a big fruit company down on Delaware Avenue near the river called R & P Fruit. The R is for Rozin. That's the father-in-law. The P is for Peck—like us. They sell unusual fruit, like bananas and pineapples and something called Chinese gooseberries that they also call Kiwi."

"Oh. Does he live down there?"

"Hah! Are you kidding? That's a bad neighborhood. He lives a couple of blocks from here on Thirty-third Street near Diamond, across from the park."

"Yeah. He drives a big car. We don't see him much," chimed in Simeon again.

"Does he have children?"

"Oh yeah. Two little girls, eleven and nine."

"No boys?"

"Nah! He makes only girls."

Jack gulped. A stab of pain passed through him as he unconsciously fondled his coin.

"Are you two married?"

"Nah. We don't want a wife. Too much trouble. We work hard. No time for a wife or kids."

Nice to meet you uncles. Maybe someday I'll tell you who I am.

Jack paid and thanked the storekeepers and took his baked goods.

"Thank you very much. I know I'll be seeing you again," he said as he left.

* * *

Jack bought a corned beef sandwich and a sarsaparilla at Weinstein's delicatessen. Then he made his way to Thirty-third and Diamond. There was a large, flat grassy area on the west side of Thirty-third Street. About two hundred yards back, a large hill with a pointed wrought-iron fence at the top marked the wall of a city reservoir. Scattered benches surrounded by grass faced the street. A few mothers with small children played on the grass. The kids were constantly trying to climb the hill, and their mothers kept scolding them and telling them to come down.

Jack sat on a bench near the corner of Diamond Street. He had no idea which of the large three-story houses across the street belonged to his father, but he wanted to familiarize himself with the neighborhood. He spread a newspaper on his lap, unwrapped the sandwich, and began to eat. It was about noon.

A few minutes later, pedestrian traffic picked up as neighborhood children left the elementary school for their lunch break. A dozen or so passed by, but none turned into any of the homes across the street. Straggling behind, though, came two pre-teen girls holding hands. The taller one was tugging at the younger one in an effort to make her move faster. Jack could hear their high, tinkling voices.

"Hurry up, Gita. We're late for lunch. Mama will be worried."

"Don't pull so hard, Lily. You're hurting me!"

"Well, move faster then."

Jack watched as the girls entered the third house from the corner and disappeared inside. A pang of jealousy traveled up his spine. He noted the address: 2105 North Thirty-third Street.

Stifling a completely unexpected and surprising sob, he thought, *I'm not ready to meet that son of a bitch yet, and I don't know when I will be. But, sooner or later, he'll pay for what he's done.*

Shaking with thoughts of revenge percolating through his brain, Jack stumbled to the streetcar stop and caught the Number 9 trolley back to his hotel.

Chapter Twenty-Six

Jack spent the next few weeks exploring his new city. He wandered through South Philly, where most of the newly arrived Jewish and Italian immigrants settled. He walked the waterfront by day, watching the busy docks where longshoremen loaded and unloaded large freighters. He took note of the corners that were occupied by bookmakers and the floating craps and poker games that appeared and disappeared. Nothing missed his keen eye.

He strolled the waterfront at night as well, observing the patterns of prostitutes picking up their tricks, the prices they charged, where they took their customers, and how many were controlled by pimps. Sizing up the situation in this way was relatively easy for Jack to do, as hordes of sailors returning from the war were waiting for their ships to be repaired in the nearby Philadelphia Naval Yard.

Mulling over his plans for the future, Jack reflected, *I know my activities have been against the law, but they're the only thing I've known how to do since I've been six years old. And by now I'm really*

good at them. I try not to hurt people, and I know I often help them out.
I guess you can't teach an old dog new tricks.

Having made his decision, Jack set out to build his new career. By the time he had been in Philadelphia for three weeks, he had familiarized himself with the city's crime structure, including the gangs that dominated each of the various operations.

He made it a point to walk past the R & P Fruit Company frequently. The business occupied a large warehouse on Delaware Avenue across from the river. The port area was close by. Each afternoon, large wooden crates filled with pineapples, bananas, and other fruits would be delivered and repacked into smaller boxes. Each morning, a small fleet of R and P trucks would deliver the fresh fruit to food and produce stores. The high level of activity suggested a very successful operation.

The first week that Jack spent time observing the fruit company, he saw no one resembling his father moving around outside the warehouse. He did see an older man barking orders to the workers whom he assumed to be Rozin, Aaron's father-in-law.

Reasoning that he'd have a better chance of spotting his father at quitting time, Jack staked out a vantage point across the street at 2 p.m. on a Friday to catch him leaving if the business closed early for the Sabbath. Jack had rented a car for this purpose.

His patience was rewarded. At 3 p.m., he saw Aaron climbing into a black Ford sedan parked in front of the warehouse and drive away. At the first glimpse of his father, Jack again began to shake uncontrollably, and the tears flowed.

My God. I never thought I'd see him again. He looks the same. He's just a little fatter and his hair a little grayer. How can I feel so excited to see him after what he did to me?

Despite his emotional reactions, Jack had not admitted to himself how much he ached for his father's love and acceptance. Once more, the reawakened pain of his rejection ran through him like an electric current. He fingered the pouch around his neck. Then he got out of his rented car, threw the glass bottle of sarsaparilla to the pavement so that it broke into a hundred pieces, and kicked the hard tires of his car.

I can't let that affect me. He'll never be any different. But I'll find a way to pay him back. I have to—for my own sanity. He wiped his eyes and returned to his hotel.

Jack's analysis indicated that the most likely chance for success breaking into the Philadelphia crime scene was the sex trade. There appeared to be no dominant gang, and he expected to meet little resistance from the few disorganized pimps whom he had observed operating in the city.

He started off by identifying a girl whom he had watched over the past few weeks interacting with returning sailors. He had noticed that other girls looked to her when they were faced with problems on the street.

* * *

One evening, he approached her. "My name is Jack," he said. "I'd like to talk to you. What's your name?"

"You can call me Jane but I'm not interested in talkin', mister. There's nothin' in it for me."

"I'll pay you for your time, Jane. How's twenty bucks for an hour?"

"Twenty bucks! Are you crazy or somethin'? I only get five bucks an hour."

She's exaggerating. She works for two dollars an hour.

"Okay," said Jack with a smile, "we'll make it five dollars an hour."

"Never mind," she replied sheepishly, "twenty will be fine."

Jack invited her to join him for coffee at an all-night café. He assured her that he was not looking to hurt her in any way and explained that he had had some experience in helping prostitutes increase their income and decrease their risks. He asked whether she thought that her fellow workers might be interested in learning more about his ideas.

"I guess so. I never thought about it."

"How would you feel about bringing a group of your friends to dinner with me? I'd like to meet them."

Jack rented a private party room at the Old Original Bookbinders Restaurant at Second and Walnut. He plied the girls with drinks and good seafood—the specialty of the house. Most of them had never been to such a fine restaurant and very few had ever tasted lobster. Certainly, no one had ever showed this kind of an interest in them before. They were duly impressed.

The handsome young man explained some of his ideas to them. Like all of the other women with whom Jack came into contact, they were charmed and ready to go along with whatever he proposed. He asked them lots of questions, wanting to confirm or correct the conclusions that he had drawn about the sex trade in the city. At the end of the evening, he was ready to move forward with his plans.

* * *

Jack opened his first Philadelphia bordello at the corner of Second and Arch. It was designed much like the one in New York, only larger and more luxurious. For the opening night, he sent out engraved invitations to all of the major crime figures in Philadelphia. The food and drinks were free, but the girls were not. Jack had hired a beauty consultant to help dress them appropriately, style their hair, and teach them how to apply make-up. The transformation was startling. The customers didn't mind paying fifteen dollars an hour for girls they would never have looked at on the street.

His profit in Philly was even greater because Jack ran the operation himself. There was no madame who took a ten-percent cut. By the end of the first year, the Philadelphia house was making more money than the one in New York. As 1920 rolled around, Jack opened two more bordellos, one in South Philadelphia and one in the Olney section of North Philadelphia. Both operations were profitable from the start.

The young entrepreneur became a well-known figure in the underground Philadelphia gangster society. He was a highly desirable guest at parties given by the rising stars of organized crime. He dressed impeccably and was always well-groomed. His wardrobe became the standard of local fashion. Jack was especially well-liked by Harry Rothenberg, the dominant figure in Philadelphia crime and an associate of New York's Melvin Meyers. .

"When you gonna get married and settle down?" Harry would ask.

"What wife would let me hang out with all these beautiful women? I'm not getting married for a long time."

Jack rented an expensive apartment on Rittenhouse Square. His neighbors were affluent businessmen and professionals. Jack never talked about himself or his work. To them, he was a charming mystery man.

"He must come from money," went the gossip.

* * *

Once a month, late on a Saturday morning, Jack would drive his Packard convertible to Strawberry Mansion. He would stop at Pecks Bakery, kibitz a little with Lemel and Simeon, and leave with a supply of bagels and schnecken. Then he would go next door to Weinstein's for his usual corned beef sandwich and a drink. The Jewish merchants were fast becoming Americanized. They no longer felt it necessary to close on the Sabbath, which became one of their busiest days.

Jack then parked at Thirty-third and Norris so as not to be noticed and walk the block to his bench across the street from 2105.

About 12:30 p.m., Aaron and his wife and daughters would leave Sabbath services at the B'nai Jeshurun Synagogue two blocks north, after which they would slowly make their way home for the Sabbath midday meal.

Jack watched his father playfully interacting with the girls, pulling their pigtails and picking up the little one and giving her a kiss.

Why couldn't he have been that way with me?

The pain and jealousy never diminished. The wound remained raw even after all these years.

Why do I do this to myself? It only gives me grief.

Nevertheless, each month, he continued to make his trip to the park bench.

Chapter Twenty-Seven

In 1919, the world of organized crime was galvanized when Congress passed, and state legislatures ratified, the Eighteenth Amendment to the Constitution, which prohibited the manufacture, sale, or transportation of alcoholic beverages anywhere in the United States. Many chafed under the new prohibition laws, especially those wanting to celebrate the return of an invigorated economy and general exuberance following the end of the war as well as the end of the Spanish Flu epidemic which had affected practically every family in the country.

Not long after Prohibition went into effect in January 1920, Harry Rothenberg invited Jack to lunch.

"There's a tremendous opportunity here to take advantage of this new law," he told the younger man. "We're gonna be trucking booze across the Canadian border and opening up a bunch of nightclubs here in the city to drink it in. You've had lots of experience running bars and entertainment. We'd like you to partner with us in this venture. We'll provide the booze, you provide the night-clubs, and we'll split 50-50."

This could be a gold mine.

* * *

By 1923, their partnership had come to include more than twenty speakeasies in the greater Philadelphia area. Their empire extended to South Jersey, northern Pennsylvania, and Delaware.

One Monday afternoon, Jack received a phone call from Harry.

"Melvin Meyers wants to see you. Why don't you take the train into New York tomorrow?"

Jack was curious. Usually, any business between him and Meyer always went through Harry.

I wonder what he wants.

* * *

When Jack walked into Meyer's office the next day, he was shown to a conference room where the entire New York syndicate had gathered around a table. Surveying the room, he did a double-take: Needles Needleman was seated at the far end of the table. Needles saw Jack at the same moment and, rising from his chair, pulled a pistol from his pocket and pointed it at Jack. For a split-second, Jack froze, panicked.

Then Needles holstered his gun and laughed. "You've come a long way, boychik!" he smiled.

The others in the room laughed nervously.

Jack was taken aback and speechless for a moment.

"It's a good thing you left when you did," Needles continued.

"I was so angry at you I would've killed you. But I'm over it."

There was a pause.

"Do you ever hear from Rose? How is the boy?"

In fact, Jack heard from Rose regularly. He sent her a money order every month to cover her living expenses. She had met and married an old boyfriend shortly after her return. Richard was adjusting well. He never asked about his father.

"They seem to be doing all right."

"I'm glad. I don't know what I would've done with him, anyway."

He's really mellowed over the past four years.

"Let's get down to business," said Meyer. "You've done a great job putting together the speakeasy operations in Philly," he said to Jack. "We want you to do the same thing here in New York. It could be structured like your deal in Philly."

"I don't think that would work, Mr. Meyers. Someone needs to be present every day to keep a close eye on things. It wouldn't be fair to you. But I think I know a way around it."

"What's that?"

"Instead of giving me a piece of the action, why not just hire me to supervise whoever you choose to run the operation? I could come into New York once a week and go over each plan and transaction. That way, it'll cost you less and you'll still get the result you're looking for."

"You think that would work?"

"I'm sure of it."

* * *

Jack came through on his promise. The syndicate hired him
as he proposed, and the New York speakeasies turned out to be
as successful as the ones in Philadelphia. Melvin Meyers was
very pleased. Jack received an enormous retainer to remain on
call for the project as well as a bonus at the end of each year the
operation exceeded projections.

The twenty-four-year-old mystery man was making more
money than he knew what to do with, and he decided to acquire
some legitimate businesses that would serve as fronts to
launder the enormous amounts of cash flowing into his many
bank accounts. He started off by taking a silent majority stake
in Shein's Coat and Linen, the largest linen supply company
of its kind in Philadelphia. Its size allowed it to knock out
any competitors for the business of servicing the area's major
hotels, hospitals, and restaurants. Jack thought of the business
as a cash cow; it only gave him greater amounts of accumulating
cash that he had then to reinvest.

So, Jack began to purchase large tracts of waterfront property.
His ownership was hidden under corporations so that his role
could not be traced. Many of the city's largest businesses
operated along the Delaware River, but few of the owners also
owned the property on which their businesses were located.
Jack was able to establish a monopoly on rents in the area so
that he could destroy many successful men on a whim should he
so choose. The R & P Fruit company was among the firms that
rented one of his warehouses.

Having purchased these properties, Jack turned his

attention to the import-export business. He had learned that, to operate successfully outside the law, he needed to be able to ship materials into and out of the country surreptitiously. After his usual exhaustive research, Jack bought the Norton Art Company, the oldest and most respected dealer of artwork in the city. Norton had been in business for so long and had such a clean record that customs officials cleared its crates without bothering to examine the contents.

Jack knew that the Philadelphia and New York syndicates were getting ready to mount a new smuggling operation bringing uncut heroin in from the Orient. Two kilograms cost them twenty-five hundred dollars. They could sell it through their distribution networks for thousands more once it was cut and processed.

Jack didn't want to be a part of the narcotics trade. He disliked heroin, having witnessed its devastating effects. However, after he thought it over, his greed got the better of him. Also, he didn't want to anger the mob. Accordingly, he decided to allow the syndicate to utilize his transportation facilities. He would be paid handsomely, and, in the worst-case scenario, his company could always claim ignorance of what had been packed in an objet d'art since he had been careful to maintain plausible deniability. He pushed his feelings of guilt to the back of his mind.

The money kept rolling in.

Chapter Twenty-Eight

E xcept when he was out of town, Jack continued his monthly
Saturday morning routine. In fact, he looked forward to
it. He loved kibitzing with Lemel and Simeon, who told him
never-ending stories about the old country. Jack especially
liked the ones that mentioned his grandfather. He devoured
any information that gave him some connection to his family,
though his uncles didn't know who he was.

Jack had bought the block of buildings that housed the
bakery and the neighboring businesses. He wanted to make sure
that no other landlord could raise their rent or otherwise take
advantage of them.

One Saturday, Lemel said to Jack, "We must have a very
stupid landlord. All my neighbors are paying a lot more rent,
but ours is staying the same." Jack laughed in agreement. He
was happy that he was able to do something good for them. It
didn't matter that they were unaware of his role.

Jack had been making his monthly pilgrimage now for six
years. Every time he thought that he would stop, he found

himself back on the same old bench in the park.

It's a wonder that they haven't noticed me in all these years.

Gita was fifteen years old and going to high school. She was a high-spirited child and seemed to be laughing whenever Jack happened to see her.

Lily had ripened into a beautiful young woman. She was built like her paternal grandmother—tall and slim. Jack could see traces of his mother's green eyes in her. She would have been Lily's great aunt.

The seventeen-year-old beauty would be graduating from high school at the end of the school year. Jack knew that it wouldn't be long before some young man would fall in love with her and ask for her hand in marriage. Her father would fuss over her, buy her a large dowry, and pay for a large wedding. Maybe her husband would even join her father at the R & P Fruit company—*a role that rightfully belongs to me.*

Where did that come from?

Jack was surprised at the vehemence of the anger that boiled up inside him. God shouldn't let his father get away with his disgusting and dishonorable behavior of abandoning his first family. Aaron had never sent them one red cent, even after he could easily have afforded to mail them occasional support.

For God's sake, even Lemel and Simeon sent my grandfather some money to make his life a little easier—at a time when they could barely afford to support themselves.

Jack would argue with himself. *Shit! I'm twenty-five years old. I should be able to get past all this and let it go. I could buy and sell*

Aaron and his R & P Fruit Company a hundred times.

However, he could not let it go. As Lily's high school graduation approached, he found himself visiting the park bench more often. The intensity of his resentment seemed to increase with each visit. Eventually, the pressure was so great that he felt compelled to take some action.

If God isn't going to punish Aaron for his despicable behavior, then I will!

Jack thought about his next move.

It's time to meet the family. I want to get to know the daughter and her father.

The subtle description of his father as her father escaped Jack's notice. It came too close to reminding him that Lily was his sister.

A plan of action was taking shape in his mind.

* * *

"This is the most beautiful home in the neighborhood," bubbled Willard Taylor, the real estate agent, as he showed Jack through the large, single-family home on Thirty-third Street past Dauphin. "It's one of the few houses that has its own lawn. The lot is really quite large. There's a half-acre of land. The trees are old and tall. The gardens are lovely in the spring. Crocus, hyacinths, and tulips, you know."

I wish he'd shut up!

"Let me show you through the house."

Jack was, to his surprise, impressed with the architectural gem. It was perched majestically on a gentle rise overlooking the park across the street. Beautifully proportioned fluted columns stood on either side of the front steps. The porch was spacious and shady, with an intricately carved wooden balustrade running its entire length.

As he entered the house, Jack found himself in a large foyer with a many-faceted crystal chandelier hanging from the second-floor ceiling. The exquisitely crafted wooden staircase curved from there to the second floor.

On the downstairs level was a formal parlor and a dining room, each of which could be closed off by sliding wood-paneled doors. The floors were oak. The spacious tiled kitchen boasted a six-burner gas stove and two deep sinks with an upholstered breakfast nook in one corner. In addition to the ceiling-hung cabinets, a center island provided storage underneath. A large ice-box stood against one wall. Adjoining the kitchen was a butler's pantry with another sink, ice-box, and additional cabinets for storage.

Upstairs were five large bedrooms, each with its own toilet and bath—an unheard-of luxury. Next to the master suite was an intimate library paneled with mahogany. Roomy closets were positioned in every bedroom and throughout the house.

The realtor continued to sing the praises of the property.

"The owner of this house, sir, is the president of the Pennsylvania Railroad. He's moving out to Haverford because he desires more land for the purpose of breeding horses."

Jack realized that he knew the present owner indirectly. He had been a client of the bordello on several occasions and tended to shoot his mouth off as soon as he had had a few drinks.

What Taylor did not mention was that the white, Anglo-Saxon Protestant millionaire had become uncomfortable with all of the upwardly mobile Jews moving into the neighborhood and decided it was time to leave.

"And what is the asking price?"

"It's rather high, sir. But you will admit that the house is worth it."

"What is 'it'?"

"The owner wants thirty-five thousand dollars." Taylor unconsciously lowered his eyes. He knew that the price was inflated.

Jack smiled.

"He may want thirty-five thousand, but the house isn't worth any more than twenty thousand. Go back and tell Mr. Pennsylvania Railroad that I'll give him that amount in cash tomorrow if he wants to sell. Otherwise, I'm not interested. Here's my phone number. If the man wants to make a deal, call me tomorrow. If not, don't call me again."

Jack turned and left. He knew that there weren't many people who could raise that amount of money overnight. He figured the house was really worth thirty thousand but that he would let Mr. Railroad stew for a long time if his first offer was rejected.

The next morning at 9, Jack received the expected call.

"Your offer has been accepted, sir. The owner would like to close tomorrow."

Ah! Testing me out, are you?

"How about this afternoon?"

"I'm sorry, sir," sputtered Taylor. "I don't think the owner can have the papers prepared that quickly."

"Tell him I'll wait until tomorrow but no longer. Maybe he needs a better lawyer. Make sure to tell him I'd be happy to make mine available to him if he so desires."

"Yes sir. I certainly will."

That should fix you, you antisemitic son of a bitch.

* * *

Jack engaged the interior designer who had worked on his other projects.

"Just don't make it look like a whorehouse," he told her, only half in jest.

He spent another twenty thousand decorating his new home. Artists were brought in from Paris to paint murals on the ceilings and walls. Carpets and flocked wallpapers were commissioned that incorporated his initials discreetly into their design. Italian marble was chosen and shipped by sea along with Italian craftsman to cut and install it. Antique pieces were brought in from Norton's vast inventory. No expense was spared.

Who am I trying to impress?

* * *

But, of course, he already knew the answer. He was trying to impress his father—and maybe Lily, too.

Six months later, Jack moved in.

That same week, he phoned Rabbi Seymour Goldstein of the B'nai Jeshurun Congregation for an appointment. Jack planned the meeting carefully.

The following Tuesday, Jack stood looking up from the pavement at the impressive structure. The synagogue was constructed of hand-hewn golden Jerusalem stone and had a vaguely Moorish design. A circular stained-glass window, its sections separated by elaborately carved wooden dividers, was installed just above the heavy double front doors. Four rectangular stained glass windows ran along each side of the building. Two flights of wide cement steps led up to the locked entrance. The main doors were unlocked only for services.

Jack walked around to the side of the building, where the administrative offices were located. Proceeding inside, he was greeted by Rabbi Goldstein, who had been waiting for him.

I haven't been inside a synagogue since the day my father left us in Vilna.

He smiled to himself.

Though I did sit through many church services afterward.

"Can I get you a cup of tea, Mr. Perle?"

"I'd like that, rabbi."

They sat at the rabbi's desk sipping the tea.

"What can I do for you? Are you experiencing some kind of problem?"

"No, rabbi. The question is, what can I do for you?"

Rabbi Goldstein was startled by this unexpected response.

"What do you mean?"

"Rabbi, I've recently moved into the neighborhood. For many years, I've wandered away from the fold. Lately, though, I've been feeling the need to become more active in my religion. I'd like to make a substantial donation to the synagogue. But, before I do, I'd like to meet with your board of directors to discuss what the synagogue's needs might be."

"They'd be delighted to meet with you, Mr. Perle. I'll discuss the matter with them and give you a call. We can set up the meeting here in the synagogue at your convenience."

"Wonderful," replied Jack. "I'm looking forward to it."

* * *

On the night of the meeting, Jack chose his most expensive, but most conservative, wardrobe items. He wore no jewelry except for a single diamond stickpin in his silk cravat. He wanted to nurture the aura of wealth and mystery for which he had gained a reputation.

The group of five directors met in the temple's boardroom. The rabbi made the introductions.

"Mr. Perle, I'd like you to meet our board." He went around the table from left to right.

"This is Zev Landau, the president of Blue Star Appliance Company." Blue Star was the largest retailer in the city of electrical appliances.

"Next is Abraham Weiss, the president of the Shein Coat and Linen Supply." Jack owned eighty-five percent of the company through a dummy corporation, though Weiss had no idea of his identity.

The rabbi introduced two more prominent businessmen in the community, to whom Jack nodded.

"And, last but not least, this is Aaron Peck, the president of the R & P Fruit Company.

"Pleased to meet you," said Aaron.

"Likewise, Aaron," replied Jack.

These are the first words I've spoken to my father in eighteen years.

For a moment, Jack thought that he would lose control of himself and struggled to contain the rising tears.

The group went on to discuss the needs of the synagogue and how a large donation could do the most good. They finalized an outline of their plan and ended the meeting.

Before the group broke up, Jack called for attention.

"I've recently moved into your neighborhood. I'd like to invite each of you, along with your families, to dinner at my home in celebration of our new relationship."

The members of the group beamed at each other. They had all heard about Jack's new mansion. One had dubbed it 'Perle's folly.' They were eager to see the house for themselves. The men couldn't wait to tell their wives about the invitation. This would be a real social coup.

* * *

Jack considered the details of the dinner carefully. He hired the city's finest kosher caterer and, unsatisfied with the regular selections, had a new haute cuisine continental menu designed. The appetizers included beluga caviar with onions and chopped egg, sweetbreads, stuffed artichokes, and heart-of-palm salad. There was consommé with tiny matzo meal dumplings stuffed with chopped liver. The main course included rack of lamb and breast of capon served with miniature potato pancakes and candied carrots. Dessert consisted of various fruit pastries made with phyllo dough and served with raspberry sauce. Candies and nuts adorned every table. Two staff members served each table. The dishes were of the finest Royal Dalton English porcelain, and the crystal was Baccarat.

A bar and bartender were set up in the foyer, and the finest white and red French wines were paired with the appropriate courses. Despite Prohibition, Jack had decided to serve wines and whiskies. He knew the guests would be shocked but pleased.

The party numbered twenty-four in all, including Jack. The rabbi and his five directors brought their wives and eleven children among them. Jack seated the children—except for Lily and Gita—at a large round table. The directors were seated with their wives at two smaller round tables, with name cards indicating the seating arrangements. Jack seated himself at a round table for five with the Peck family. Aaron was on his right around the table and Sadie sat to his left. Lily was on Aaron's right and Gita sat to the left of Sadie.

"And so, Mr. Peck, how long have you been in this country?" Jack's question was not unreasonable since Aaron spoke with a strong accent, though his English was intelligible.

"Sadie and I came here with her parents about eighteen years ago. Lily was born here. Her father and I started our company together. He passed away two years ago."

"Do you have any other children?"

Jack thought he detected a slight wince in Aaron's eyes.

"No. Just the two girls."

You lying prick.

Jack unconsciously felt for the pouch he always wore under his shirt.

"What part of Europe did you come from?"

"We lived in a small shtetl in Lithuania called Jelzai."

"Oh! And were you childhood sweethearts?"

Aaron looked at his wife and smiled wanly but didn't answer. Jack continued.

"My family had relatives in Vilna. I think they were tavern keepers. Have you ever been to that city?"

Jack could tell that Aaron was beginning to get uncomfortable. He was unsure of how to answer the question.

"Uh—yes. I spent some time there at the yeshiva. But I didn't frequent any taverns. I studied all the time.

You self-righteous bastard.

Jack turned to address Lily. "And you, young lady, are a beauty. You must have a thousand beaux chasing after you."

A deep blush appeared on Lily's cheeks. Her eyes lowered.

"Well, I am seeing someone very seriously. We'll probably get engaged in a few months."

A stab of anxiety ran through Jack.

"Congratulations! And what does the lucky young man do for a living?"

"Well, his parents are pushing him to be a doctor. He's very smart. But he says he can't stand the sight of blood. I have no brother who can take over the business when papa's ready to retire. David has a flair for numbers. He thinks he can expand the business to two or three times what it is now. I think he'll end up going into papa's business."

Another stab of anxiety hit Jack. This time, it was mixed with hot anger.

Not if I can help it.

Jack bade his guests farewell at the door. As they gushed over his beautiful home and the lovely that time they had had, Jack was thinking about his next move. He wished his mother were alive to help him plan the revenge that he was so desperately seeking.

Chapter Twenty-Nine

Sean O'Reilly stood in the hot sun directing the unloading of a freighter from the Caribbean. The cargo was perishable and had to be moved immediately into the shady warehouse to prevent spoilage.

"Get those crates off the dock, you lazy bastards! You want to stay here all night?"

Sean was well-liked by his men. He overlooked the times when they came to work late and hung over from the night before. When one of them needed extra money for a family emergency, he would advance it out of his own pocket until payday. And he loved his job. He enjoyed the feeling of sweat running down his face and body, though he complained about it all the time. He loved taking care of his men and having titans of business dependent on him to unload and deliver the products that they needed for the survival of their businesses.

Sean and Jack had been friends since the early days when Jack first came to Philadelphia and had roamed the waterfront asking questions of everyone. Since that time, Jack had often treated his friend to dinner and the use of one of his girls for the night. Sean would fill Jack in on the latest gossip at the docks. Often, Sean knew what the bosses of the longshoremen were planning far in advance of anyone else. Once, Sean had warned him of an impending strike, and Jack was able to clear a load of art objects containing smuggled heroin just before it went into effect, which saved him and the syndicate weeks of delay and lost revenue.

As Sean jumped down from atop the large crate on which he was standing, he spotted his old friend waiting in the shade of the warehouse. As usual, despite the heat, Jack was impeccably attired. This day, he wore a cotton shirt and tie under a lightweight tropical suit.

Sean walked over to him.

"Hello, my friend. What can I do for you today?"

"I have a favor to ask of you," replied Jack.

"Anything you want, my friend. Your word is my command."

* * *

"Where's today's shipment?" Aaron called from the back office.

"It hasn't arrived yet," the manager yelled back.

"What the hell could be taking so long?

"Don't know. I'll call the dock."

Jimmy Thurlow had worked for the R & P Fruit Company since its founding; the next spring would mark his eighteenth year in Aaron's employ. During that time, he had learned every facet of the business. Aaron knew that, if he were gone for a week or two, Jimmy could carry on with no problem.

Aaron took good care of Jimmy, paying him well and giving him yearly bonuses based on the company's profits. The bonuses had grown larger every year.

He picked up the phone and called the transfer agent at the dock.

"Hey, Paul. Where's today's delivery?"

"What? You didn't get it yet? Hold on."

Paul came back on within two minutes.

"Our foreman has a couple of guys out today so they couldn't unpack everything. You'll get it first thing in the morning."

"Are you kidding? That won't give us any time to repackage and deliver it."

"Sorry. There's nothin' I can do about it."

The next morning, the crates of fruit were delivered to the company.

"For God's sake", said Jimmy. "These bananas are turning black already. And the pineapples are too ripe. I can't send them out this way."

The customers of R & P Fruit Company didn't get their delivery that day.

* * *

The next delivery was due in two days. Once again, it was held up at the docks.

"Sorry about that," Paul told Jimmy. "Our foreman said that Customs held up the paperwork. We'll get it out as soon as we can."

The pattern continued. For every delivery that came on time, some problem delayed two or three others. The reasons were seldom the same: "The government is changing their procedures," "The crane is out of order," and so on.

Aaron was receiving an increasing number of complaints about the company's products and service.

"Aaron, I don't know what's wrong, but the quality of your fruit has gotten terrible. The customers won't buy it," said Charles Corbin, the owner of Corbin's Supermarket chain, which was one of Aaron's oldest and largest customers.

"If things don't get better quickly, we're going to have to look somewhere else for our tropical fruit."

Aaron was starting to panic. He visited the docks.

"Paul, these delays are killing me. They're going to put me out of business."

"Let me call in Sean."

Sean reassured Aaron that everything possible was being done to straighten out the problem.

For a while, deliveries returned to normal.

Aaron didn't understand what was going on. Nothing like this had ever happened before. He checked into the possibility of unloading his products at a port in Delaware, but the inconvenience and the added travel time made that solution impractical. Now that things were almost back to normal, he hoped that they would stay that way. He had already lost two of his most important customers.

Chapter Thirty

The plight of the R & P Fruit Company was not made known to Sadie or the girls. Aaron didn't want to worry them with his problems. He knew that Lily was depending on him to pay for a big wedding and to provide employment for her husband-to-be.

Sadie wasn't sure that David Moscowitz was the right choice for Lily. She broached the subject to her husband that night as they were getting ready for bed.

"He's got no profession," she told Aaron. "What's he gonna do for a living? His father's got nothing. He doesn't wanna go to medical school even though he's smart enough to get in. He thinks we're very rich and will take care of him. And if they have any children, he'll expect us to take care of them. Next thing you know, Gita will be getting married, and she'll want us to support her husband, too."

"You didn't seem to mind when your father took me into the business."

"That was different. I was ugly and fat. He knew that nobody would marry me unless he paid them to do it. I knew what he was doing. And I know you only married me because you didn't have anywhere else to go after you ran away with that woman and she had your baby. You think I'm stupid?"

Aaron winced. This was the first time that Sadie had ever brought up that subject. He hadn't realized until now that she knew about Rebecca and Jacob. And he didn't know that she could be so blatantly honest about herself and her circumstances.

"What ever happened to her and the kid? You treated them like dreck the day they came to see you at my father's house. After what you did, I wasn't sure I wanted to stay married to you."

Aaron was stunned.

"It's a damn good thing you were so dependent on my father's money. Otherwise, you might've done the same thing to me and the kids."

My god. What's gotten into her? I never knew she could talk like that. I always thought she was stupid. But she's known everything all along.

"I don't know what happened to them. For all I know, they could be dead by now."

"Some father you are!"

Sadie stormed out of the bedroom.

Chapter Thirty-One

A t his wife's insistence, Aaron reciprocated Jack's invitation. They invited him for Sabbath dinner.

Jack had flowers delivered to the Peck household on Friday afternoon. Sadie had never before laid eyes on these kinds of blooms. There were two separate bouquets. The first was an exotic arrangement of birds of paradise, protea, and orchids. It was addressed to Aaron, Sadie, and Gita Peck. The note on the card said, "Looking forward to the pleasure of your company."

The second bouquet was somewhat smaller. It was a delicate arrangement of tiger lilies and was addressed to Lily. The card said, "For the most exquisite Lily of them all."

Lily didn't know what to make of the note and the flowers. She wasn't thinking about Jack as a potential suitor. After all, she had told him about David and their plans to become engaged.

Sadie was ecstatic. She was hoping that her daughter would break off the relationship with her young, directionless boyfriend. She had fantasies of Lily marrying this rich, handsome, and charming bachelor. As she put the last-minute touches on the dinner table, she thought about it.

Why shouldn't he be interested in my Lily? She's beautiful, she's smart, and she's talented. She comes from a good family. We've had no scandals. No one knows about Aaron's past. She'd make him a fine wife.

Sadie hummed as she wiped her good crystal for the third time. The song she was humming was her favorite, 'My Blue Heaven.'

This time, when Jack pulled up in his Packard convertible, he parked right in front of 2105. Gita had been looking out the window waiting for him. Before he could knock, she flung the door open and pulled him in.

Jack laughed.

"Thanks for the great welcome."

Sadie caught the action.

"Gita, don't be such a pest. Stop bothering our guest."

"I don't mind at all. I don't like being treated like a guest. I'd much rather be treated like one of the family."

I am one of the family.

"Come sit down," Sadie said. "Have a glass of wine and some chopped liver."

Gita sat down next to him and moved closer. She had developed a crush on the handsome stranger and didn't mind letting it show.

Lily came down from upstairs. She was wearing a simple black velvet dress trimmed in lace. It was closely fitted around the bodice and hung straight from her waist.

"Thank you for the flowers. They're lovely." She was clearly uncomfortable and didn't know what else to say.

"I'm glad you liked them."

"Why didn't you send me flowers?" asked Gita with the open honesty of youth.

Jack was caught off-guard.

"Uh—I did send flowers to you and your parents."

"That's not the same," Gita pouted. "I know. You like Lily. But she already has a boyfriend, you know."

"Gita! That's none of your business." Sadie's tone was sharp. "Go to the kitchen and tell Saphronia to put the appetizers on the table."

"Don't worry. I'm not offended. It's just the brashness of youth." Jack smiled at his hostess.

Sadie relaxed. She liked the fact that he was willing to shrug off Gita's comments.

That girl will never find a husband if she doesn't learn to keep her mouth shut. No matter how many times I tell her, she never listens.

Aaron came downstairs. He had come home late from work. He had had a flurry of calls at the last minute from customers wanting reassurance that their deliveries would be on time for Monday morning. Luckily, he had already received Friday afternoon's shipment, so he could confidently confirm their orders.

"So, Mr. Perle, how do you like living in Strawberry Mansion?"

"I'm very happy with the neighborhood. I especially like the local bakery. I believe it's run by relatives of yours?"

"Yes. They're my brothers from my father's first marriage. I never knew them until we came to America."

"It must have been nice to have some family around who already knew the ropes."

"To tell you the truth, we've never been very close."

"Did your father stay in contact with them after they came here?"

"Every once in a while they would send him a letter, and I guess he would answer."

Their money put you through school, you ungrateful bastard.

"Are your parents still living?"

"No. They passed away in an influenza epidemic just before Sadie and I came to this country."

"I'm sorry to hear that. Do you have any family left over there?"

Aaron's eyes met Sadie's. There was a slight hesitation in Aaron's reply.

* * *

"No. Other than my two brothers, I have no family left."

"Ah, but you have a lovely wife and two lovely daughters. Did you ever miss having a son?"

Beads of sweat were forming on Aaron's forehead.

Why is he asking me all these questions?

"I guess it would have been nice having a boy around the house."

Jack shifted his position and directed his attention to Sadie.

"Maybe you're wondering why I'm asking all these questions. Both of my parents died when I was very young. My father died when I was six. My mother died when I was twelve. I've been on my own since then. I never had a real family life. Whenever I see a wonderful family like yours, I get jealous. I wish I knew what it felt like."

Listening to Jack's words, Sadie began to cry. Her mind returned to the scene of Aaron sending little Jacob away to grow up alone and fatherless.

Jack saw her tears falling. He somehow sensed what she was feeling. He had always thought of her as the heartless woman who stole his father away. That image was changing.

I'll bet she didn't have anything to do with it. It was all him. I owe her an apology.

"Dinner's on the table, ma'am," Saphronia called from the kitchen.

"Let's eat!" cried Gita. "I'm starved."

* * *

Aaron sat at the head of the table with Sadie to his right and Jack to his left. Lily was on Jack's left, and Gita sat next to her mother.

All of them were lusty eaters. There wasn't much conversation as they dug into the gefilte fish, matzo ball soup, roast chicken, and brisket.

Jack enjoyed himself. He wasn't kidding when he said that he missed having a real family life. This was as close as he had come in years.

After dinner, they sat around the living room. Sadie wanted to know more about him.

"Where did you grow up?"

Jack knew that, sooner or later, people would ask him about his past. He had developed a consistent story that couldn't be checked out. It was built around his only visible business operation, the Norton Art Company.

"I was raised in New York City. I was an only child. After my mother died, I moved around, staying with different friends. When I was fifteen, I went to work as a janitor in an art gallery. They let me sleep in the basement. It was there that I learned all about paintings, sculpture, and antiques. I saved my money and began to buy and sell objects of art. Over the years, I became very successful. When I heard that the Norton Art Company was for sale, I bought it and moved to Philadelphia."

"You've never been married?" asked Sadie.

"No. I haven't yet found the right girl. But I'm still looking. I very much want to have a family of my own. It's something I've really missed in my life."

Jack turned to Lily and smiled. Lily blushed.

"I'm available," exclaimed Gita. "I'd love to marry you."

Everyone at the table was so startled by the brashness of Gita's outburst that they broke out laughing.

"Why are you laughing at me?" Gita pouted. She got up and started to leave the table.

Jack stood up.

"Don't leave. We're only laughing at your honesty. I like you very much, Gita, but you're a little too young to think about marriage."

"I'm fifteen years old."

"You have to graduate from high school. You're a very beautiful girl. You'll have lots of good-looking guys running after you."

Gita seemed somewhat mollified.

"Not if she doesn't learn to think before she opens her mouth," said Sadie. "She'll scare them away. Most men are not as tolerant as you."

"A real man will want to hear what she has to say. He'll love her for her honesty. If he doesn't, she shouldn't marry him," replied Jack.

Gita ran around the table and gave Jack a kiss on the cheek.

"Thank you," she said. I've always thought the same thing."

Lily said nothing. She was still confused about what Jack wanted and why he was there.

The rest of the evening was spent in general conversation. Growing bored, Lily left the dining room to telephone David. A few minutes later, Gita also tired of the discussion and went to her room to do schoolwork. Aaron and Sadie were left to entertain their guest and answer his many questions.

"How did you happen to get into the tropical fruit business?" asked Jack.

"In the old country, my wife's father was active in importing and exporting fruit. When we got to America, he was impressed with the wide variety of available tropical fruits that were not familiar to him. He figured there would be a large market for them once people tasted them and realized how delicious they were. So, he traveled to two of the Caribbean islands and cornered the market on shipments to Philadelphia. Unless a retailer was willing to travel to New York, he would have to buy these products from R & P."

Aaron was clearly proud of the company's business strategy and its marketing success, but now he silently worried

I only hope it doesn't fall apart on me now.

Jack listened in silence.

Well, old man, you're about to suffer one of the biggest disappointments of your life—a disappointment that you richly deserve. And it will feel like slow torture.

Chapter Thirty-Two

For the next few months, business at R & P Fruit Company seemed to return to normal. Deliveries once again became regular, and the customers settled down. Aaron's relief was palpable. He still didn't understand what had happened, but now it didn't matter—so long as it didn't happen again.

Since the evening of Jack's first visit for dinner, Sadie had made up her mind that she would do everything possible to encourage a relationship between Lily and the rich, mysterious Mr. Jack Perle.

A week after Jack's dinner with the Peck family, she received a phone call.

"Mrs. Peck, this is Jack Perle."

"Hello, Mr. Perle. Please, call me Sadie."

"Only if you'll call me Jack"

"All right, Jack."

"Sadie, I'm calling to invite all of you for dinner a week from Saturday night. There's a wonderful new restaurant opened up on McKean Street called Lefkowitz's Steak House. I heard they serve out-of-this-world rib steak. I'm sure Aaron will love it. If you agree, I'll pick the four of you up around seven. I just got a new Rolls-Royce sedan, so we'll all be able to fit in one car."

Jack didn't mention that he had recently given the budding restauranteur, Rubin Lefkowitz, fifty thousand dollars to open the new dining spot in return for a fifty-one percent ownership position.

"I'll check with Aaron. I don't think we have any plans Saturday night. He's a real meat-and-potatoes man. I'm sure he'll love the idea."

* * *

Aaron, however, was ambivalent about their developing relationship with Jack.

"There's something about him that makes me nervous," he said to his wife. "Why is he so interested in us?"

"You should know the answer to that. It's because he's interested in Lily."

"But Lily already has a beau."

"Men! Sometimes you're so thick-headed. Do you think a man like Jack is gonna be put off by a nebbish like David Marcowitz?"

"But she says she loves him."

"Do you really think a seventeen-year-old girl knows what love is? She's a baby, for God's sake! And so is he."

Aaron tried to stand up to his wife. "Lily has a mind of her own. You won't be able to force Jack Perle down her throat."

But Sadie, with her sensitive intuition regarding the female psyche declared, "You mark my words. If Jack Perle makes up his mind that Lily is what he wants, he won't stop until he finds a way to get her. And, eventually, she'll see that that's what's best for her."

Aaron gave up arguing.

What you think is best for her.

* * *

"Lily, we're all having dinner with Jack on Saturday."

"But Mama, David is supposed to take me to the Broadwood. The YMHA basketball finals are that night."

"Well, you'll have to go a different night. Jack is a prominent man in the community, and it's important for your father to cultivate his friendship."

Sadie eyed her daughter critically.

"I think you need some new outfits. Your old ones are going out of style."

"What are you talking about, mother? They're last year's dresses."

"I know, but you're getting older and should have a more sophisticated look."

Lily knew that Sadie was doing it for Jack's benefit. But she also knew that nothing or no one could force her to marry against her will.

I'll go along with her. I always love new clothes.

She accompanied her mother downtown to Frank and Seder, the department store with the largest selection of ladies' fashions in the city, and let her mother buy her three new dresses. She was secretly delighted with the way she looked in her new outfits. The-tight fitting dresses showed off her well-proportioned figure. Wearing them, she felt she possessed a commanding presence—older, cultured, and worldly.

* * *

A few days later, Lily tried on her new wardrobe for David.

"Aren't they beautiful?" she crowed as she danced around the room twirling her skirts for David to appreciate. "Mama thinks I don't know why she really bought them. But I wanted to look beautiful for you."

"You're beautiful to me no matter what you wear," the young man replied. "We're going to have a beautiful life together."

"Mama thinks you should go to medical school. I heard her talking to papa the other night."

"What did your papa say?"

"Nothing. He didn't want to argue with her."

"Do you think he'll take me into the business?"

"Of course. When he realizes we're going ahead with our plans, he'll do anything he knows will make me happy."

David kissed her on the lips.

* * *

On Saturday, the whole family loved Lefkowitz's steaks. Even more, Sadie loved being picked up and delivered in a Rolls-Royce. There were several members of the synagogue waiting for tables when the Pecks stepped out of Jack's car and were immediately shown to their seats by Rubin Lefkowitz himself.

"Hello, Sadie!" called Myrna Katz, who was waiting for a table with her family.

Sadie graciously nodded to them as she swept by. She was in her glory.

Aaron had to admit that it felt good to be treated like someone important. Maybe Jack Perle would make a good son-in-law after all.

* * *

Sadie telephoned Jack to invite him for Sabbath dinner again two weeks later, but he told her that he would be out of town for a while on business. They set a date in four weeks.

As he hung up the phone, Jack smiled to himself. He knew his plan for retribution was working.

Chapter Thirty-Three

Four months after Jack's initial dinner at the Peck home, Jimmy Thurlow walked into Aaron's office. He was obviously upset.

"There's a new outfit opened up near South Street. They're sellin' the same fruit as us, and they're sellin' it for less."

"How is that possible? We've got the market cornered in Barbados and Jamaica."

"We'd better go down and have a look."

The two men walked the few blocks to South Street. The old, broken-down warehouse that used to stand on the corner had been torn down. In its place stood a new, one-story building with a large, fenced-in yard. Half of the yard was covered by a wooden roof that protected crates of fruit underneath from the sun. Aaron saw large bunches of bananas and piles of pineapples laid out on enormous tables. Workmen were sorting the fruit and repacking it into smaller containers. Another table held colorful cans of coconut milk and packages of coconut candies.

A freshly painted sign hung above the warehouse entrance reading

EXOTIC FRUIT COMPANY
TROPICAL FRUITS AND PRODUCTS

Aaron began to worry.

* * *

Each week, one or two of Aaron's customers called.

"I'm sorry, but Exotic is offering us special deals that we just can't turn down. And they have products that you don't carry."

"But, Harry, we've dealt with each other for seventeen years. How can you just turn your back on a relationship like that?"

"I know, Aaron. But business is business. Our margins are much higher with Exotic. We can charge the same price, but our cost is considerably less."

"Harry, don't you realize that they're just doing this to get your business? Once they get the customers, they'll raise the prices."

"Well, I'll worry about it then. In the meantime, I'm making a fortune."

Aaron was able to determine that Exotic's products were being shipped from Puerto Rico and Hispaniola. He hadn't even known that those islands had begun exporting fruit; the main crop was sugar cane. The amount of fruit exported from these islands was negligible overall, but it seemed that most of it was coming directly to Philadelphia.

The ownership of the new company was a mystery. The manager and foreman had been brought in from New York to run the operation. At one point, Aaron pretended to be a potential new customer in order to meet with the manager. He was only able to discover that the company was owned by a holding company, Alliance Investments, that was incorporated in New York. The manager said that he dealt by telephone with a Mr. Jackson, whom he had never met.

Aaron tried to investigate Alliance Investments. He checked the Pennsylvania Records of Incorporations, public tax records, anything he could think of, and met dead ends wherever he looked.

Within three months, Exotic had managed to capture most of R & P's customers. In an effort to reduce his costs, Aaron visited Richard Sherrard, the owner from whom he leased the warehouse. Aaron knew that Sherrard's family owned large tracts of waterfront property and could afford to be flexible with an old client.

"Mr. Sherrard, I've come to ask a favor."

"Yes, Mr. Peck."

"I've been your tenant for seventeen years. I've never been late with my rent. Right now, my business is having some temporary problems, which I'm certain will be resolved in a few weeks. I'd like your permission to hold off the payments for two months, just until the business can get back on its feet."

Sherrard felt bad about the situation. His voice softened.

"Mr. Peck, I thought you knew. Four years ago, the family sold all its property to a private investment corporation. We got a very good price. We are still, however, acting in a management capacity for the new owners. I'll see what I can do."

Two days later, Sherrard phoned Aaron.

"I'm sorry, Mr. Peck, but the new owners would not approve your request. However, they authorized me to grant you a two-week extension. If the rent isn't up to date by then, they'll be forced to take legal action if you don't vacate the premises."

He could hear Aaron's pain in the silence that followed.

"I'm sorry, Aaron."

As Aaron hung up the phone, Jimmy Thurlow knocked on the office door. His eyes were downcast. He couldn't look his employer in the eye.

"Boss, this is hard for me to say. I've worked here for seventeen years and loved every minute of it. You've always been good to me and treated me fairly. But I know the situation, and I can't work here anymore. The business is dead, and I have to support my family. Exotic offered me a job as manager. I'll be making a little more than what I'm getting here. I took the job."

Aaron stood up and came from behind the desk to shake Jimmy's hand.

"I understand, Jimmy. You've been a good employee. Good luck to you."

Jimmy began to sob. "I'm sorry boss."

Aaron hugged him until the sobbing trailed off. "We'll be okay."

When Jimmy left, Aaron looked around the office that he had occupied for eightteen years and began to cry.

What will happen to the family and me? There's nothing left.

* * *

Aaron had been keeping the company afloat by injecting his personal funds into it. He now saw that his efforts were useless. Now, both he and the company were on the verge of bankruptcy.

He had been keeping any knowledge of his financial problems from Sadie and the children. He no longer had a choice; they had to know what was going on.

Chapter Thirty-Four

"Hello Sadie, nice to see you," said Minnie Landau. "Hello, Minnie. How is Zev? Unless there's a synagogue affair, we never get to see you anymore."

The women were at the butcher shop picking up food in preparation for the weekend.

"I'm sorry to hear about Aaron's troubles."

"What troubles?"

"Oh, I'm sorry. I must have the story wrong."

Sadie felt a rush of panic.

"Minnie, tell me. What is it you heard?"

"It must have been somebody else."

"Minnie, tell me!"

"Uh, Zev told me that a new fruit company had moved into town and was stealing some of Aaron's customers."

"When did this happen?"

"A few months ago."

"Thanks, Minnie. I guess Aaron was trying to protect me."

"I'm sorry, Sadie," Minnie repeated. She realized that she had put her foot in her mouth again.

Sadie left the butcher shop without her order, her heart pounding and palms sweating, and went directly home.

* * *

"Why didn't you tell me?"

"I thought things would get better. I didn't want to worry you."

"How bad is it?"

"Very bad. I'm afraid we're going to have to close the business."

Sadie's heart sank.

I can't believe Aaron let this happen to the business my father handed him on a silver platter. Oh, papa! I wish you were still here. You'd know what to do.

Sadie tried to maintain a cheerful front.

"Well, we can live off the bonds that papa left us. That should carry us for a while. By the time they run out, you'll have figured out what to do."

"They're gone, Sadie. All of them. I used them to try to save the business."

"Oy Gott. What are we going to do?"

She broke into tears and sank into a chair.

Aaron walked over and tried to put his arm around her.

"Get away from me. We're ruined. God is punishing you for what you did. Bringing you to me was my father's one mistake. Now I'm paying for it."

"How can you say that, Sadie? We have two beautiful daughters."

"And how will we pay for their weddings? And who will want to marry them now?"

She broke into sobs again.

* * *

Aaron arrived late to the next board of directors meeting at the synagogue.

"Hello, Aaron. How are you?" asked the rabbi.

"Well, to tell you the truth, I could be better."

"What's bothering you."

"Nothing you could help me with, rabbi. Just run-of-the-mill business problems."

"The board members and I were just discussing that before you came in. We know you're under enormous stress. It's no good for you to also have to worry about the problems of the synagogue."

Abraham Weiss, the president of the board and CEO of Schein Coat and Linen, took over the discussion.

"We think it would be a good idea if you resigned from the board until things settle down for you a little. When you straighten things out we'd love to have you back." The phony smile on his face couldn't cover his real message.

The other members of the board nodded in agreement.

Aaron heard the unspoken message. *They only want rich members representing our synagogue. You two-faced sons of bitches. I thought you were my friends. Now I see that you're all phonies.*

You like to kick a man when he's down. "I'm glad you're all such compassionate people and are all so worried about me," he said sarcastically. "I expected more from all of you—especially from you, rabbi. I see now just where your compassion lies and what it's based on."

Aaron choked as sobs began to rise in his throat. He turned and left the room. The others, embarrassed that their motivation was so transparent, silently stared down at the table.

"I think we should call it a night, gentlemen," Zev Landau finally said.

* * *

"Oh, David, I don't know what we're going to do," Lily was crying on the telephone. "We have no money. Papa just stays in his room all day and sleeps. If we don't pay the bills soon, I'm afraid they're going to cut off our phone and electricity. Please come over. I need somebody to cheer me up."

"I can't make it tonight, Lily. Maybe tomorrow."

"I haven't seen you in a week. Where have you been?"

"To tell you the truth, Lily, I've been rethinking our relationship. I really don't want to go to medical school, and, if I can't go into business with your father, I have to figure out what other possibilities there are for me. I wouldn't be able to support you the way things are now."

"But I thought you loved me. We don't need my father's business. We could both go to work.

"I'm sorry Lily. That's not the kind of life I want."

Lily slammed down the receiver.

Mama was right. David saw me as a ticket to an easy life. How could I have been so stupid? I believed everything he said.

* * *

Except for bill collectors, the Pecks' phone had stopped ringing. Jack Perle was the only person who called occasionally to keep in touch.

Gita picked up the telephone.

"Hello, Gita. This is Jack. How is everyone?"

Gita started to cry.

"What's wrong?"

Gita sniffed back her tears. "Things here are terrible. We have no money to pay the bills. Papa just sits around all day. He doesn't eat, he sleeps a lot, and sometimes he talks about wanting to die."

"And how is mama holding up?"

"She cries a lot, too. She yells at papa, trying to get him to do something, anything—but all he does is sit and stare. She spends a lot of time on the phone talking to all the people we owe money to. They want to cut off the electricity and the telephone service. She had a little bit of household money saved up. She's using it to buy food. We've been eating a lot of rice and beans."

"She's a strong woman," said Jack. "I really admire her."

"And how is Lily?"

"Lily's in bad shape, too. When David found out that papa had lost the business, he broke up with her. She's heartbroken. I think it's more because she realized that he was more interested in papa's money than he was in her. She had a rude awakening. She's wondering if anyone will ever love her for herself."

"Ah, the pain of life's lessons is not easy to bear" he replied.

"And you, Gita. How are you?"

"I'm trying to help mama as much as I can. Somebody around here has to keep their head on their shoulders and think straight. I've decided to drop out of high school and go to work. We've got to get some money from somewhere."

"Gita, don't do anything rash. It's important for you to finish high school. You're a smart girl. Maybe you should even go to college. Let me talk to your mother."

Gita put Sadie on the phone.

"Oh, Jack. I don't like to talk to you when I feel like this. I'm not myself. I don't know what to do."

"I'd like to help out however I can. I'm going to arrange for a loan to tide you over these bad times."

"That's very nice of you, Jack, but Aaron is too proud to accept money."

"Aaron doesn't have to know. We'll keep it between you and me."

Jack hung up and was flooded with ambivalent emotion.

My plan is working well, but it's beginning to affect people I care about. I'll try to protect them, but that old man is just starting to suffer payback for what he did to my mother and me.

Chapter Thirty-Five

S adie invited Jack for Sabbath dinner.
    This time, two bouquets arrived along with a potted palm. The first bouquet was for Gita, consisting of a bunch of forget-me-nots with a note reading "I forgot-you-not."

Lily received an arrangement of calla lilies. Jack had written, "Still the loveliest of them all."

The areca palm was for Sadie and Aaron. "Palms survive by bending with the wind" was written on the accompanying card.

"What's that supposed to mean?" asked Aaron.

"It means that we'll get through this if we don't break," replied his wife.

Aaron was impressed with Sadie's strength and resiliency. He was learning new things about his wife every day. She had been correct in her assessment of David Moscowitz, and she was somehow managing to keep creditors off their back.

"How are you managing to pay the bills?" he would ask.

"I saved some of my household money every week just in case of a rainy day."

Who would have thought this woman would turn out to be such a treasure? I'm very lucky.

* * *

Aaron slowly began to rouse himself from his depression. Sadie was relieved to see her husband begin to pull himself together.

"I need to do something, Sadie. I've got to bring some money in. I can't let my family starve. But I don't know how."

"Maybe one of the directors from the synagogue needs a good man."

"Those hypocrites? I'd rather starve than ask them for anything."

Sadie thought for a few moments.

"What about your brothers at the bakery? Maybe they could use some help."

"That's a good idea."

Aaron walked over to the Pecks' bakery. He hadn't been there in several years. He was amazed to find that the bakery had expanded and taken over the two properties next to it. Weinstein's delicatessen had also expanded and had moved across the street.

"My God, Simeon, when did all this happen?" asked Aaron in wonderment as he gazed at the large retail area in front and the larger baking area in the back.

"Our friend Jack Perle suggested that we begin selling our bread to local grocery stores and markets. We now have over a hundred shops that carry our products. We even have two trucks that make the deliveries. Jack helped us arrange to rent the buildings next door. The cost is very reasonable. He convinced Weinstein's to move across the street and suggested that they add a restaurant to the deli. They're doing fabulously well, and they use a lot of our rye bread for their sandwiches."

Jack Perle seems to be everywhere.

"Maybe you could use some help around here. My fruit business went kaput, and I need to make some money."

Lemel eyed his half-brother with a cynical expression.

"Simeon and I will talk it over. We'll let you know."

After Aaron left the brothers discussed Aaron's visit.

"When he had a lot of money, he thought he was too good for us," observed Lemel.

"Now that he's poor, he suddenly remembers that he has a family," echoed Simeon.

Nevertheless, the two brothers decided to not allow their resentment to prevent them from helping out their half-brother. Since Aaron had had experience organizing and delivering orders, they placed him in charge of that aspect of the business. He also relieved the employees in the front when they took breaks. They paid Aaron twenty dollars a week, at Jack's suggestion. This was just enough to cover his monthly bills but didn't leave much for any luxuries.

Aaron was grateful to his brothers for their help. He felt that, at least, he was able to provide the basics for his family. As he became busier and saw his skills pay off in growth in the business, his self-esteem began to return.

One Friday afternoon as the Sabbath was approaching, Libby Weiss, the wife of Abraham Weiss, came into the bakery to buy her usual Sabbath challah and pastries. Aaron was on duty at the front counter.

"Oh, hello Aaron," said Libby. "I knew you were working with your brothers, but I didn't know you worked the sales counter."

Aaron's face grew red with embarrassment. He tried to find a way out of this distressing situation.

"Well, I usually handle the administrative end of the business, but two of our workers called in sick today, so I had to help out here.

From then on, Aaron tried to avoid working in the front of the store so that he wouldn't run into anyone he knew.

As things settled down in the Peck household, Jack began to spend more and more time there.

"He's the only one of our friends who has remained loyal. Having rich friends isn't important to him," Sadie commented to Aaron one day.

"It's because he likes Lily."

Sadie became irritated with her husband.

"Aaron, sometimes you're pretty stupid. Jack might like Lily, but he's been a good friend to us. And, anyway, would it be so bad to have Jack Perle as a son-in-law? I would be very proud."

* * *

Lily had changed her attitude toward Jack. Now that defending her relationship with David had ceased to be part of a power struggle with her mother, Lily increasingly appreciated Jack's good looks and the attention that he paid to her. Each time he visited the house, he brought a small gift for her and one for Gita. Once it was a bottle of French perfume, another time a box of imported chocolates. She couldn't get over his attention to the smallest detail. If she happened to make an offhand comment about a particular food, or perhaps a new book that she had heard about, Jack would invariably remember and make sure to present it to her at a later date. Occasionally, Lily wondered what went on inside his head.

Sometimes, I think he tries too hard to get me to like him. He can have any girl he wants. Why me?

Lily had grown up in the past year. She was no longer the doted-on daughter of a wealthy man. Though not as brash as her sister, Lily was never one to mince words. She didn't like to play games with people.

"Jack, why do you spend so much time with my family? And why are you taking such an interest in me when I know you can have any girl you want?"

Jack liked her spunk and the way she asked questions without beating around the bush.

"I told you, Lily, I grew up without a family of any kind. When I'm here, I feel like I'm at home. It's the closest I've ever come to feeling like I'm part of a family. As far as you're concerned, I think you're smart and beautiful. I like the way you aren't afraid to say what you really mean. And I like the way you stand up for your beliefs even if everyone else has a different opinion.

I've had a lot of girlfriends over the years. They fawn over me and try to flatter me. You've never done that. I like the fact that you're not impressed with my money. If you like me, I want it to be because of me, not because of what I have."

Lily could empathize with that. It was precisely the way she felt after her experience with David. And yet, despite Jack's seemingly honest response, she had an inexplicable feeling that there was more to the story than he was telling her. She couldn't quite put her finger on it.

Jack and Lily spent most Saturday nights together. They might go to a picture show or perhaps a basketball game and then for a bite to eat. At the end of the evening, Lily would give him a peck on the cheek and thank him for a wonderful evening. Jack didn't try to force her into a more intimate physical relationship. He knew that, the moment he started to push too hard, she would bolt.

One Saturday night, before she got out of the car, Jack decided it was time for a serious talk.

"Lily, we've been seeing each other for a while, and I've tried hard not to push you. I sense that you're not ready to commit yourself to a relationship with me. Am I right about that?"

"Oh, Jack. You've been so good to my family and me. I hate to hurt your feelings. I'm just not sure what I feel. I don't just want to get married and be a housewife for the rest of my life. I'd like to accomplish something—do something useful.

"Like what?"

"I'd like to go out and get a job—see what it's like out there in the real world."

"I could easily arrange for you to work down at Norton's. Do you think you'd like that?"

"No, Jack. I want to do it on my own. I want to succeed or fail on my own merit."

"All right, Lily. Under the circumstances, I think it would be better if we stopped seeing each other for a while."

As Lily exited the car, she was in turmoil.

How can I do this to him after all the good things he's done for my family? Am I so selfish that I would throw away a chance for real love for a fantasy of my own independence? But I know I won't be happy if I don't at least try to find out who I really am.

She walked into the house knowing that her mother would think she was crazy and try to talk her out of her decision.

Jack drove away stunned. He reeled with the acute feeling of rejection. He was not used to women turning down his advances, though he respected Lily for her honesty.

I can't allow this to get to me. I know I can get over it. It's probably better this way. What was I thinking when I pursued this relationship with my own sister?

At home a few minutes later, he opened a bottle of illegally imported Glenfiddich scotch whiskey and finally went to bed when it was half-empty.

Chapter Thirty-Six

Lily answered a newspaper ad for an executive secretary position. Even with no previous job experience, her high-school secretarial skills, combined with her beauty and common sense, secured her a job as the executive assistant to Jonathan Lieberman, a successful, middle-aged insurance broker.

Jonathan's twenty-five-year-old son Ben worked for his father as a life insurance salesman. He was a good-looking and nattily dressed man about town. He drove a Stutz Bearcat and enjoyed being seen with beautiful women. Ben liked challenges.

"My father's new secretary is a gorgeous piece. I'll have her in bed within a month," he told his best friend Bernie.

"Ten bucks says you don't," replied Bernie.

Though he usually spent most of the day meeting with clients outside the office, Ben began to appear at the office every afternoon at about 4. He would spend the last hour of the day hanging around Lily's desk trying to kibitz with her.

"Ben, I'm trying to get my work done. Your father will fire me if I don't have this paperwork finished before I leave tonight. I can't get it done if you sit here bothering me."

The insurance office was located in North Philadelphia, near Broad and Olney. Lily had to take two streetcars and the Broad Street Subway to get there.

"I'll tell you what. If you let me drive you home, I'll stop bothering you."

"All right."

Lily was not particularly attracted to Ben but thought that he was pleasant enough.

At least I'll get a ride home.

* * *

Ben appeared at the office two or three times a week offering to drive Lily home. Because she was relieved not to have to ride the crowded public transportation, Lily usually accepted his offer.

About the second week, Ben began to put his arm casually around Lily's shoulder in the car.

"No, Ben," she would say as she pushed him away, "it's not that kind of relationship."

"I'm only trying to be friendly."

"I'm not that kind of friend."

Soon the interaction became a kind of ritual between them. He would try to put his arm around her, and she would remove it.

"Look, Ben, I've told you over and over. If you don't stop this little game I'll never get in the car with you again."

"Okay, Lily. I'm sorry. I won't do it anymore. But I'd like to see you sometime outside of work. If you agree, I promise not to try to touch you in any way. We'll just go out and have a good time. Swear to God."

I haven't been out in months. Not since the last time I went out with Jack. It might be fun. If he starts to get fresh, I'll just leave.

"All right."

* * *

"Where are you going all dressed up?" asked Sadie.

"I'm just going out with Ben Lieberman—my boss's son."

"Oh. Is he your new boyfriend?"

"Stop it, mama. I have no new boyfriend. It's just that I haven't been out for a very long time—since I stopped seeing Jack. I thought I could use a little fun for a change."

"Well, whose fault is it that you stopped seeing Jack?"

"Mama, you know it was my decision. Right now, I just don't know what I want. It wouldn't be fair to lead him on."

"You're not gonna find too many men like him waiting around for you. And I don't think he's gonna wait too long either."

"I don't expect him to, mama. That's the chance I take."

Ben picked Lily up at 6. They went to Horn and Hardart's Automat for dinner, then to the Boyd Theater to catch Al Jolson's Jazz Singer, a talkie movie that neither of them had yet seen.

After the movie, Ben headed back toward Strawberry Mansion. However, instead of going straight home, he drove through Fairmount Park and pulled over on George's Hill, a spot where young couples parked to 'neck.' That night, the spot wasn't too crowded, and Ben found a private parking area away from the rest of the cars.

"What are you doing, Ben?"

"I thought we could just sit here and enjoy each other's company."

"I don't want to sit here. I want to go home."

"Not yet, baby. I want some action."

"Action?"

Before she could move to get out of the car, Ben had slid over and pinned her in her seat. She tried to push him away, but his strength was overwhelming.

"Let me go!"

"You know you want it. Why don't you just lay back and enjoy it?"

Lily tried to scream, but Ben put his hand over her mouth. While holding her against the seat with one hand and the weight of his body, he ripped her blouse with his other hand and placed his hand on her breast. As she continued to struggle, he slapped her across the face. While she was momentarily stunned, he shoved his hand under her skirt and tried to pull down her panties.

"Get off of me!" she tried to scream, but he put his mouth over hers and tried to force his tongue into her mouth. As he did so, she bit down as hard as she could on the soft muscle. He screamed.

"You fuckin' bitch! I'll fix you."

But the pain and flow of blood from his mouth could not be ignored. As he pulled a handkerchief from his pants to staunch the blood flow, Lily managed to open the car door and jump out.

She ran over to the closest car and banged on the window.

The couple in the front seat was startled in the midst of their necking.

"Help me, please! I've been attacked."

They looked at her and saw her torn blouse stained with Ben's blood.

"Of course! Get in."

The young man started the engine and drove away. In the headlights, Lily could see Ben staring at her with his handkerchief against his mouth.

"Do you want to go to the police station?"

She thought about having to spend the night answering questions and bringing her family into it.

"No. I'd appreciate it if you could just take me home. It isn't very far."

* * *

Sadie was still awake when she heard Lily come in the door. Aaron was still working at the bakery.

"My God! What happened to you?"

Lily sank onto the sofa. Now that she was safely at home, she allowed herself to cry. Sobs racked her body.

Gasping for breath, she attempted to explain to her mother. "He tried to rape me."

"What do you mean?"

As Lily calmed down, she described the night's events to her mother.

"I don't know what to do," said Sadie. "I'm going to call Jack."

* * *

Jack had just returned home from dinner with Melvin Meyers. They had been celebrating the successful completion of a recent smuggling operation. Jack's 'leasing' fee was twenty thousand dollars, which he received in cash.

"I'll be there in five minutes." He placed the money in his bedroom vault, jumped into his car, and drove the four blocks to the house on Thirty-third Street.

He took one look at Lily and wrapped her in his arms. She received his embrace willingly, crying softly on his shoulder.

"I'll fix the son of a bitch so that he won't ever be able to do this again."

"No, Jack. Promise me you won't use violence. I don't want you to get into any trouble on my account. That won't do either of us any good."

"All right, Lily. But I'm going to go over there and scare the hell out of him."

* * *

Jack drove to the home of Jonathan Lieberman, where Ben lived with his parents. There were no lights on. Jack rang the doorbell and pounded on the door as loudly as he could. He saw a light go on upstairs.

"What the hell do you want?" asked the elder Lieberman. "Why are you pounding on my door at this time of night?"

"I want to see your son. Where is he?"

"What business is it of yours?"

Jack looked him straight in the eye.

"It's about time you knew the kind of son you've raised.

Tonight your son attempted to rape your assistant, Lily. If it weren't for her quick thinking, he would have succeeded. Now where is he?"

Jonathan's face had turned a ghostly white. He knew his son's reputation for womanizing, but he didn't know it included violence.

"Wait here."

Jonathan marched up the steps. A few minutes later he came back down pulling Ben by the sleeve behind him. Ben was still holding a wet, blood-stained washrag to his mouth.

Jack pushed Ben by the shoulders across the room to a chair.

"Sit down," he commanded.

Ben sat.

"You're very lucky that Lily asked me not to hurt you. I would have beaten you so badly that you'd have been in a hospital for weeks. If I ever find out that you've touched Lily or any other woman when they did not want to be touched, I swear to you that I will come back here and beat the shit out of you like I should be doing right now. I want you to tell your father what happened tonight."

* * *

Ben was silent.

Jack pulled him to his feet by the front of his bathrobe.

"Now!"

"All I wanted was to play a little."

"Is that what you call playing?" asked Jonathan. "I'm ashamed that I could have ever raised a son like you."

"I'm sorry," Ben said to his father.

"I want you out of this house tomorrow," said Jonathan. You're fired from the business. And you're to write a letter of apology to Lily. She's the best assistant I ever had. I hope she doesn't quit."

Jack turned and started to leave.

"Remember what I said," he said to Ben. "I mean every word of it."

Chapter Thirty-Seven

L ily did not want to return to work at Lieberman's agency.
I'd live in fear that Ben was going to show up one day. I don't want to put myself through that.

All of the family—and especially Jack—was relieved that Lily had made this decision. They didn't want her taking those kinds of chances either.

Jack and Lily began to spend a lot of time with each other once again. Jack could sense that the emotional wall that Lily had erected around herself was crumbling. When he called, he could hear the joy in her voice. When he came over to visit or to take her out, she was visibly excited to see him.

Jack questioned his own motivation for resuming the relationship.

I know I'm allowing myself to get back into the same complicated situation, but I can't help it. I love her.

Even Aaron could tell that Lily was happy. He was pleased by her happiness, though he continued to have a vague sense of uneasiness whenever Jack was around.

Sadie noticed his discomfort.

"What's the matter with you? You're always so suspicious. Why can't you accept Jack and be happy at your daughter's good fortune?"

"I don't know. It's just that, since Jack came into our lives, everything seems to have gone wrong."

"And you think it's his fault? If it weren't for him, we wouldn't have gotten through these bad times. He's been a good friend. What other friend stuck around when we began to have trouble?"

"I guess you're right. I'll try to act better."

* * *

In early July, Lily received a phone call from her friend Ceil.

"Lily, Sol and I want to go to Atlantic City this weekend. I told my mother we would be double-dating with a friend and that the girls would have a separate hotel room. Otherwise, she wouldn't let me go. How about you and Jack joining us?"

Lily thought about it.

I've never been away from home overnight with a man. But I'm nineteen years old. I think I can handle myself. Besides, Jack is a gentleman. He'd never force me into doing anything I don't want to do. Actually, it's kind of exciting to think about being away alone overnight.

"All right Ceil, I'll talk to Jack about it."

* * *

"Are you sure you feel comfortable going away with me for

the weekend?" asked Jack.

"If I didn't, I never would have asked you."

"I'd love to spend the weekend with you. We'll stay at the Chalfonte Haddon Hall Hotel. It's right on the boardwalk. And I know a really good nightclub that has a wonderful band."

"Do you mean one of those speakeasies?"

"Yes. It's run by one of my friends." Jack didn't say anything about his ownership of the establishment.

"Oh, so I'll finally get to meet some of your friends! I didn't think you had any."

"I have lots of friends. But I'm not sure you would approve of all of them."

"Are they bad people?"

"Oh, no! But many of them operate on, shall we say, the fringes of the law. Do you think you're able to handle that?"

"I'm a big girl now. I'm looking forward to meeting some new and interesting people. And I want to find out more about you, too."

"I'm a pretty dull guy. But being with you makes me feel like I'm getting a breath of fresh air."

"Why thank you, Jack. That's a wonderful compliment."

"You're a wonderful girl."

* * *

On Friday evening, the couples checked into their hotel. The Chalfonte Haddon Hall was located on the boardwalk overlooking the Atlantic Ocean just a few minutes from Steel Pier. Their room was luxurious, with a large bed, wide brocade draperies with a matching bedspread, and a large bathroom with both a tub and a shower.

The couples split up for the evening. Jack walked Lily a few blocks north to Virginia Avenue just off the boardwalk. There, they descended three steps to enter an unmarked basement that looked like the other basement entrances in the area. Jack knocked three times, paused, and then twice more. The door was opened by a tuxedoed maitre d' who smiled when he saw who had knocked and bowed as he invited them inside.

"Good evening, Mr. Perle. Welcome back. Let me show you to your usual table."

"Thank you, Raymond. This is Miss Peck. She's a very special friend."

"Glad to meet you, Miss Peck. You must be very special. He's never said that about anyone else he's brought here."

Lily blushed.

"So, you bring all your girlfriends here?" asked Lily after they had been seated.

"No, only the ones I like."

"And how many of those are there?"

"Only one, at the moment."

The room took up the full basement. There were fifteen tables for four with white linen tablecloths. Crystal wine glasses and champagne flutes had been placed at each seat. The elaborately carved wall sconces were set with electric lighting that cast a dim but intimate glow over the room.

Lily smiled as they were seated in the most secluded area.

She was enjoying this new experience. Getting out of her usual 'good girl' role gave her a sense of freedom and sophistication. She looked across the table, noticing the ease with which Jack interacted with the waiters and other clientele.

I don't know the first thing about who he really is or what he's all about.

"What would you like to drink?"

"I don't know. Why don't you order for me."

The waiter brought Lily a creamy green drink in a cocktail glass.

"Umm. It's delicious. What is it?"

"It's called a grasshopper. It's made of crème de menthe mixed with sweet cream."

"I've never tasted anything like this before."

"I'll bet there's a lot of things you've never tasted before."

"Yes. And I want to taste them all."

"You'd better be careful, Lily," warned Jack. "Don't jump into things you don't know anything about."

"How else am I going to learn?"

* * *

Lily loved the music. She had never danced to live music except at weddings and bar mitzvahs. This was different. The alcohol and the atmosphere were making her high.

"You're a wonderful dancer, Jack."

"You're not bad yourself. Where did you learn?"

"Gita and I used to dance to the music on the Victrola. I used to pretend I was dancing with the man I loved."

Jack was silent. Lily didn't finish her thought.

"Time to go back to the hotel," said Jack.

"I want to spend the night with you."

"What are you talking about?"

"Ceil is going to be in the room with Sol. They want to be alone."

"Lily, do you know what you're getting yourself into?"

"Yes, Jack. Like I said, I'm a big girl now. I've been thinking about this for a long time."

"Are you absolutely sure?"

"Absolutely sure."

* * *

Lily accompanied Jack to his tenth-floor room. It had two windows facing the ocean. Jack turned on the lights and opened the window. A cool summer breeze rustled the curtains. The sound of the surf filled the air.

Jack sat down on one of the comfortably upholstered chairs, not sure what to do next. Lily sensed his discomfort.

"Are you this uncomfortable with other girls?"

"I don't care about other girls."

"Does that mean you care about me?"

"It means I care about you and I'm not sure you know what you're doing."

Lily came over and sat on his lap. She unknotted his cravat, removed it, and unbuttoned his shirt. Then she placed her warm hands inside his shirt and began to massage his bare shoulders. As she massaged, she brushed her lips on his.

She interrupted the kiss as she felt a thin string around Jack's neck.

"What's this?" she asked.

"It's the only thing I have left from my father. I never take it off."

"Tell me about it," she said as she examined the pouch and coin.

"My father received this from his parents as a bar mitzvah gift. The pouch was sewn by my grandmother. It's an heirloom meant to be passed down from generation to generation."

"How wonderful. They must have been wonderful people. Someday, you'll pass it on to your own son or grandson. Too bad your father didn't live to see the success you've made of your life."

Tears sprang to Jack's eyes. It was the first time Lily had witnessed any vulnerability in his self-confident manner.

"I'm sorry. I didn't mean to make you feel bad. You must have loved him very much."

Jack couldn't speak.

Lily gently pushed the pouch aside and continued to massage him.

Jack relaxed in spite of himself. He could feel himself involuntarily responding. Lily noticed it too. She was pleased not only because he found her attractive and sexually desirable but also because he had trusted her enough to cry in her presence.

Lily unbuttoned her own blouse and removed it. She took the pins from her hair and let it cascade around her shoulders. She unbuttoned Jack's pants easing the pressure in his loins. The bulge there was growing noticeably larger.

Standing up, she stepped out of her skirt and petticoat, leaving her curvaceous body clad only in a bra and panties. She kneeled at Jack's feet and took off his shoes and socks. Pulling him to a standing position, she led him over to the bed and removed his tank top undershirt. She lay him down on the bed and unhooked her brassiere, allowing her breasts their freedom. Wrapping her arms around him, she pressed her body against his and gave him a loving kiss on the lips.

Jack lay there aware of himself responding. He was surprised at her considerable skills in arousing him. He knew that she was a virgin and had no extensive experience at lovemaking.

Where do women learn how to do this? Or is it an inborn talent?

As his passion grew, Jack could no longer remain rational and detached from what was happening. He pressed her close and returned in kind the stroking and touching. His kisses were deep and probing. Jack's sensual touch and gentle exploring hands evoked sensations much different from anything she had ever experienced with David.

Slowly Jack took over the initiative, throwing his reluctance to the wind. He gently pulled down her panties and then his own trousers and underwear. He could sense Lily's surprise and pleasure at each new sensation she was experiencing. He made love to her like he had never made love to anyone else. Even with other women he cared about, Jack enjoyed sex because of the pure erotic pleasure involved. But with Lily it was different. Her pleasure came first. Knowing that she was enjoying their lovemaking was what stimulated his excitement. Her pure innocence was far more arousing than any physical stimulation. Recognizing the trust she placed in him made him love her even more. He allowed her to set the pace, matching her increasing levels of arousal as he sensed them escalating. Moving together in sync, he mounted her and held off his own release until he felt her approaching crescendo. Climaxing together, they collapsed on the bed in exhaustion. Panting and gasping, sweat mixing with sweat, they held each other tightly.

"Thank you for being so gentle with me," gasped Lily once she was able to speak.

"I thought I knew what to expect. But this experience can never be described."

"Are you sorry?"

"Oh no. I feel like I'm now a complete woman."

"You are a complete woman."

The two couples checked out of the hotel after having treated themselves to the hotel's lavish Sunday buffet of smoked salmon, roast beef, bagels, whitefish, and other delicacies. As they drove on the White Horse Pike through south-central New Jersey, they passed fields of tomatoes, corn, and other crops. They stopped at a local fruit stand to sample ice-cold watermelon, which slaked their thirst on a hot summer afternoon.

As they resumed their return drive to Philadelphia, Lily caught occasional glimpses of Ceil and Sol necking in the back seat.

That's something Jack would never do. It's much too public for him. He's far beyond that.

They dropped the couple at Ceil's house and drove to Thirty-third Street. Jack didn't go inside. He didn't feel like facing Sadie and Aaron. For the first time, he felt like he wouldn't be able to look them straight in the eye.

*   *   *

Lily didn't notice any change in Jack's attitude. For the next few weeks, they continued to see each other on the weekend and, at Lily's initiative, spent time alone at Jack's house making love. Jack began to feel increasingly guilty.

My plan is going exactly according to schedule. And yet, I'm finding no satisfaction in revenge. All I'm succeeding in doing is to hurt other people. I can't go on like this. I'm growing to love her more every day. But where can this go? She's my sister. I've got to cut this off.

The next Saturday rolled around, and Lily, as usual, met Jack at his Thirty-third Street mansion. She knew something was wrong by the troubled look on his face.

"What's wrong, Jack"?

"Lily, I'm sorry to say this but things are going a little too fast for me," he lied. "I'm not ready to get serious, and I'm taking up all your time. I think we'd better cool it off a bit. I think you should go out with some other nice young men."

"But I thought you loved me! I thought we were a couple."

"I'm sorry if I led you on. I didn't mean to hurt you. I don't know what else to say. I don't want to see you for a while."

I love her but I can't let this go on. I just can't tell her that she's my sister.

Lily did not reply. She was stunned and too hurt to offer any resistance. She couldn't think at all and was paralyzed with despair.

Jack forced himself to control any show of emotion as he drove Lily home. She sat next to him silently sobbing and not uttering a word. When they reached her home, she walked robot-like into the house and didn't look back.

Chapter Thirty-Eight

"I told you he was no good," said Aaron to his wife. "He's broken her heart—your wonderful Jack Perle."

Sadie sat there crying. She didn't know what to say. This development was completely unexpected; the possibility of it never occurred to her.

Gita was angry.

"That son of a bitch used you," she told Lily. Gita guessed that the relationship had progressed to a sexual one, though Lily never explicitly told her.

"He's a bastard. You're lucky you found out now."

Lily just sat in her room staring at the wall. She refused to come out for meals or to join Gita and her friends for a trip to the talkie movies. She was too numb to think.

* * *

A few weeks after Jack broke up with her, Lily noticed that she had missed her period and that her breasts were becoming swollen and tender. Unlike Jack's mother, Lili was a sophisticated young woman who understood the implications of her symptoms.

Oh no! That can't be possible. What would I do?

But, indeed, it was possible. Lily finally decided she had to tell her mother.

Sadie was furious with Jack and angry with Lily too.

"How could you let him do that to you?"

"Mama, it was me who started it. Jack just went along. It wasn't his idea."

"How can you say that? It's always the man who takes advantage. Stop trying to protect him."

"I'm not trying to protect him, Mama. I'm just trying to tell you the truth."

"I want you to call him up immediately. Tell him you're pregnant and he must marry you."

"Mama, I won't marry him under those circumstances. I won't blackmail him. He doesn't want to get married, and I'm not going to force him."

Try as Sadie might to knock some sense into her daughter, Lily remained firm in her resolve.

Finally, Sadie gave up.

"All right. Maybe we can find a medicine that will get rid of it."

"No, mama. I won't drink any poison. It never works anyhow."

Sadie was getting more frustrated by the minute.

"Lily, you're very stubborn. Okay. I'll try to find somebody who will get it out of you."

"Listen, Mama. I don't want to go to a filthy abortionist. You know what can happen to girls who go there. I want to have this baby."

"What? You must be crazy! What will you tell everyone?"

"I'll move to a different city and make a new life. I'll have the baby there."

"And you'll give the baby up for adoption?"

"No, mother. I'm not giving away my baby. I'll stay there and make a new life."

"Oh, no, darling. I don't want to lose you. Aaron! See if you can talk some sense into her."

Aaron had been standing in the other room listening to the argument between his wife and his daughter.

Dear God. I went through this once. Do I have to go through it again? Why are you doing this to me? Haven't I been punished enough?

He walked into Lily's bedroom.

"Papa, I know I'm hurting you terribly. You've had enough problems. I feel terrible doing this to you."

"Lily darling, what would it hurt if you should call Jack and tell him what's going on? Maybe he'll do the right thing by you and the child. Maybe he'll marry you."

"Papa, I already told mama. I don't want him to marry me for that reason. I'd rather be alone."

"Darling, at least humor me a little. Call him and tell him what's going on. He's the father. He deserves to know what's happening."

Lily thought about what Aaron had said.

Papa is right. Jack's the father. Even if he doesn't want to marry me, he has the right to know."

* * *

The next day, Lily called Jack at home.

"I need to talk to you."

"I'm sorry, Lily. I told you that it's best if we don't see each other."

"But there's something I have to tell you."

"All right. Meet me at my office at Norton's tomorrow morning at 10. I don't want to see you at home."

Lily was shown into Jack's office as scheduled. It was the first time that she had been there. The office was paneled in redwood. The large desk was burnished mahogany. On the wall were paintings by Renoir, Matisse, Van Gogh, and Rubens. She had never seen original paintings by such famous artists except in a museum.

Lily wasted no time with small talk.

"Jack, I'm pregnant, and I'm going to have the baby."

Jack was taken aback. He paced the floor for a few moments, then looked at Lily sitting defiantly in the straight-backed chair.

"Lily, I can't marry you."

You're my sister for Christ's sake.

"I didn't come here to ask you to marry me. I came here to tell you you're going to be a father."

Jack was stunned and could not reply.

The very thing I worried about has happened. What should I do now?

Lily interpreted Jack's silence as lack of concern. The proud young lady stood up, turned, and left.

* * *

Lily found herself strangely calm and clear-thinking under these painfully stressful circumstances. As she returned home on the Number 9 trolley, she busied herself trying to figure out exactly how she would manage her next moves. She found her parents pacing up and down the living room, anxiously awaiting her return. They pounced on her as she entered the house.

"So, what did he say?" asked Sadie.

"He said he couldn't marry me."

"And what did you say?"

"Nothing. What was there to say?"

"That bastard!" cried Sadie.

* * *

That evening, Lily began to make plans to leave Philadelphia.

"I'm going to New York, mama. There's a hospital there run by an organization for unwed mothers. I can stay there until the baby's born. Then I'll get an apartment and find a job."

"Who'll stay with the baby?"

"I'll find a babysitter. I'll figure something out. I always do."

"But darling, I'll be too far away to help you."

"You and papa can take the train up on weekends. I want to see you as much as possible. I'll need all the moral support I can get."

"Of course we'll be there. And I'll come up when the baby

is born."

As she watched her beloved daughter preparing to leave, Sadie was inconsolable.

"How can he be so unfeeling?" she asked Aaron. "There must be something we can do. Aaron, I want you to go talk to him. Maybe he'll listen to a man. We've got nothing to lose."

Aaron didn't want to go.

How can I change a hardened heart? God has sent this man here to teach me a lesson. This man is me twenty-six years ago. Nothing stopped me then, and nothing will stop him now. My beloved daughter is suffering for the curse I have inflicted on my own family.

"Sadie, I just can't do it. I have nothing—no money, no power, no leverage to make him do anything."

"Aaron, you have the power of moral righteousness. He needs to know that what he's doing is wrong."

Aaron interrupted her. "Sadie, don't do this to me. You'll give me a heart attack."

Sadie ignored him. She finally let loose more of the feelings that she had held back all through her years of marriage.

"Aaron, you have always been too scared to face the truth. You make excuses for everything. Jack has a responsibility to God to do the right thing. Lily may have thrown herself at him, but he's much older and knew the consequences of what could happen. If he doesn't live up to his responsibility, the lives of four people will be ruined—Lily's, the baby's, yours, and mine. You and I don't matter so much, but do you want your daughter bringing up your grandchild in a strange place away from home where they will both be alone and have to struggle simply to survive?

"Sadie, please stop!"

Once started, however, Sadie couldn't stop herself. She was willing to face the reality of her apparent mistake in judgment.

"I thought he was our friend. He pretends to be an outstanding pillar of the community. But what kind of friend would do this to a vulnerable young girl who trusted him?"

"I don't know, Sadie. I feel like I'm falling apart. I can't take much more of this."

"Aaron, it's about time you behaved like a mensch. You selfishly ruined the lives of your son and first wife. Now your daughter's life is at stake. It's our last chance. Don't make the same mistake again. Once she goes to New York, it will be 'out of sight, out of mind' for Jack Perle."

* * *

Aaron couldn't resist Sadie's pressure. The next, day he telephoned Jack.

"Jack, I want to talk to you."

"What about?"

"You know what about."

"I have nothing to say."

"I want to see you anyway."

* * *

Aaron's hands were shaking as he entered the building that housed Jack's office. He felt frightened, powerless, and guilty for having somehow created the current impossible situation.

"I'm here to see Mr. Perle," Aaron said to Jack's secretary. "Tell him it's Aaron Peck."

"Just a moment, please. Would you like a cup of coffee while you wait?"

"Thank you," replied Aaron.

I'd better be careful. My hands are shaking so much I might spill the coffee all over the furniture.

Jack's secretary was curious. She wondered why he had emphatically instructed her not to interrupt this next meeting under any circumstances. This had never occurred before.

Aaron was impressed with the ornate furnishings of the reception room. The floor was almost entirely covered with a fine silk and wool Persian carpet. The paintings in large gilt frames hung on the walls. He drank his coffee carefully, sipping from one of the fine porcelain cups that hung in a magnificent antique breakfront against the wall. He didn't want to embarrass himself by spilling the brown liquid all over the expensive antique furnishings.

Where does this man come from? No one knows anything about him. His parents must have left him a lot of money. What am I going to say to him that will change his mind? I can't even think straight. He's so much smarter than I am. Why should he listen to me?

Jack kept Aaron waiting for twenty minutes. He didn't do it purposely, but his heart was racing so fast and his hands were so cold and clammy that he couldn't function properly. His usual composure had disappeared in a rush of anxiety.

This is the moment I've been waiting for all my life. Now that it's here, I don't know what to say. Should I tell him who I am? Should I tell him why I can't marry his daughter? All I've ever wanted was for him to love me. He's a fool and a liar and a hard-hearted son of a bitch, but he's my father.

Jack finally opened the door and motioned Aaron in. His vocal cords were too tight for him to speak. The two men faced each other. Ironically, each realized at that moment that they were alone together for the first time. Each felt intimidated by the other and wondered how to begin.

Jack motioned for Aaron to sit down. Aaron sat in the same straight-backed chair that Lily had occupied. Jack moved to his upholstered swivel chair behind the large desk. His throat was still so tight that he had trouble speaking. He sat waiting for Aaron to begin.

Aaron finally spoke.

"I know you know why I'm here. Lily is pregnant and refuses to even consider getting rid of the baby. She's planning to move to New York and have the baby there where no one knows who she is. She won't consider giving it up for adoption."

"What do expect me to do about it?"

"I expect you to act like a man and live up to your responsibility."

"What responsibility?"

"The responsibility of taking care of your child."

"Oh?"

"What kind of man is it that would abandon his own child

and allow the child to grow up fatherless?"

Jack drew a deep breath and found his voice. Twenty-plus years of pent-up emotion were let loose loudly and clearly.

"You speak like a paragon of virtue. Have you lived up to your own responsibilities?"

Aaron's heart nearly popped out of his chest.

"What do you mean by that?"

"Just what I said. Have you lived up to your own responsibilities?"

How could he know?

"Of course I have! I've worked to provide for my wife and children and to help others who can't provide for themselves."

"Is that right? How many children did you tell me you had?"

"T-t-two."

"Are you sure? Or are you also a liar along with being irresponsible?"

"What do you mean?"

"And what did you tell me you did when you lived in Vilna?"

"I—I attended the yeshiva."

"Oh! Did they hold classes in the local tavern? Or did you attend advanced classes while sweeping up the elementary school floors?"

What is happening here? How does he know so much?

Aaron's brain was spinning. He couldn't respond to Jack's questions.

"Aaron Peck, you're a liar and a fraud. You pretend to be an upright and righteous family man, but you're really an arrogant coward who runs away from his own responsibilities. You never attempted to make up for—or even ask about—the result of your careless actions. And yet you, a man who has deceitfully covered up the sins of his past, who has inflicted hurt too horrible for words on innocent, helpless souls of your own blood, tell me to live up to my responsibilities! What do you have to say for yourself?"

Aaron couldn't breathe. His panic was overwhelming.

* * *

"Who... who are you?"

Staring deeply and fixedly into his father's eyes, Jack's decision came without thinking. He slowly reached inside his shirt and pulled the silk cord over his head. He drew out the well-worn velvet pouch and threw it as hard as he could at Aaron.

Aaron was confused and ducked the oncoming object. It hit his shoulder and landed at his feet. Aaron bent over and picked it up, feeling the wine-colored velvet and the thin irregular round coin inside.

As his mind slowly comprehended the significance of the object, Aaron's chest constricted. He felt a sharp pain and thought he was having a heart attack.

"OOY! OOY!" He let out a loud shriek and fell to his knees. Screams and tears poured forth as he rocked back and forth on the floor banging his head repeatedly on the oriental carpet. Unable to control his emotions, he crawled on all fours around the massive desk to where Jack was sitting and grabbed him around the legs, pushing his face hard against Jack's knees.

Jack's secretary sitting outside the office door heard the loud screams. Her first impulse was to call the police or an ambulance. However, her boss had told her not to interrupt under any circumstances. She decided to wait and see what would happen next.

"I'm sorry, I'm sorry," Aaron kept repeating between sobs. "Forgive me, forgive me! Everything you say is true. I am a selfish coward who ignored my responsibilities. My guilt has tortured me for years, but I've never had the courage to do what I should have done. I've always found excuses to avoid facing my actions. I abandoned my family. I deserted you when you needed me most. I'm so ashamed of myself. I'm an evil man. Don't even look at me."

And Aaron let go of Jack's knees and dropped to the carpet, head on the floor, crying, still rocking, oblivious to his surroundings.

Jack sat silently for several minutes watching his father's unexpected display of unbridled contrition. Tears welled up in his eyes. His long-held anger and desire for revenge dissipated in that moment.

"I've been waiting to hear that for twenty years!" he cried as he finally pulled Aaron from the floor and hugged him tightly. The two men stood crying and holding each other for several minutes.

Finally, Aaron's sobs diminished.

"I can't believe you are my son. I am so proud of you. You've managed to overcome such hardships despite my despicable behavior. I don't deserve a son like you."

* * *

Jack took a step backward and looked at his father with tenderness.

"I've hated you and loved you at the same time ever since you left. You're the only close family I have. You told me you never wanted to see me again and not to try to contact you. Since I found you, I wanted to hurt you any way I could. But I realized I only ended up hurting the people I love. I couldn't go on doing it."

"I don't blame you for anything you've done, my son. I deserve all of it and more. I only pray that, someday, you can forgive me for my thoughtless and hurtful behavior."

"I forgive you—papa."

I can't believe I'm finally saying that word.

Jack continued, "We have a lot to make up for and, with God's help, we'll do it over time. But my own thoughtless behavior has created another terrible problem. I have fallen in love and impregnated my own sister. What shall I do? How can I marry her?"

Aaron looked into his son's eyes with a mixture of deep sorrow, pride, and unconditional love. He held Jack's hand tightly to his chest and didn't want to let it go. It was as if he needed to concentrate twenty years' worth of loving physical contact into this single moment.

"My son, the damage is already done. She's pregnant with your child. What would be accomplished by ruining the lives of both Lily and the child? Nothing. Only unhappiness can come of it—as we both know so well. Besides, a miracle has brought you back to me, and I never want to lose you again."

Jack wrapped his arm around his father's shoulder and squeezed him tightly. The gaping hole in his life—one that he thought would be there forever—was closing. He and his father sat as Jack often dreamed they would, getting to know one another and cementing their new relationship.

Jack spent the next few hours bringing his father up to date on the essentials of his life. Then Aaron and his son left the office and drove to Thirty-third Street together. They knew that they had difficult conversations to look forward to.

Chapter Thirty-Nine

When Jack and his father arrived at the Thirty-third Street house, Lily and Sadie were upstairs going through Lily's wardrobe to decide what to bring with her to New York. Gita was still not home from class. She was in her last year of high school.

"Sadie! Lily!" Aaron called from the bottom of the staircase. "Come downstairs."

"We're busy," Sadie answered. "Can't it wait?"

"No, it's important. We have a guest."

As Sadie and Lily descended the stairs, they caught sight of Jack standing there quietly. Both stopped in their tracks, shocked to see him and not knowing what to say. Jack and Aaron had decided on the way home that Aaron should be the one to initiate the discussion. Aaron felt that it was finally time to face up to the responsibilities that he had avoided for so long.

"Come and sit down," he said.

He first addressed Lily.

"My darling daughter. You need to know something about

me that I have hidden for many years."

Aaron went on to describe the events of his earlier life and finally, with tears in his eyes, spelled out the familial relationship between Jack and herself.

"Lily, Jack is your half-brother."

Lily gasped and her hand flew to her mouth in shock.

Aaron continued, "That's why he pulled away from you when he did. He was afraid that something like this would happen, and he didn't want ro repeat my mistakes. But he loves you very much, my darling, and he very much wants to marry you." Aaron couldn't bear the thought of other lives being ruined the way he had ruined the lives of Jacob and Rebecca. Lily, who was still too shocked to respond was thinking,

He's defending Jack because he feels so guilty himself.

Lily looked over to Jack whose face was racked with anxiety, guilt and shame. He was hyper aware that his scheme to commit vengeance upon his father had backfired and ended up hurting the very ones he loved the most. He wondered how Lily could ever forgive him for having deliberately planned the events in question until they had gotten out of hand in his overwhelming desire for Lily's love. The same obsessive thought bombarded his brain:

I shouldn't have let things progress to this point.

She was hurt, confused, and extremely angry to think that Jack would have let the situation proceed this far.

How could he do this to me knowing the truth about our family relationship? Did his need for revenge against his father blind him to its effect on me?

Lily raced upstairs to get away and think. She locked herself in her room. Over the next two days she considered her dilemma.

I remember his tears when he showed me the coin his father gave him. He must have grown up very lonely and scared when his father abandoned him and he was left on his own to take care of his mother. How could MY father have done that to him? MY father did a terrible thing and never even tried to make it better. I know Jack loves me. He's shown it in so many ways. And it really was ME who initiated the sexual relationship between us. He should have known better but I guess I am partly to blame as well. And how will I feel watching my child grow up without a father and knowing that it was finally my own decision that created that situation?

Lily spent those days letting these thoughts percolate over and over through her mind. She avoided her family and did not discuss the issue with them. The more she considered the various aspects of her situation, the more confused she became.

Jack had returned home. The more he dwelt on his behavior the more self hatred emerged. He spent much of the next two days in a drunken stupor trying to erase the memories of his dishonorable actions.

She'll never trust me again. How can she forgive me for what I did? But I love her. What can I do now? How could I have allowed myself to let it get to this point.

Sadie and Aaron spent the time hanging around the house but, at Sadie's insistence, made no attempt to engage Lily.

"Shouldn't we try to talk to her?" Aaron would ask.

"No Aaron. She's a big girl. This is her decision to make."

Gita had returned from school after Jack left the house that day and had not yet been apprised of the new information. She was aware that something was wrong but her parents would not answer any of her questions.

"What's wrong with Lily? Why won't she leave her room?"

"You'll know soon enough," they would answer.

On the third day after the confrontation with Jack and her parents, Lily called Sadie into her bedroom.

"Please ask Jack to come over and discuss the situation with us."

That afternoon Jack arrived at the Peck household in an unshaven and generally unkempt condition. The others had never seen him in this kind of state. He joined Sadie, Aaron and Lily in the living room. Gita knew they were meeting and asked to be included. They all felt she was old enough to understand the situation.

Lily initiated the conversation by asking her father to bring Gita up to date on what had occurred. Aaron obliged and gave Gita a short version of his past behavior and its implications. Gita was shocked but before she could respond Jack clumsily stood up, lurched over to where Lily sat, got down on one knee and gutterally whispered, almost crying, "Lily, I'm so sorry for what I've done. Please forgive me. I love you very much. I never meant to hurt you. Will you marry me?"

Lily sat quietly for a moment. Again her mind briefly flashed back to Jack's wet eyes as he showed her the coin his father had given him. She leaned over, put her hand down the front of Jack's open shirt and pulled out the coin. Then she kissed it. Standing up, she pulled Jack up from his kneeling position. With tears running down her face she put her arms around him. Although once again she couldn't speak, her answer was clear.

Upon recognizing Lily's acceptance of Jack's marriage proposal, Sadie was relieved and began to cry again. She had been surprised but not shocked with the new revelation. In fact, she realized that she was feeling pleased not only with Lily's decision, but with the way Aaron had handled himself as he honestly described his shameful actions to Lily and then to Gita without any excuses.

Finally he's behaving like a 'mensch'.

Sadie had seen firsthand what could happen when an unmarried woman and her illegitimate child were abandoned by the child's father and she didn't want that to happen to her daughter.

Gita could hold back no longer. "That means you're MY brother too," she declared almost shouting with delight. Then harking back to her usual direct way of cutting through a complicated situation she thoughtfully added, "but will the baby be normal?"

Jack, who had already researched the question in his search for answers replied, "There is a slight chance that the baby will have some genetic abnormality." Then looking at Lily who nodded her head, he continued, "But under the circumstances, it's a chance we're willing to take."

This seemed to satisfy Gita and she gave Jack and Lily big

hugs of approval with tears in her eyes. The family unanimously agreed that no one outside of those present in the room would ever be told the nature of the genetic relationship between Lily and Jack.

That evening they all went downtown to Shoyer's—their favorite family restaurant for a celebratory dinner.

Epilogue

The phone rang in the office of the Exotic Fruit Company. The owner picked up the receiver.

"Aaron, it's so good to hear your voice. It's really a pleasure to deal with you again. That other guy never did understand the business the way that you do."

"Thanks, Charles. I'm enjoying being back. The bakery business was okay, but this is my first love."

"We're all glad to see you on your feet again. Congratulations."

"Thanks. Your order will arrive first thing Monday morning."

* * *

Aaron checked to make sure the fruit was stored properly and separated into packages for delivery. Jimmy Thurlow stopped in to wish him a good weekend. Jimmy was excited and happy to be able to return to working for his old boss.

"You've made my life happy again," he told Aaron. "I love coming to work."

Aaron sent the employees home and locked up. As he climbed

into his car, he looked up at the gleaming new signs above the door and on the roof.

PECK & FAMILY

EXOTIC FRUIT COMPANY

TROPICAL FRUITS AND PRODUCTS

He smiled and drove home to Thirty-third Street for the start of the Sabbath.

* * *

Abraham Weiss, the president of Shein's Linen Supply, sat in his office staring at the wall. He had been surprised yesterday when he received notice telling him he had been removed from the synagogue's board of directors. This day was turning out to be even worse. He picked up the phone to answer a call from the representative of the corporate owners. It was unusual for them to call at this time. He usually heard from them only four times a year to discuss the company's financial performance.

"Mr. Weiss, this is Bob Lavan. I'm calling to let you know that the owners of the company will no longer require your services. Today will be your last day."

Abe Weiss did not believe his ears.

"That can't be. I don't believe what you are telling me. What have I done?"

"I'm not at liberty to discuss that," replied the caller. "However, to mitigate your financial situation, the owners have decided to grant you a generous termination bonus of one thousand dollars. You are to leave the premises immediately." The caller hung up before Abe could pump him for more information.

Why have I been fired? The business has been profitable. And who is it that's calling the shots? What am I going to tell my family? What will my friends think?

Abraham slowly dragged himself up from his desk and prepared to go home.

* * *

That Friday evening, Jack and Lily sat around Sadie's dining room table with Aaron, Gita, and Gita's new fiancé, Nate Gordon. Lemel and Simeon would arrive shortly, after the close of the bakery. For the past year, Aaron had made sure to include his half-brothers in any family activity.

A chubby, pink-cheeked one-year-old played on the floor of the Pecks' living room.

"Come to me 'tataleh'!" called Aaron to his granddaughter using a Yiddish phrase meaning 'little one.' She crawled across the carpet and stood up by her grandfather's chair. The child was named Rebecca, after her paternal grandmother.

"Zeda," she said, pointing at Aaron. Then she pointed at Lily. "Mama."

"Rebecca's vocabulary is almost thirty words—amazing for a little girl who isn't even a year old," said Lily with motherly pride. "And she'll be walking by herself any day now," she added,

Aaron, Jack, and Sadie gave a secret sigh of relief. Their watchful eyes had followed Rebecca's growth closely, looking for any sign of developmental problems indicating a possible genetic defect.

"Nate will be graduating from the University of Pennsylvania in June," said Gita. "He's been accepted at the Wharton School there to get his master's degree in business and finance."

"Come talk to me when you're ready to look for a job," said Jack to the young man. "We always are on the lookout for a smart young fellow to help grow our businesses."

"Thank you, Mr. Perle," said Nate, "I'll do that." Nate was still overwhelmed at the prospect of having a man like Jack Perle as his brother-in-law.

* * *

After dinner, the family walked the few blocks to the synagogue. Aaron and Jack took their seats in the first row, facing the altar. They enjoyed the sermon of Rabbi Glassman—the new, well-known rabbi who had been enticed to the congregation by a large, anonymous donation that funded his special interest in the Diaspora.

A new board of directors had been put in place with Aaron as president. His first priority was clear. He instructed the board to "make sure that any congregant who cannot afford the usual dues is fully able to participate in all synagogue activities including, if appropriate, a position on this board."

* * *

Not long afterward, Nafty emigrated from Vilna with his wife and daughters and their families. He became Jack's right-hand man, helping to manage the family's growing business empire.

A picture of the old building in Vilna where Jack and his mother had spent so many years hung on the wall of his office.

Everyone around them was surprised at the close bond that had developed so quickly between Aaron and his son-in-law. They marveled when they heard Aaron address Jack as 'son.'

"Jack must represent the son he never had," one friend commented pseudo-analytically.

Aaron and his son-in-law overheard the comment. Their eyes met, and they smiled.

Author's Note

This book is a work of fiction. The broad sweep of historical background is, however, accurate. The conditions for the Jews in Eastern Europe at around the turn of the twentieth century were as described. The migration of the Jews out of Eastern Europe is also accurately described.

While the characters and incidents in this book are purely fictional and enhanced for literary purposes, they are based on somewhat similar events in the background experiences of the author and his ancestral family.

The mass migration of Eastern European Jews to America during the period from 1850 to 1930 and their successful integration and assimilation into American culture form a saga that has been detailed many times over. The success stories were matched by stories of abandonment of wives and children who were either left behind in Europe or deserted by their husbands and fathers once they arrived in this country. There really was a column in the Yiddish newspaper—the _Daily Forward_ in which wives whose husbands had left them would publicly announce their abandonment and ask for help in locating their lost spouses. Also, the conditions of the steerage class on transatlantic ships are accurately described.

Immigrants arriving at Ellis Island really were not permitted into this country without twenty dollars to get them wherever they were going. These were difficult, yet inspirational, times.

At this particular time in the history of American immigration, it is vital to remember the rich benefits that the new blood of immigrants has contributed to the invigoration of the economy and culture of our country.

Acknowledgments

I cannot express how much I am indebted to the late Yaffa Eliach, professor of Jewish history and Judaic studies at Brooklyn College.

Her book, *There Once Was a World,* (Yaffa Eliach; Little, Brown, and Co; 1998) provided me with a comprehensive picture of 900 years of Jewish life in the shtetls of Lithuania. Her descriptions of everyday life and activities in the Jewish villages of Eastern Europe were of immense help to me in setting up the background of my novel.

I also want to express my thanks to Dr. Holly W. Schwartztol, author of *Sherry and the Unseen World* and *Along my Garden Path: Poems on the Rhythms of Life.* My dear friend Holly put me in touch with John Prince of Hallard Press, who has proven to be a tremendous resource in helping me to publish my novel.

About the Author

Dr. Barry Kaplan has led many lives within his lifetime. He has served as both a U.S. Army Captain and on the American Peace Corp staff. He has helmed mental health facilities for youth and bereavement groups for senior citizens. After rising through traditional ranks to serve as President of his regional Psychiatric Society, he worked as a consultant at the innovative Upledger Institute, renowned for its pioneering techniques in whole-body healing. Along the way, he and his wife raised and successfully launched four kids.

Barry was born in the Strawberry Mansion neighborhood of Philadelphia, PA, a once thriving community of Jewish immigrants and a featured location in *The Coin*. Like the story's protagonist, Barry's father traveled from eastern Europe to America as a child on his own. Although the character similarities end there, such courageous voyagers are a hallmark of many American families. Barry has crafted *The Coin* in memory of all those family heroes, flawed and imperfect, to whom we owe absolutely everything.

From the Author

Thank you for taking time to read *The Coin*. I hope that you enjoyed reading it as much as I enjoyed writing it. My father came to America as a child from Eastern Europe. I can't imagine how difficult or frightening that must have been.

I love to hear from my readers. If you'd like to write to me about *The Coin*, or relate your own family story, email me at bsk96918@gmail.com.

Barry

Made in the USA
Middletown, DE
07 July 2021

43759109R00225